I0629261

Privileged
Corruption

a novel by

Ursula Ringham

COPYRIGHT

DEDICATION

To my dad for being the ultimate storyteller and fueling my love of a good story at such a young age. To my mom for *always* correcting my grammar. To my husband and kids for supporting this crazy dream. And to the rest of my family and friends for putting up with hearing about this crazy dream for so many years.

CHAPTER 1
Tuesday

Walter Rudolf slammed the bedroom door and stood alone in the dark hallway. Taking a deep breath, he reached for the light switch. The yellowish glow instantly illuminated the hall as he walked towards the foyer. He hated the new ceiling light Elizabeth had bought. It was too expensive and modern.

Walking past the kitchen, Walter noticed the light above the Viking range was still on. Damn it. Why couldn't Elizabeth remember to do the simplest things? Money didn't grow on trees. He walked into the kitchen towards the range and spotted his half empty Riedel Vinum Scotch glass beading on the new granite counter top. He picked up the glass. The ice had already melted. Crap. He took a last desperate swig and reached over to turn off the light.

He walked back into the hallway. The small foyer barely accommodated Elizabeth's newly acquired antique Biedermeier console table. He had only just received the latest payment and she was already filling their house with more overpriced items. He placed his damp glass on the table and smirked.

The orange pumpkin bowl was still perfectly centered on the table. Walter selected a tiny Snickers bar, which he unwrapped and popped into his mouth. The smooth chocolate taste intensified the last dregs of scotch still on his palate.

He grabbed his wallet from the console drawer and placed it in his rear right pant pocket. Walter glanced at his older generation silver encased iPhone resting next to Elizabeth's brand new iPhone. She always had to have the latest, greatest, most expensive gadget. He picked up his phone—eight o'clock. The battery only had 15% life. Shit. He'd forgotten to charge it. Would it have enough juice? Screw it. He put the phone in his left breast shirt pocket then snatched the end of a worn, brown leather fob attached to a large grey Land Rover key.

Walter closed the console drawer, took two steps toward the front door and called out, "If you care, I'm leaving." Hearing no response, he heaved a big sigh then walked out the front door, slamming it behind him.

Turning the ignition of the Range Rover, Walter revved the engine. He adjusted the rear-view mirror and took one last look at his childhood home; a modest one-story ranch his wife had transformed into a garish trophy. Doric white columns now flanked an oversized portico while newly boxed windows jetted out from the kitchen and living rooms. As Elizabeth's designer had said, "a modest touch up" to fit in with the now affluent neighborhood. He shifted the car into drive and released the brake.

Flooring the gas pedal, he sprayed pea gravel in all directions as the Rover bolted out of the driveway onto Ridge Road.

CHAPTER 2

The Range Rover soared across the San Tomas Bridge onto Creek Drive. Walter looked in the rear view mirror then across the creek. The headlights illuminated the swollen creek from the previous day's rain and the patch of the undeveloped land beyond known as the meadow.

Why did he let greed cloud his better judgment, setting in motion the plan that would forever change this last pristine piece of land?

Walter's phone rang.

He grabbed it and looked at the display. It was Elizabeth. He had made up his mind. He was going to show Nate the video. Walter returned the phone to the center console then lowered his window.

The cool air and smell of damp marsh grass from the creek slightly settled Walter's nerves. He unbuttoned the top of his shirt then ran his fingers through his gray hair.

Nate lived on Creek Drive but which house?

Walter grabbed the phone then glanced at the road ahead. He passed the intersection of Elder Ave, noticed the yellow Dead End sign and continued on Creek Drive. As he scrolled through his contacts, Walter saw headlights from another vehicle in the rear view mirror. He spotted Nate's number and placed the call.

Voicemail.

Walter clenched the steering wheel and glanced at his side mirror. He wanted to talk with Nate in person. Tell him why he didn't show up for the debate. He didn't know Nate well but felt he could trust him, especially after showing him the video.

The car behind came closer and turned on its high beams.

Walter squinted as the headlights reflected off the rear view mirror and temporarily blinded him. He tapped the brakes lightly as the Rover crossed the center median of the damp winding road.

"Jerk!" Walter blurted out as he swerved back into the right lane.

The lush vegetation cast deep shadows and intermittent houses along the creek left little light for Walter to judge the road ahead. The car tailing him only made his inability to see and increasing anxiety worse.

The headlights disappeared from the rear view mirror and moved to the center of the road. A black jeep, accelerated past. Walter threw up his middle finger and yelled, "Asshole!"

The jeep sped ahead, rounded the bend and disappeared from view.

Walter reached for his phone again. He glanced down to place the call, raised the phone to his left ear then looked ahead as he turned the steering wheel, anticipating the bend in the road.

Red brake lights. The black jeep was stopped in the middle of the road next to a pedestrian bridge.

Walter's heart pounded as adrenaline took over.

Grabbing the steering wheel with both hands, Walter slammed on the brakes, swerving into the center median and then back across the road towards the creek. The tires screeching across the wet pavement jolted Walter back to reality. He pumped the brakes one last time.

The anti-lock brakes abruptly sent vibrations through the Rover as it came to a sudden stop on a ledge next to the pedestrian bridge. The front passenger wheel dangled above the creek.

Walter did not move. He held his breath.

The dirt ledge collapsed.

The three-ton Rover slid forward then rolled on its side. Walter felt the "thud" and "crunch" of each turn as the heavy vehicle repeatedly toppled over its side. The loud whoosh of the side air bags deploying distracted Walter. He looked back over his shoulder and saw a red glow of taillights. The loud "crack" of wood splintering twisted the car upright and sent it plunging towards the creek. Walter looked back at the front windshield as the Rover slammed headfirst into water deploying the front airbags.

Walter screamed. The cool Nylon pummeled his face then tore his right arm from the steering wheel, smashing it into the passenger headrest. The Rover pitched up into the air, landing belly up on a partially submerged tree it had taken out.

"What the fuck?" Walter said as he found himself pinned against the seat belt, suspended upside down, his left arm hugging the airbag while his right dangled in the air.

Walter felt pain in his right arm. He jabbed at the airbag with his left hand until it was batted down enough for him to touch his right arm. A hot flash of pain seared through his body. He didn't have to see it. His arm was broken.

He looked around for his phone but then saw water pouring in through the open window. He frantically grabbed at his seat belt with his left hand but could not release it.

The cold creek water brushed up against his hair and then brow. Walter raised his torso into the air and grabbed the steering wheel with his left hand for support as he lifted his head out of the water.

The water leveled off.

"Oh my god," Walter said as he surveyed the tight quarters. The vehicle was ruined. Elizabeth would be furious.

The sound of splashing water made Walter turn his head toward the open window.

"Are you okay?" a woman's voice called out.

From the shimmery glow of the headlights bouncing off the water, Walter saw a figure wading through the creek towards the Rover.

"Thank God," Walter said. With his left leg, he tried to

shimmy his foot up, past the airbag to kick at the door latch. The door wouldn't open. He was stuck.

"I broke my arm. I can't get out," Walter called out.

"Let me see what I can do," the woman offered.

Walter smiled as the woman swam up to the Rover and grabbed onto the window frame and looked into the car. From the light of the instrument panel, he saw a young woman with long, wet, dark hair, blue eyes and scarlet smile that somehow comforted him.

The woman glanced at Walter then peered behind him into the back of the Rover. "Anyone else with you?"

"No, just me."

"Do you have an phone, we can call for help?"

Walter looked down into the murky water and shook his head.

The woman tried to open the door then paused and looked to the front and then back of the Rover. She disappeared from view.

Walter felt the car rock back and forth as the cold creek water splashed up into his face. "What the hell?"

The woman returned to view. "Sorry. There's a branch blocking your door and the car's pinned in. You think you can get out through the window?"

"I can't. Seatbelt's stuck. And my right arm's no good."

The woman pursed her lips then ran her tongue over her porcelain white teeth. She looked up at Walter and slowly cocked her head to the side. "How'd you end up down here?"

"There was a jeep. Stopped in the middle of the road. I swerved. You must've seen it?"

"It's a shame." The woman stroked the Burl Walnut paneling on the inside of the door.

"What?"

"Such a nice car. A Rover?"

"Yeah...a Range Rover."

The woman leaned back and looked off at the embankment. "Sorry to tell you this buddy, but it's totaled."

"I figured but can you help me get out?"

The woman's smile disappeared as she leaned in towards

Walter and said abruptly, "They wanted the car undamaged."

"They?" Walter froze. "Who are you?"

Without answering, the woman swam back to the embankment and with cat like reflexes, leapt up onto the tree branch holding the car in place and feverishly jumped up and down.

The car swayed back and forth as the tree branch slowly fragmented. Walter could hear the nail-scraping-chalkboard screech of metal tearing away from wood.

The Rover trembled as it broke away from the splintered branch, slid off the tree onto its side, submerging the entire driver's side compartment.

Walter tried to scream but only gulped in the muddy creek water. He clawed at the airbag, the dashboard and tried to grab onto the leather-trimmed seats. He kicked at the gas and brake pedals. He flailed his left arm at the door latch but suddenly felt his chest become very heavy. The water was clogging his throat. He wasn't breathing. He was choking. Walter blinked his eyes several times as his arms and legs became sluggish and unresponsive. He gulped one last time and then became still.

A single string of air bubbles came to the surface of the creek and then there was nothing.

CHAPTER 3

"God damn it." The blue-eyed, brunette cursed as she lifted her mud encased Ferragamo boot from the steep wet embankment of the creek. Making her way back to the road, she shook her foot, sending streams of dark brown muck in all directions.

When she reached the black jeep, the woman opened the driver side door, illuminating the interior of the car. She leaned inside and pulled the rear view mirror toward her. "Fucking A!" She wiped her face on the wet sleeve of her black, velvet Anthropologie blazer. The woman stomped back to the trunk, and opened the flatbed, pulled out a Louis Vuitton duffle bag and rummaged through it. She laid out a pair of True Religion jeans, a black camisole, a raven Burberry velour jacket, and black Reef sandals.

Slipping out of her muddy boots, she stripped off her wet clothes to reveal deep tan lines around two perfectly augmented breasts and a manicured patch of dark hair down below. She wiped the excess moisture from her toned body and shivered. As she quickly dressed, she heard the sound of her phone.

The woman grabbed the pile of wet clothes, stuffed them into the trunk, closed the flat bed, slipped on her sandals then dashed to the driver side door and hopped in as she heard the fourth ring.

She clawed at her brown leather Fendi handbag and pulled out a skull and crossbones silver bedazzled Samsung phone. A Glock 26, 9mm pistol with a 12 round extendable magazine peeked out from under the purse. She looked at the phone display "Ruby," and rolled her eyes. She hesitated before answering. "Hello."

"Courtney?" a low, hoarse voice whispered.

"Yep. It's me, Ruby." Courtney closed the car door. "I can barely hear you."

"Deal with it. I've got people around me."

Silence.

"So is it done?" Ruby whispered.

"Yeah. But not exactly as we'd planned." Courtney placed the phone on the dashboard and hit the speaker button.

"What happened? Did the wife get in the way?"

"Not exactly. When I got to his house, he was already in his car." Courtney grabbed a black ponytail band from the center consul and angled the rear view mirror in her direction. She put the band in her mouth as she used her hands to slick back her wet hair.

"What did you do?"

Courtney pulled her hair into a tight, low ponytail then wrapped the band around. "You told me not to let him leave the house without getting his phone so I followed him. He drove down to Creek Drive–"

"That's where Nate Crawford lives," Ruby blurted out.

"Nate Crawford?" Courtney questioned.

"Shit. The video," Ruby muttered under her breath.

"What video? Is that why you want Walter's phone?"

"Never mind that. Did he make it to Nate's house?"

"I got ahead of him and parked in the middle of the road. I thought he'd stop. But he lost control and crashed down into the creek."

"The car is damaged?"

"Why do you care about the car–"

"Is he dead?"

"Isn't that what you wanted?"

Silence.

"How did you do it?" Ruby whispered.

"He was stuck upside down in the car with an open window. It'll look like he drowned."

"Then he's really dead?"

"Yeah but I'm pissed off." Courtney looked back at the creek. "My clothes are destroyed and I didn't get any pleasure in –" She looked at the road ahead as she adjusted the rear view mirror back in place. "You better reimburse me for my outfit."

"Shut up you spoiled little brat. You'll do exactly as I say or I'll get your daddy to cut off his pampered debutant for good."

Courtney narrowed her eyes. "Don't make idle threats you can't back up. You don't even know my dad."

"You owe me. I don't know your father but one call from me and that trust fund of yours will disappear."

Courtney closed her eyes and rolled her tongue over her teeth. "I'm just mad because Walter was a good looking man. The things I wanted to do to him—"

"Do you know if Walter told Nate anything?"

"Who is Nate?" Courtney started the car and lowered the driver side window.

"What about Walter's phone? Did you get it from the car?"

Courtney shook her head and smirked. "No phone could have survived the creek."

"I'm not asking you to speculate. I need facts."

Courtney looked back at the creek then at her fresh, dry clothes. "If Walter had it, it's in the car under water. We don't have to worry about it."

"You took care of Walter and now I need the phone. I want it found wet or dry. We're not done until I have it in my hands."

Courtney bit her lower lip and lied. "Okay. I'll go look for it now."

"Good. Then take care of the wife."

"I'll go back after I look for the phone." Courtney released the parking brake.

"Can you get the wife to talk? *Without* killing her?"

"Definitely. I don't swing that way." Courtney smiled as she ended the call.

A cool breeze drifted through the car as Courtney made a U-turn, punched the gas pedal and sped back up Creek Drive towards the hills above Oakview.

CHAPTER 4
Wednesday

Kate Crawford adjusted her eyes to the dim morning light then glanced at her heart rate monitor, 6:30 AM. Her long strawberry blonde hair was pulled tight into a ponytail with a thin black headband just above her hairline. She didn't like the feel of wispy bangs against her face when she ran. She yanked Dillon, her fluffy blonde golden retriever, by the leash as they continued running down the street. Gray clouds danced in the translucent sky as a light wind gathered in the trees along the creek and swayed the branches from side to side. Kate was on Creek Drive, not far from her childhood home, out for her usual morning run heading towards the pedestrian bridge.

She couldn't stop thinking about the NDA. Why would something so routine go missing? Brett couldn't answer her questions, which was strange. Since they had started dating, he had never withheld information from her even though it was against company policy. It must be the IPO.

As she neared the bridge, Kate spotted the yellow caution tape and was instantly reminded of the previous night's events. Her father was the newly elected member of the Oakview City Council and his opponent, Walter Rudolph, was dead. The officer arrived at her parent's front door right after the election results were announced.

Dillon barked at the tiny black birds perched on the bridge handrails, scattering them in all directions. Kate stopped under the streetlight and exhaled a groan at the sight of a black jeep parked by the steps. She hated when people blocked the entrance to the bridge.

Before continuing, Kate decided to check out the scene. She slowly stepped over the yellow tape, past the deep tire grooves embedded in the wet ground. Looking over the embankment, Kate spotted a jagged crown of a tree stump half way down.

Something splashed in the water under the bridge. Dillon's ears perked up. He broke away from Kate, jumped over the caution tape and ran down the embankment. Kate followed Dillon with her eyes but soon lost his silhouette in the dark shadows.

Kate called out for Dillon but he did not return. She cautiously stumbled down the dark, muddy embankment until she came to a small ledge just above the water. Dillon lay crouched on his hindquarters barking at the water. Kate laughed when she saw he was barking at his own dark reflection. She knelt down and stroked his back.

"Enough," Kate laughed. "Let's go for that run."

Climbing back up, something lodged in the embankment twinkled in the streetlight. Kate knelt down by her foot and saw a silver rectangular object fixed in the mud. She reached past a clump of brown leaves and pulled out a silver encased phone. Taking a closer look, she saw that it was an older generation iPhone. She pushed the power button but got no response. Kate put the phone in her pant pocket.

Dillon tried to return to the creek. Kate grabbed his leash and pulled him up. When they reached the road, she took one last look at the creek then turned and squeezed past the black jeep onto the bridge.

As Kate and Dillon ran across the bridge, a dark figure emerged from the murky water and watched them pass over.

CHAPTER 5

Stratus clouds gathered from the east and turned a dusty rose as Kate and Dillon emerged from the dense vegetation along the creek. She deliberately paced herself to beat her internal clock of seven minutes per mile. It wasn't as fast as her cross-country days in college but it was the motivation she needed. The recent rain left muddy pockets of small puddles along the dirt trail leading across the open field. Dillon leaped in and out of the small reflection pools as they passed.

Red and yellow leaves gave way to dying brown grass as the path veered away from the creek and split the meadow in half, the oxidized wire mesh of the community garden on one side and the vacant land once occupied by the Convent on the other.

A white crane stood in the middle of the field. It slowly moved its long neck from side to side as if to gain a better view of the intruders then flapped its wings and effortlessly lifted itself up into the air and disappeared into the trees.

Kate released Dillon from the leash and watched him gleefully sprint ahead. She inhaled the fresh smell of wet earth and exhaled her morning grogginess.

Halfway across the field, she passed the old cement foundations of the Convent. Tall clusters of yellow and white yarrow raised their flat petals above the burnt grass and thick green empty pumpkin vines that wound around the patches of cement blocks. She sometimes stopped here to remember her sister but today she was behind schedule. Kate wiped away beads of sweat dripping down the side of her face as she ran towards the service road.

The service road was the dividing line between the town of Oakview and Altamont Heights and ran the length of the meadow. The rooftops of the Sinclair Shopping Center buildings were just visible above the trees behind the road. The service road snaked through oak trees then disappeared into a canopy of sycamore behind an old red brick wall that surrounded St. James Seminary.

Keeping her pace, Kate gazed onto the vast open space. She could hear birds chirping as they began to wake in the trees. A deer grazed in the distance. The muffled sound of Dillon's paws pacing across the dead oak leaves and redwood needles reminded her of the solitude this area provided. How could the Sinclairs want to develop it into a gigantic office park? Kate glanced in the direction of the service road then back at the remains of the Convent. She decided to forego her usual run through the shopping center.

Her eyes came to rest on the entrance to the Seminary. Two brick pillars supported a rusted wrought-iron gate. Kate had never dared step foot on the grounds of the Seminary. She stopped and looked back at the dilapidated cement ruins. Even after twenty years, she couldn't believe her sister committed suicide. Kate may have been only five at the time, but her memories of Jenny were happy, bright and joyful. Why would she have thrown herself off the roof of the Convent because of a boy, even if he were Logan Sinclair? If the Convent was this close to the Seminary, why didn't someone hear or see something the night Jenny died?

Kate ran to the brick wall then headed along the perimeter back towards the creek. The wall came to an abrupt end five feet from a natural ledge above the water. Time and erosion had taken its toll as pieces of brick had splintered from the wall and crumbled down into the creek. Kate looked over her shoulder for Dillon. He was completely consumed by the smells in the meadow.

She easily hopped over the crumbling wall and walked towards the back of the Seminary. She passed through a grove of oak trees and dense low shrubbery that nipped at her left arm. Distracted by the scratch on her arm, she walked into something hard and stumbled backward. She looked down and spotted a dark gray rectangular headstone. She looked around her surroundings and spotted at least five more. Kate was standing in the middle of an old graveyard.

Crouching down for a better view, Kate could barely read an inscription hidden behind years of grime. She rubbed the stone with the corner of her shirt. In the dim morning light, Kate read the epitaph:

Rupert Sinclair (1863-1910)
An Eye for an Eye
Now All is Right in the World

A Sinclair was buried in this distant, forgotten area of the Seminary grounds? Kate looked up and saw through the trees the back of the Seminary with its gray, shingled roof, and off-white trimmed dormers. She stood and continued to walk towards the building.

Upon reaching the clearing between the grove of oak trees and the back of the Seminary, Kate stopped. She was surprised to see no manicured lawns or gardens. Dead amber grass grew right up to the side of the gray foundation of the brick building. Three floors of windows led up to the off-white dormers. Looking closer, she realized the dormers and the entire structure had not been cleaned or painted in some time. The building was slowly decaying with the surrounding landscape.

Kate glanced at her heart rate monitor. 7:00. It was time to head back and get ready for the day. She took one last look at the Seminary, hoping it could provide some answer about her sister's death.

A hooded figure dressed completely in black appeared from the side of the building. The shadow started to walk towards her. Something didn't seem right. Kate instinctively turned around and ran back to the brick wall. She called for Dillon and ran through the meadow towards the old concrete foundation of the Convent.

Jumping over a crumbled cement block, a hard object struck the back of Kate's knees. As she fell forward, Kate felt pressure against her right shoulder pushing her deeper into the damp earth.

Someone was on Kate's back. She pushed her palms into the ground and lifted her body up as she felt a hand grab her right thigh.

Kate twisted her body around to face her attacker. She glimpsed a dark hooded figure as she was slammed back down to the ground on her back.

He was trying to straddle Kate's pelvis with his knees as he held down her arms with both his hands. Drops of water fell from her attacker onto Kate's face.

Kate kicked her knee up into his groin but nothing happened. Instead he held both of her hands with one of his as he reached down and touched her right thigh.

Kate looked back over her head onto the dry leaves and screamed, "Dillon!"

Dillon sprinted over then stopped. He started barking ferociously at the pair rolling around on the ground.

"Dillon. Help! Get him! Get him" Kate pleaded.

Dillon instantly jumped on the attacker and latched on to his arm.

The dark figure rolled off Kate then kicked Dillon in the gut. When Dillon released, the figure got up and ran away.

CHAPTER 6

Kate sat at her desk, staring at the brick office building across the street and the yellow leaves of the trees below. She spun around and looked outside her office door into the hallway at the bank of cubicles occupied by the inside sales team. Over the past four years, the software company Obsidian had expanded onto five floors of the Bank of Bay building in the trendy Altamont Heights downtown area but was now busting at the seams. Kate tried to concentrate on her work but she was still on edge by what had transpired earlier that morning.

Dillon had always been her front line of defense. She never imaged anyone would attack her while he was by her side. Then she remembered Dillon had been off his leash. Brett had insisted on calling the police but she couldn't tell them much. Had she kneed the guy in the groin? Or was it Dillon who saved her? All she saw was someone in a dark hooded sweatshirt. There was nothing the police could do but take a report and alert the public. Thank God she had been left unharmed.

Her mind focused back on the missing NDA for Cayenne and the meeting with Fortunato. She reached down for her brown leather valise and pulled out her laptop. A silver twinkle at the bottom of the bag caught her attention.

Kate reached in and grabbed the silver iPhone she had found at the creek. She opened a desk drawer and located a compatible cable and charger. She walked over to the file cabinet in the corner of her office and plugged it in the outlet behind. If any good could come of this morning it would be to figure out the owner of the phone and return it to them.

A ringing sound came from Kate's purse. She returned to her desk, pulled out her brand new white iPhone and smiled at the caller ID. "Jessica."

"I hate to say it but I didn't expect your dad to win. What a total, major upset," Jessica responded.

"I know. Crazy."

"You've got to tell your dad congratulations. But what about Rudolph? How did that happen?"

"I know. The cops showed up last night to ask us questions."

"You guys? Did they suspect foul play?"

Kate spun around and looked outside at the cityscape. A line of young children dressed in rain jackets and boots paraded across the intersection below. "No, no. You know the creek by my parents' house?"

"Yeah."

"He crashed his car down into it and drowned."

"That seems kind of odd."

"Don't get all Sherlock and make something out of nothing."

"Sorry. It's the reporter in me. Doesn't it seem odd that Walter Rudolf would die the night of the election?"

"If Walter was alive today, he still wouldn't be able to vote for the Cross Creek project. He didn't win."

"Maybe he knew too much about Cross Creek so the Sinclairs got rid of him."

"You can't be serious?"

"Maybe your sister Jenny knew something about the Sinclairs and they got rid of her?"

Kate tapped her index finger on the arm of her chair. "Did you find any evidence to support that? Because all I've ever been told is Jenny killed herself."

"Well no. But I've only been searching for stuff on the Sinclair family since you called me on Monday."

"So what did you find out?"

"I couldn't find anything online about their real estate deals prior to 1986; the files haven't been digitized yet."

"What do you mean?"

"You have to go the San Jose Daily offices or the California room at the King Library in downtown San Jose to view the originals or at least the microfiche."

Kate spun around in her chair and looked at the calendar on her laptop. Her manager Amy had sent her a meeting request. Without looking at the context she replied "Yes."

"What about Logan Sinclair, William Sinclair's son?"

"He's a ghost. He graduated from Altamont Heights and then nothing. The only information I was able to find about a Logan Sinclair was on a web site for an Italian company called Fortunato."

Kate already knew this bit of information but couldn't let Jessica know.

"According to the website, he has a Computer Science doctorate from the University of Trento. That's it. No bio. Not even a photo," Jessica said.

"Anything else?"

"Is there something you're not telling me?"

Kate hesitated. Jessica was her best friend. They'd known each other since the first day of 6th grade at Valencia. Attending an all-girl school for seven years had made them life-long friends. But Jessica was a reporter for the Seattle Tribune and she couldn't disclose the real reason Logan Sinclair was of interest to Kate after all these years. If Cayenne hadn't left a voice message inquiring about their NDA, she might have overlooked the similarities between Cayenne and Fortunato's products. But making accusations now would do no good if she had no proof. She'd lose her job. "Maybe next time you're down here to plan the wedding we can go look for those newspaper articles?"

"Kate, what are you hiding? You don't sound right."

Kate let out a deep sigh. "I was attacked this morning while running in the meadow."

"What? Are you okay?"

Kate noticed the time on her laptop monitor. 10:05 AM. She looked over at her calendar application. "Shit!" She stood up at her desk and started toward her office door.

"What?"

"I'm fine, fine. Just a little shaken. Listen, I've got a meeting with my manager right now. I've got to go."

"No worries. Be careful."

"I will. Let's catch up later. Bye." Kate ended the call and ran down the hall towards her manager's office.

CHAPTER 7

Nate Crawford sat quietly in the sleek, sterile tenth floor lobby of Sinclair Enterprises as he arched his back trying to lessen the pain. With salt and pepper hair highlighting his olive skin and caramel colored eyes, he was roguishly handsome at sixty. Deep wrinkles in his forehead made him appear very serious, but when he smiled his eyes lit up. In that moment, you could still see the young man despite the weathered road he had traveled earlier in life.

He scanned the lobby for a familiar face. He had just won a seat on the Oakview City Council, but had never stepped foot inside these offices. But everyone knew all about the family and the building. Though the Sinclair name remained on the gold plaque outside, the Altamont Heights address was all a facade. Two years before, Verano Industries had acquired the building but allowed the Sinclairs to retain the office space through the deal. Renee Verano, Nate's business partner and the Sinclair's nemesis in all things real estate, considered it her greatest triumph. Nate agreed.

A glass receptionist desk, two white couches, and four white chairs filled the lobby. Architectural drawings, photos and models of projects the Sinclairs had developed over the years decorated the walls and corner spaces.

What was taking so long? Nate had been waiting for over twenty minutes. They had called him. They wanted to meet.

Looking around the lobby, Nate recognized the projects on the walls. He smiled as most had been completed over a decade ago.

Nate's iPhone rang. He looked at the display: Renee Verano.

"You're meeting with William?" Renee asked slowly.

"How'd you find out?" Nate whispered as he stood and walked into the corner away from the receptionist.

"I called your house. Vivian told me. What's going on? Does this have anything to do with Kate being attacked this morning?"

"I doubt it. William's assistant called around 9 AM. She asked if I could meet with him today."

"Who would want to attack Kate?"

"The police think it was just random," Nate said as he massaged his lower back.

"Random. Just like Jenny. It stinks of the Sinclairs. That's why William wants to see you this morning. Why else would he contact you so quickly? We thought he'd wait until after you were installed. He must be more desperate than we thought."

"I hear what you're saying. Before we jump to any conclusions, let's see what he wants."

"Be careful what you say."

"Renee, you don't have to worry. He's scrambling because of the election. I'm sure he just wants to establish some form of relationship since I'll be the swing vote on Cross Creek."

"Amazing!"

"What?"

"How quickly he called you today when he never returned any of your calls back when Jenny died."

Nate clenched his jaw then slowly gnashed his teeth from side to side. "I know. But I can't play that card just yet."

"Now you have the upper hand. Bring up the past and use it to get what we want."

The young blonde receptionist approached Nate. "Excuse me Mr. Crawford. Mr. Sinclair will see you now."

23

"I'll call you back later," Nate said as he abruptly ended the call.

"Follow me," the receptionist said.

The receptionist opened the door to William's office and motioned for Nate to step inside.

The office had the same style elements from the lobby except for the large mahogany executive desk in the center of the room. With its leather inlay surface, intricate paneling and the hand carved "S" detail on the legs it looked like an antique. A silver computer monitor, banker desk lamp and two pewter frames finished off the top.

One frame contained a close up profile image of Maria Sinclair with her Cindy Crawford mole above her right lip. Maria was looking away from the camera and laughing. She wore a white tunic with a swirling peach, yellow and orange design. Her signature jaw length blonde bob was perfectly styled.

The other photo had William shaking hands with Sander Walker? Nate took a double take. The man in question wore rectangular black-framed glasses and was standing behind a large Obsidian sign. It had to be Sander. The men were both dressed in formal black suits and appeared to be on stage at a party. Why would William have this photo in his office?

William walked up to Nate and shook his hand. "Congratulations on your win last night."

William commanded attention with his imposing 6' 4" frame. He enjoyed talking down to people as it made him feel important. He easily played the role of a seemingly wealthy titan with his brown leathery skin and white hair. But it was his incessant smiling that often made you wonder what he was really thinking.

"Thank you," Nate said.

William walked over to the receptionist, placed his hand around her waist, winked and said, "That will be all for now."

The receptionist closed the door behind her. William and Nate stood apart from one another in uncomfortable silence.

William walked back over to his desk, turned around and faced Nate. He spread his lips to reveal an overly white smirk and proceeded to stare at Nate without blinking.

Nate didn't move.

"It was my great grandfather's," William finally said breaking the silence.

"Excuse me?"

William tilted his head back. "I saw you eyeing my desk when you first walked in. It's a real antique. Brought all the way from Pennsylvania in the late 1800s."

"It's quite impressive," Nate said.

"Thank you. Please take a seat," William motioned to a white chair in front of the desk. William leaned up against the desk and sat on the edge in front of Nate. "It's unfortunate that your win comes under such tragic, unexpected circumstances.

"Walter Rudolf?"

"Yes. He was a good friend of ours. What a shame he had to go like that."

"Yes it is." Nate coughed in his hand as he arched his back, straining to relieve the lower back pain. "How's that Cross Creek project coming along?"

William looked away from Nate and focused on his hands. "You get right to the point don't you?" He slowly twisted a gold ring with a silver crest in the shape of an 'S' on his right hand ring finger. "How's that son of yours?"

Nate narrowed his eyes. "Why did you ask me here this morning?"

"We've never formally met. I thought considering the circumstances we should get acquainted."

"Now that we've met, what do you really want?"

"I don't want anything." William stood and walked behind his desk to the floor to ceiling windows. He looked out across the Altamont Heights skyline towards the San Thomas Hills and threaded his fingers together behind his back. "I just wanted to personally invite you to our annual fundraiser. Maria's worked on it all year. It's called the Din for Grins Gala and it's tonight. All proceeds benefit Maria's foundation that mends cleft palates of the poor youth of Central America.

We're asking $2,500 a head. There will be dinner, dancing and a silent auction."

"Thank you for the invitation but I'm—"

"I'd like to invite your whole family to join Maria and me as our guests."

Nate remained silent.

William walked back and sat on the edge of the desk. "No strings attached. Just a nice gesture. All the Oakview City Council members have been invited. They'll all be there tonight as our guests—gratis."

The two men stared at each other, wondering who would make the next move. Nate looked at the photo of Maria and then Sander. "I can't guarantee my entire family can make it, but I will definitely be there."

William padded Nate on the shoulder and gestured for him to stand. The meeting was over.

As they walked towards the door, William said, "After you take office next month, we should get together for lunch and discuss business."

The two men shook hands.

"Yes. I look forward to the opportunity," Nate said.

"Good. My girl will call to set it up," William said as he opened the door. "Thanks for stopping in today. I look forward to seeing you and your family at our fundraiser tonight."

CHAPTER 8

"Sorry I'm late," Kate offered as she closed the door to her manager's office, nicknamed, The Palace, for its elaborate furnishings and décor.

"Please sit down." Amy was sitting with her back to Kate in a tight black mesh Herman Miller Aeron chair.

Kate was careful not to step on the expensive Ghom silk rug that lay under the L shaped desk as she maneuvered into the facing chair. The rug was placed to keep subordinates at a distance yet attract the attention and envy of peers and executives. When Amy was promoted to director these expensive accessories appeared and were strategically placed in plain view. Her close relationship with Sander was immediately scrutinized. Had she really earned the promotion?

As Kate sat down, her phone vibrated. She glanced at the display, Hashim Abbasi of Fortunato.

"Shouldn't you get that?" Amy spun around to reveal a new hairstyle of auburn shades and blond highlights cut into a blunt layered bob. Wearing a black Prada suit with her signature amber and ruby beaded necklace, Amy looked polished though a little severe. She glanced down at her open leather bound Samsung tablet and read some notes.

Kate ignored the comment. "I like your haircut," she offered as she put her phone in the front pocket of her skirt.

"Thanks," Amy said without looking up. She picked up

her Android, hit the vibrate button, placed it back on her desk then looked at Kate. "I see you were late getting in today."

Kate felt her face getting flush. She thought about the attack that morning. By the tone of her voice, Amy would see the incident as just another excuse Kate had dreamed up to distract from any inefficiencies at work. "Sorry. I won't let it happen again."

Amy sat back in her chair, resting her elbows on the armrest. "How's Cayenne doing?"

Kate stared at Amy like a deer in headlights. She couldn't breathe.

"They left me a number of messages. I just forwarded them to you. I expect you to handle your own accounts."

Kate's heart skipped a beat. She tried to find the words and finally blurted out, "Why are they calling you?"

"Kate you've got to be on top of your clients. Is that product of theirs close to being done? Or have they decided to scrap it?"

Kate thought about the NDA and the voice message Cayenne had left on Monday. That non-disclosure agreement was supposed to protect Cayenne's unreleased product, make it impossible for Obsidian to create a similar product. Knowing that the document was now missing, she wanted to check with legal before telling Amy anything. An NDA doesn't just go missing. "Soon."

"We need a precise date. You should be in contact with them every day. When was the last time you went up to Seattle?"

Kate was baffled. Amy had not asked about Cayenne for several months. And she rarely cared about any account Kate was handling. "Back in August."

Amy raised her hands. "When we both went up there? That's not good enough. You are overdue for another visit."

Should she tell Amy about the voice message the guys from Cayenne left her last night? Kate hesitated.

Amy noticed Kate's hesitation. "What is it?"

"I'm meeting with them later today."

Amy narrowed her eyes and studied Kate's face.

Kate stared back at Amy without batting an eyelash. She wasn't intimidated, just annoyed.

"Why didn't you say something sooner?" Leaning back in her chair, Amy looked out the window. "How well do you know Sander?"

Kate did not know how to respond. "Excuse me?"

"Have you socialized with him outside of work?"

Now Kate was baffled. "No."

Amy pursed her lips and looked back at Kate. "That's right. You're seeing Brett."

Kate refused to discuss her personal life. That line of questioning was insulting enough. "Why all the questions?"

Amy leaned forward, cocked her head to the side then looked directly at Kate. "I'm just wondering how someone like you gets assigned an account by Sander himself."

Kate tried not to smile. Sander assigned Fortunato to her personally? Kate had been in meetings with Sander but had never spoken to him. "I didn't know that."

"Well I'm telling you now. What do you know about Fortunato?"

"Not much–" Kate began to say.

Amy rolled her eyes. "If Sander personally assigned this account to you, you better know everything about the company. You better have the pulse of the engineering team. And you better know why Sander has taken an interest in them or it'll make me look bad."

"Fortunato is out of Italy. The founder is Logan Sinclair. He's the son of the Sinclairs of Altamont Heights."

Amy stared blankly at Kate without responding.

"The Sinclairs are wealthy real estate developers here in the Bay Area," Kate added.

"I don't care about his lineage. Have you spoken with him?"

"Not yet. But I did speak with his lead engineer, Hashim Abbasi. Their product is called Mirage and it sounds similar to what Cayenne's doing."

"I doubt that."

"It's a social photo and video collaboration product.

Hashim says it's a game changer that will blow Instagram and YouTube out of the water when you combine it with our products, Facebook and Twitter. It will disrupt entertainment as we know it."

Amy nodded her head.

"And I've scheduled the meeting for tomorrow."

Amy's eyes opened wide. "Why wasn't I invited?"

Kate felt her cheeks become hot. Amy never attended first meetings. She began to stumble over her words. "I...I...intended to."

"If Sander's going to be in the meeting, I need to be there."

Kate sat paralyzed by this new information. She slowly asked, "Sanders going to be in the meeting?"

"Yes. That's why I called you in here. He sent me a message about it this morning."

Kate gulped. Her CEO never attended early meetings with a new account. He's going to see the similarities between Mirage and Cayenne's products. Now finding the NDA for Cayenne was even more important.

"Don't mess this one up. Fortunato must be important for Sander. Don't make me look bad by not doing your homework. Everything must be perfect."

Kate stared directly at Amy determined not to be unnerved by her patronizing comments. "Amy. I can handle it."

"I hope so." Amy typed a note on her tablet. Looking Kate squarely in the face, she continued, "In the future, "cc" me on all correspondence with Fortunato and Sander." Amy swiveled her chair around to the other side of her desk. Their meeting was over.

Kate walked back to her office in a blur of confused excitement. Amy was jealous. She was the gatekeeper with Sander. Now it seemed Kate would be able to communicate directly with him. She was thrilled as no other account manager in their group had been allowed this opportunity.

Knowing that Sander had personally selected her to mange Fortunato made Kate smile. Amy usually gave her the least strategic accounts. For once Kate actually felt valued. And by Sander himself.

Through all this excitement, Kate was puzzled by the sudden disappearance of Cayenne's NDA. Especially since Fortunato's product sounded so similar to Cayenne's product. Unprotected ideas in Silicon Valley are stolen every day, but if something happened under Kate's watch with her signature on the NDA, she would be held accountable. It could not only cost her job but Obsidian's lucrative stock options.

She grabbed her phone and sent a text to her boyfriend Brett:

Call me

CHAPTER 9

"You're going to have to clear your schedule for the next month," Sander Walker said to Brett McCormick.

"What?" Brett asked as he looked up from his iPad. He ran his fingers through his thick dark brown, messy layered mop. His previous employer had frowned upon this sort of style. At Obsidian, no one cared. He was trying to focus on what Sander was saying, but was distracted, thinking about Kate. He should have been with her this morning on her run. Work was getting in the way of their relationship.

The two men were meeting in a conference room outside of Sander's office. Brett sat at the head of the long oval table surrounded by eight chairs. His legs were extended and feet crossed resting on the edge of the table. After six months, he had adjusted quite well to the casual work environment at Obsidian. With all that had happened this morning, Brett still looked Valley chic in khaki slacks and navy blue Polo. Sander stood casually dressed in a white button down shirt and straight leg Citizens of Humanity jeans. He adjusted his signature rectangular glasses as he stood by the floor to ceiling windows. His dark brown hair had just enough curl to make a preppy rocker style work.

Gazing out the window, Sander slowly twisted the beaded chain on the beige vertical blinds concealing then revealing the outside world. "I want you to join me in New York on Tuesday when we ring the opening bell for the NASDAQ."

"Seriously?" Brett responded enthusiastically as he took his feet off the table and sat up in his chair.

Sander walked around the table and sat on the edge next to Brett. He leaned over and placed his hand on Brett's shoulder. "You're the first to know."

Brett looked down at Sander's hand but dared not move. "How'd you make that happen?"

Sander released his hand and crossed his arms. "Let's just say someone owed me a favor."

Brett set down his iPad. "I don't know how you do it. This is great news. What a way to launch our IPO. I can see the headlines–"

"Let's keep this quiet for now. I want to create a buzz and there's nothing better than a surprise like this for our employees and investors. Let's wait to release any press about it until Monday."

"Good point."

Sander walked over to the windows and looked onto the San Thomas Hills. "We'll fly out Monday afternoon and then–" Sander paused.

"And then?"

Sander looked back at Brett, "Will Kate mind?"

"Kate?" Brett was confused. He had gotten to know Sander pretty well over the last six months but they had never spoken about their personal lives.

"Kate Crawford. How did you land her?" Sander laughed.

Brett sat back in his chair. "Excuse me?"

"Don't be such a prude McCormick. What's the big deal? She's smoking hot. Just wondering what it's like, you know, to bang her."

Brett felt his blood pressure rise at the callousness of Sander's remark, but tried to stay calm. He considered his words carefully. "Kate's a great girl. I'm really lucky."

Sander narrowed his eyes then smiled. "I'm just fucking with you."

Brett breathed a sigh of relief. Sander could be mercurial,

but this was a side he had never seen.

"I do need to know I can trust you; that I can tell you anything and you won't tell Kate.

Brett nodded his head as he sat forward and placed his hands on the table. "Trust me? Sander, that's my job. You know I can't disclose anything to the press or within the company without your knowledge. According to the confidentiality clause I signed, I'd be held liable."

"But girlfriends are different. They can get you into trouble."

Brett smirked as he relaxed into his chair. "Kate's no trouble. I wouldn't worry about her."

"You may think differently after you hear what's going to consume the rest of your year." Sander stood directly over Brett. "Sometimes girlfriends are not as understanding when you can't tell them what's really going on."

Brett looked up at Sander slightly annoyed by this line of questioning. "I've been working for Obsidian, managing PR for the last six months. Have I ever given you a reason to question my loyalty or commitment to Obsidian?"

Sander smiled as he sat in the chair next to Brett. "I knew when we recruited you away from Accenture that you were the right choice."

"Thank you," Brett responded slowly. Something was different about Sander. Why the paranoia? Perhaps it was stress from the IPO.

Sander placed his hands on the table next to Brett's iPad and spread his fingers as wide as they could go. "Here's the deal. We're buying another company. I don't want to go into specifics yet. The principals arrive this week to show me the final version. I'll need you to create the PR around it."

Brett smiled. Kate would be happy. She had assumed correctly that Cayenne had finally finished their product.

"They have an incredible product that will take Obsidian in a whole new direction. With this acquisition and the IPO, you're going to be pretty busy through the end of the year."

"That shouldn't be a problem."

"Kate is managing the company."

Brett played along. "That's why you've been grilling me about Kate. Does she know you're going to buy them?"

"Not now but soon. It must remain confidential until next month until we're out of the quiet period."

"Right, makes sense."

Brett looked down at his iPad, "But why keep Kate out of the loop? She must know there has been talk of an acquisition."

Sander relaxed his fingers and looked over at Brett, studying him. "I assigned the account to Kate on Monday. She doesn't know anything."

Brett tried to hide his confusion. Cayenne had been Kate's account for the past six months. He didn't want Sander to see that he and Kate did talk business.

Sander hovered in front of Brett. "The company is called Fortunato. Their product is Mirage."

Brett remained silent trying not to show any emotion as he felt Sander breathing down his neck.

"The CEO is an old friend of mine. Logan Sinclair."

CHAPTER 10

Vivian Crawford stood silently in front of the fireplace mantel. Her customary dark clothing clung to her willowy body emphasizing her slim figure. Her long dark hair with streaks of gray was slicked back in a low ponytail that accentuated her large grey eyes, gaunt cheekbones, pale skin and creased forehead. She wiped the last picture frame with the dust cloth then placed it back on display – a shrine to a family torn apart. Photos of Eric and Jenny in Halloween costumes dotted the mantel among the holiday and birthday celebrations. There were no framed childhood photos of Kate, only graduation photos from high school and college. Vivian stopped to look at one photo. It was the last one taken of all three children together.

Kate's strawberry blonde hair was up in pigtails. She wore a pink-checkered dress. Her nose already had the signature freckles. Eric held her hand. He stood tall in a yellow polo with the collar turned up and khaki pants, his hair slicked back to the side in a preppy style. Jenny stood next to Eric in a navy-blue pleated skirt with a pink polo shirt. Her long auburn hair held back from her face by a navy blue headband. The photo was taken in front of their craftsman style home on the twins' fifteenth birthday.

Nate walked into the room.

Vivian noticed but did not acknowledge him. Instead, she started to dust the picture frames again.

Nate sat down on the sage couch facing the fireplace and adjusted the crimson throw pillows behind his back. He folded his right leg over his left knee. "I decided to go."

Without turning around, Vivian asked, "Did you meet William Sinclair?"

"Yes. I did." Nate reached behind to adjust another pillow.

"What did that son of a bitch want?" Vivian threw the dust cloth on the mantel then turned around and rigidly sat in the worn brown leather chair next to the fireplace.

Nate started to laugh.

"What?" Vivian asked.

"He invited us to their damn Din for Grins fundraiser."

"That's tonight."

Nate grabbed another of the crimson pillows and held it tight to his chest. "What do you think?"

"I'm not going to give that Sinclair scum my money."

"We don't have to pay anything. We'll be their guests—all of us."

Vivian narrowed her eyes. "Seriously?"

"All four of us."

"Eric and Kate? You want Eric at this event? He's only been out of rehab for three weeks. Is that wise?"

"He's part of our family. He'll be fine. I'll keep an eye on him."

"No. I will." Vivian gripped the arms of the chair and then sat back. "What's William's motive?"

Nate arched his back and grimaced. "For what? Inviting us gratis to their fundraiser?"

"Exactly! Did he even mention Cross Creek? Did you bring up Jenny?"

"This was our first meeting," Nate said as he adjusted the pillow behind his back. "I couldn't walk in accusing his son of murder."

"But why invite us to the fundraiser? And why involve the rest of the family. Why Kate and Eric? Something doesn't seem right."

"At least I've got his attention."

"I don't like it. Now that Eric's back in our lives and you're campaigning against Cross Creek, Kate's bound to find out everything."

Nate stood and walked over to the fireplace as he massaged his lower back. He leaned on the mantel and looked at the photo of Kate's graduation from college. "When the time comes, we'll tell her. The important thing is for me to build a relationship with William."

Vivian rolled her eyes and shook her head. "He'll never tell you what really happened to Jenny."

"Don't be so sure. This Cross Creek project is everything to him."

Vivian guffawed, "Yeah right!"

Nate smiled and turned to face Vivian. "Cross Creek is William's last chance at maintaining the Sinclair image. I think that's why they're so willing to sell out the Seminary. They're desperate."

Vivian held up her hand. "I know what you and Renee have done."

Nate glanced at the photo of Jenny sitting on a pink bicycle, grinning from ear to ear. It was the twins' fifteenth birthday and this bike was her world. And it would be her last birthday gift. "Renee's the one who helped me get back on my feet after Jenny died. You weren't around."

Vivian winced. "That's a low blow."

Nate closed his eyes and sighed. "You're right. I'm sorry." He opened his eyes and looked at Vivian. "Let's concentrate on the present."

"I just want you to be careful."

"We always are."

"But look what happened to Walter. And why was Kate attacked this morning?"

"You think someone killed Walter and also went after Kate?" Nate returned to the couch and slowly sat down.

"Why not?"

"I doubt either of those things had to do with Cross Creek."

"Seems too coincidental. Especially since you also fell on your back the night of the debate." Vivian stood and walked to the large windows overlooking the redwood trees in the backyard. "What gardener over waters the flowerbed under the overhang in front of the civic center? Especially when it's been raining all day."

"That was my own fault."

"Really? This whole plan of yours puts me on edge."

"Walter drowned by accident. Kate, unfortunately, was randomly attacked. And I was just careless. These incidents have nothing to do with Renee's and my plans for the Sinclairs."

"Then why did Elizabeth Rudolf call you last night before Walter was found dead and bring up Jenny's death? I think you should go tell the police."

Nate shook his head. "It'll be just like last time. The police aren't going to listen to me. They won't do anything."

"You were elected to the city council. That should warrant five minutes of their time." Nate looked at his wristwatch. "Maybe tomorrow I can stop by city hall."

Vivian walked over to the couch and sat next to Nate. "Just promise me you won't involve Kate or Eric in your plan."

"I wouldn't do anything to put the kids in danger, okay?"

Vivian frowned. The last time Nate had said something like this, Jenny ended up dead.

Nate placed his hand on Vivian's shoulder.

Vivian flinched.

"Can you do me one thing?" Nate asked sincerely.

Vivian looked up at Nate.

"Vivian, I know sometimes you can't stand the sight of me. But we made a pack to stay together. I rarely ask anything of you."

Vivian looked down at her hands.

"Attend the fundraiser with me."

Vivian shook her head.

"Please be there by my side."

"Come on Viv. I really need your help"

Vivian slowly looked over at Nate. "You haven't called me Viv in a long time."

Nate offered her his hand. "Don't you think it's time we broke down this wall between us? We're so close to figuring this all out."

Vivian sighed and let Nate take her hand in his. "It'll never be the same between the two of us."

Nate looked down at their hands but did not say anything.

"You'll never forgive me," Vivian continued.

Nate looked up at Vivian. "It's been a long time since Jenny died. We decided to stick together. With Eric back in our lives and Kate coming over more often, it's given me hope that we can all become a family again.

Vivian nodded.

"We can't let the Sinclairs win. I need you by my side."

Vivian squeezed Nate's hand. "I won't like it, getting all dressed up but I think I still have a couple outfits that'll work. And I'll have to get my nails done. But I'll be there for you."

The stress on Nate's face melted away. "You think there's hope for us?" Nate's phone beeped. He released his hand and grabbed his phone from his pants pocket and looked at the display. "It's Renee."

Vivian nodded.

As Nate began to walk out of the room, he turned around. "Have you spoken with Kate since the attack?"

"No."

"Call her. Make sure she's okay. Then convince her to attend the fundraiser. It will be a nice distraction."

Vivian nodded her head as Nate exited the room. She remained on the couch, staring up at the photographs of her children on the mantle.

CHAPTER 11

Kate closed her eyes and massaged her temples. The attack that morning had left her emotionally exhausted. She had wanted to take the day off but there was too much at stake. She had to focus on preparing for the meeting with Fortunato but also find the NDA before her lunch with Cayenne. She had wasted her entire morning looking through every document in her file cabinet and searching her computer and company servers. If Sander was now interested in Fortunato, why did her loyalty to Cayenne make a difference? She really liked Russ and Clive, but was she willing to sacrifice her career over a friendly business relationship?

Kate didn't want to bother her contact in legal again as it could draw attention and then she might lose her job anyway. She opened her eyes and squinted at the monitor. She spotted a new email from Hashim Abbasi of Fortunato:

Ms. Crawford,

I wanted to inform you that Logan Sinclair will be joining me for our meeting tomorrow. At 11AM. Correct?

Kate's heart dropped. She couldn't breathe. After all these years, Logan Sinclair was back. Was he the reason Jenny killed herself? This changed everything. Kate didn't have to care if it looked like Fortunato stole Cayenne's product idea. But if she could prove the NDA went missing to benefit Logan, maybe he would tell her exactly what happened that fateful night twenty years ago.

She thought about her meeting with Fortunato. What would she say to Logan? What did he look like? Kate wasn't ready. She grabbed her phone. Jessica's fiancé had attended the same high school as Logan Sinclair. Kate sent a text:

Kent went to Altamont Heights? Yearbook photo of Logan Sinclair?

Kate would at least know what he looked like. She hit "Send" and went back to her email to Hashim Abbasi:

Hashim,

Thank you for letting me know Logan will be attending the meeting. My manager, Amy Bourdon and our CEO Sander Walker will be attending. See you tomorrow at 11 AM.

She hit the send button as her office phone rang. Kate looked at the caller ID and saw that it was her parents' phone number. Why hadn't they called her cell? "Hey, Dad!"

Silence.

"Hello? Dad?" Kate repeated.

"It's your mother."

Kate always made that mistake as her mom never called her. "Sorry. Hi, Mom."

"Do you have a moment? Dad told me about what happened this morning. Are you okay?"

Kate closed her eyes and tried not to remember. "For now...yes."

"Wasn't Dillon with you? He should have protected you."

Kate twisted the phone cord around her finger. "He was with me, but I had just let him off his leash. He jumped the guy, so I got away."

"Thank God."

"I know."

"Why do you insist on running over there, in the meadow? Nothing good can come of that place."

Kate rolled her eyes. "Seriously? It's a beautiful and peaceful area. You don't find many places like that on the Peninsula."

"You're right. There aren't many places to visit where your sister died."

Kate frowned. She now realized the similarities between her brother and mom. They were both blunt and disregarded your feelings when making a point. "I'm going to be fine but thanks for asking."

"Good. Your dad wants you to come with us to a fundraiser tonight."

"Tonight?" Kate opened her calendar application.

"Yes. We've all been invited to the Sinclair's fundraiser, Din for Grins at the Altamont Heights Country Club."

Kate stared at the date. "You're kidding?" She couldn't believe the coincidence: a meeting with Logan tomorrow and dinner with his parents tonight. "Why would Dad want to hang out with the Sinclairs?"

"The entire Oakview City Council was invited."

"Can I bring Brett?"

Vivian immediately countered. "Kate, I really don't think that's appropriate. We are guests of the Sinclairs."

"It's fine. He's probably working anyway." Kate spun around in her chair and looked out the window. "What time does it start?"

"Seven o'clock. Try not to be late."

"I won't."

"And don't forget we're still having dinner on Saturday."

It was only Wednesday and her mother had already reminded her three times about their weekly Saturday dinner. "Wouldn't miss it."

"Bye Kate."

"Bye."

Kate hung up her office phone then grabbed her iPhone and sent another text to Brett:

call me

Brett immediately responded:

meet n stairwell. 5 min

CHAPTER 12

Courtney lay against the pillows of her bed in the Regent hotel room as she wiped down Walter's laptop with a sanitizer towelette. She wadded it into a ball then threw it in the garbage can next to the nightstand. She tapped the track pad and opened the web browser. She logged into Walter's iCloud account and waited. The Find My iPhone icon came up. She clicked this option then re-entered Walter's password. The location services could not find his phone. It was either broken or turned off.

She Googled Nate Crawford. The search popped up two articles on the San Jose Daily site, Crawford Squeaks by Rudolf and Tragedy Strikes Oakview Community. Courtney smiled devilishly and clicked on the one about the election.

The article disregarded the death of Walter Rudolf. It focused on the last month of the Oakview election campaign. She clicked on the article about his death. There was a photo of Walter sitting in the Oakview City Council Chambers. The article recounted how Oakview hadn't seen a tragedy like this since Nate Crawford's daughter, Jenny, committed suicide twenty years earlier.

Courtney stopped reading. Nate Crawford had two daughters? When she had questioned Elizabeth Rudolph, the grieving widow had told her the video on Walter's phone concerned Nate's daughter. Courtney had assumed it was about Kate. What if it was the other one? What was Ruby hiding?

There must be a newspaper article about her death. Courtney entered the words, Jenny Crawford, Oakview, suicide in the San Jose Daily search field.

"Shit," Courtney mumbled. The search results came back empty. She clicked on the link: "Looking to find content prior to 1986?"

Articles prior to 1986 were housed on microfiche at the main branch of the San Jose Public Library.

Dead end. Courtney read over the article again about Walter's death. Jenny had a twin brother? That could be her in. Men were easy to manipulate. She could get close to the twin, Eric, and find out where Kate was hiding Walter's phone. After her failed attempt to take the phone, Courtney dared not show her face to Kate should she be recognized.

Her Samsung phone was ringing. She looked at the display, "Ruby." She reluctantly answered the call.

"Have you located Walter's phone?"

"Not yet. I check Walter's iCloud account every hour. The phone is either broken or Kate hasn't turned it on."

"As soon as you know anything, call me."

"Don't worry, I–"

Ruby ended the call before Courtney could say another word.

CHAPTER 13

In the stairwell between the eleventh and twelfth floors of the Bank of Bay building, Brett stood on the landing, texting as he waited for Kate.

"I have so much to tell you," Kate eagerly offered as she approached Brett from the floor below.

"Shhh. We have to keep it down. There's an echo in here." Brett shoved his phone in his back pant pocket as he put his other hand on Kate's shoulder. "I don't have a lot of time. How are you holding up?"

Kate smiled. In the midst of chaos, there was always Brett. "Better."

Brett wrapped his arms around Kate and kissed her forehead. "The police will catch that asshole and then you can put this all behind you."

Kate looked up into Brett's eyes. "I'm glad you're here."

"Always." Brett squeezed tight then took a step back.

"Wait." Kate pulled Brett back towards her. "Sander assigned Fortunato to me."

Brett remained focused on Kate but did not respond.

Kate smiled from ear to ear with excitement. "I didn't think he even knew my name."

Brett closed his eyes and bit his tongue.

"You know Sander, why would he suddenly do that?"

Brett opened his eyes. "Maybe Amy's told Sander some good things about you."

"Yeah right. I doubt that. Amy was pissed about the whole thing. She even asked if I knew Sander outside of work because I must have done something to get the account."

"Did you tell her about Cayenne and the missing NDA?

Kate lowered her head. "No."

"I thought about it this morning and I think I can help."

Kate raised her head and looked at Brett with anticipation.

"You have to understand, in my position I can't have anything to do with this. So don't text, email or call me about it."

Kate smirked.

"I'm serious." Brett said a little too harsh.

"Okay. I get it."

Brett handed Kate a white envelope. "I was going to surprise you with this."

Kate took the envelope and looked up at Brett. "What is it?"

"Tickets to the Sharks game on Friday."

"Oh cool. I've been wanting to–"

"Kate–I can't go. Sander is holding me hostage before the IPO. I want you to give them to someone."

Kate narrowed her eyes.

"You know Rick Moore in legal?

"Yeah. We talked at that cocktail thing in September."

"He's a hockey fanatic. Ask him to mine legal's servers."

"Do you think he'll do it?"

Brett gave Kate a quick kiss on the lips then started back up towards the twelfth floor. "Trust me. He'll help you. Just don't tell him I sent you. Be smart."

"I will. Thanks. Oh, one last thing."

Brett waited.

"William Sinclair invited my family to their Din for Grin's fundraiser tonight."

Brett turned around to face Kate. "William Sinclair?"

"Can you believe it?"

"I thought your family hated the Sinclairs? Why are you going?"

Kate grabbed onto the handrail. "William invited the entire Oakview City council so we kind of have to go."

"Do you want me to come?"

Kate lied. "No, I'll be fine. I'm more concerned with meeting the son tomorrow?"

"Logan?"

"Yep. How did you know his name?"

"I'm sure you mentioned it before."

"Well he's coming on site to show Sander a demo of their product I told you about."

Brett looked blankly ahead as he mumbled, "Fortunato?"

The imperial march ring tone echoed throughout the cavernous stairwell. Brett grabbed his phone. "Speaking of Sander. I've got to take this." He waved at Kate, jogged the last few steps then exited the stairwell.

As the door to the twelfth floor closed with a loud metallic click, Kate stood in silence. Why had Brett been so short with her?

The sound of another door opening a couple floors above startled Kate. Hearing footsteps coming down the stairwell, her heart beat a little faster. She quickly walked back onto her floor.

CHAPTER 14

Kate shut the door to her office as her landline rang. She sat on the edge of the desk and held the handset to her ear. "Hey there."

"Guess who?" A familiar voice sang.

"I know it's you Russ," Kate responded.

A muffled voice could be heard saying, "How does she always know it's us?"

"What's up?" Kate laughed.

"Kate you are so brilliant. Just brilliant. Why don't you come work for us? We need more competent, psychic people like you," Russ said.

"You know I have caller ID?" Kate joked.

"That's not fair," Russ replied.

"Russ, please. You are too kind. Why don't you put Clive on?"

"Do tell, why should I?" Russ questioned.

"Because I'll never find out what you guys are up to," Kate insisted.

"You can be such a bitch Kate," Russ quipped.

Kate heard a "thud" and someone scramble to pick up the phone. "Ouch...that hurt."

"Hello? You guys still there?" Kate asked.

A breathless Clive responded, "Yeah. It's me. Just had to put Russ in his place."

Kate looked at the clock on her computer. 1 PM. "I was wondering when you were going to call. The message you left last night was a little cryptic. Something about food?" Kate said.

"What are you doing right now?" Clive asked.

Kate pursed her lips as she looked around her office. "Working."

"Are you hungry? Do you have time to join us for lunch?"

Kate had too much going on but she had to find out why the unexpected visit. "What's the occasion?"

Russ chimed in. "You'll just have to wait Miss Crawford. We can't just tell you over the wireless airwaves."

Kate hesitated to respond. Would they ask about the missing NDA? "What's the plan?"

"Meet us in your lobby right now. We're just pulling up," Clive said.

"I'll be right down." Kate ended the call as she walked out of her office. She was feeling slightly on edge.

CHAPTER 15

The Bank of Bay building lobby housed a three-floor atrium with a glass enclosed elevator shaft at the back. On the wall above the entrance was a large mural depicting a silhouette of a steel worker hammering at an iron—a homage to the time period the building was erected. An invisible security line on either side of the receptionist desk, two self-registration kiosks and badge detectors surrounded the elevator area. Colorful modern interactive artwork designed using Obsidian's photo editing products filled the walls of the lobby containing several groupings of black leather couches and chairs.

Kate's phone vibrated for the tenth time as the elevator descended into the lobby. Who was sending her a constant flow of text messages? Kate rummaged in her purse for her phone. And then she spotted Russ Weber.

Russ was leaning up against the receptionist desk, pouting his lips with his head tilted down but his eyes looking up at the elevators. His corkscrew bleach blonde hair jiggled up and down as his fingers feverishly moved over his iPhone keypad. A typical loud orange T-shirt with a black skull and cross bones adorned his chest. When their eyes meet, Russ flung his right hand back and mouthed, "Who me?"

Kate rolled her eyes and shook her head as the vibrations from her phone stopped.

Clive Peterson stood next to Russ. In his svelte black suit

he was the conservative counterpart who kept the team on tract.

"Kate, Kate, Kate! Don't you look extraordinary today?" Russ gushed as he raced up to Kate and gave her a hug.

Clive casually strolled over to Kate, gave her a hug then a kiss on the cheek. "Extra-extraordinary."

Kate inhaled Clive's fresh, clean scent as she admired his smooth bronzed skin and dark thick hair.

"Boys, you are too kind." Kate replied, relieved to have a momentary distraction.

"We only converse in true talk." Russ took Kate by the arm and led her towards the lobby door.

"Is that some new kind of speak?" Kate asked sarcastically.

Clive walked ahead and opened the door. "Enough of this bickering. I'm hungry." He bowed before Kate then offered his hand, "Your chariot awaits."

"Chariot? I thought we were going local." Kate anxiously followed them out of the building.

Russ nudged Clive.

"Not when you can travel in style." Russ led Kate towards a new green Jaguar X-Type that was illegally parked with its hazard lights on.

"Is this some new toy?" Kate asked Clive as he opened the door and helped her in.

Russ got in the back seat as Clive made his way around to the driver's side.

"It was the best car the rental place had so we had to take it," Russ said.

"It's better to arrive in style," Clive added as she shut the driver side door.

"Whatever makes you two happy," Kate smirked.

Clive started the engine and pulled out into the street. "Just having you with us makes us happy. Right Russ?"

Russ leaned forward and rested his chin on the armrest between Clive and Kate. Looking up at Kate, he batted his eyes, "Kate won't you move up to Seattle and work for us. Or we could simply get married."

Kate pushed Russ's head back with her hand. "How tempting."

Clive drove down Paseo Grande towards Highway 101. He turned to Kate. "Obsidian is getting too small for that building. Any plans for expansion?"

"Not that I know of," Kate responded. "Clive, where are we going?"

Clive ignored Kate's question and concentrated on the road as he entered the highway.

"We heard your dad won the election last night," Russ said.

Kate looked back at Russ who shrugged his shoulders. She turned back to Clive, "Yeah he did. Where are we going?"

Clive looked at Russ in the rear view mirror.

"Don't worry Kate. We just have a surprise for you," Russ said reassuringly.

"What kind of surprise?" Kate asked.

"Let's not ruin it. Wait until we get to the restaurant." Clive floored the gas pedal and accelerated into the fast lane of the highway. He looked down at the radio and pushed the 'on' button. Social Distortion's cover of the Johnny Cash song "Ring of Fire" was playing.

What ring of fire had Kate fallen into? Normally, she wouldn't care about Russ and Clive kidnapping her for lunch but after her attack, and knowing they may confront her about the missing NDA, she was on edge. She could feel her face beginning to flush.

An awkward silence ensued as the song came to an end. Kate looked from Clive to Russ. "Okay, you guys are beginning to scare me. What's going on? And where are we going?"

"We're almost there." Clive moved the car into the slow lane and then pulled off at the next exit.

Kate had never been to this part of San Mateo. It was an Asian warehouse district near the bay with a few shops.

"We're here," Clive exclaimed as he pulled up in front of a small restaurant with a dilapidated black and white sign above the door that read, White Lotus.

Kate froze. Her legs remained glued to the seat. What if they asked about the NDA? Before she could think, Russ opened the passenger door and offered his hand.

CHAPTER 16

Vivian loathed Bella Salon in the Sinclair Shopping Center. Although it was a beautiful spa, it catered to a specific class of ladies. The ones who did lunch, not work, hired nannies to care for their kids, and spread gossip faster than butter on a warm piece of toast. Vivian had never been part of this crowd. She only went to this salon when her usual place wasn't available.

With the Sinclair fundraiser hours away, every nail salon in town was booked. Bella Salon called with a last minute cancelation, so she reluctantly drove over.

The nail room was located behind the main receptionist area. The room's tranquil aqua and pink hues contained two semi-circular pods that were positioned back-to-back and separated by tall bamboo shoots. Eight customers were seated in each pod. Each lady sat in a plush pink pedicure chair with ergonomic controls for massage and lumbar support.

Vivian was in the first chair closest to the receptionist desk with her back to the bamboo divide. After selecting the massage settings, and placing her feet in the warm water, Vivian picked up a People Magazine and perused the articles as she subtly scanned the room.

Two trophy wives sat next to Vivian in pink designer sweat suits with their perfectly styled blonde and auburn manes. They were trying to whisper to each other about the latest happenings around town but Vivian couldn't help but overhear their conversation.

"Elizabeth was here last week," the blonde said.

"Can you believe her husband is dead?" the brunette replied.

"I heard she is in seclusion, not talking with anyone," the blonde offered.

"Kinda sad that Walter also lost the election," the brunette added.

Vivian rolled her eyes. She glanced back at the magazine and tried to block out the low murmur of chatter.

The manicurist started to massage Vivian's feet. She put down the magazine and closed her eyes. Concentrating on the mechanical rhythmic massage on her back, Vivian began to relax. She took a deep breath and exhaled.

"Logan."

Vivian immediately opened her eyes. She slowly scanned the room without moving her head. She had not heard that name in a long time. The women next to her were still talking about the Rudolf accident. She closed her eyes again.

A woman's low voice could be heard again from the pods behind Vivian. "He flew in this weekend. William's already had some kind of confrontation with him."

Vivian sat up. Had she heard those names correctly? William and Logan? She tried to look behind but the bamboo shoots blocked her view. With the manicurist still holding her feet, she did not want to draw attention to herself. She sat silently and tried to concentrate on the conversation behind her.

This time a woman with a high-pitched voice joined the conversation. "How do you feel?"

The woman with the lower voice responded. "I'm frustrated. William abandoned him. If it weren't for me, Logan would have been lost years ago."

"Does William know what you've done?" The brunette asked.

"Are you kidding? He's so bent on seeing his Cross Creek project through, he's blind to what's really going on."

Cross Creek? Vivian strained to hear more of what the women were saying. She moved closer to the side of her chair, turned her head towards the bamboo.

The manicurist guided her feet back into the water.

Vivian smiled at her then raised her arms above her head in a stretch. The voices became more audible.

"And you've known all along?" The woman with the high-pitched voice asked.

The woman with the lower voice responded. "Who do you think pushed him to develop that product? It's his ticket back and will help all of us—including you."

Vivian's eyes became wide as she continued to listen in on the conversation.

The woman with the high-pitched voice continued. "Did you know that Father O'Connell is back?"

Vivian kicked up her right foot and almost hit the manicurist in the face.

"I'm sorry." Vivian apologized to the manicurist as she settled her foot back down onto the foot cushion. She turned her head again towards the bamboo but could not hear any voices. Instead, two women emerged from behind the back pod and walked towards the receptionist desk. One wore her hair in a low ponytail while the other had a chin length blonde bob. This woman turned around.

With her upturned nose, tight smooth skin, thin arched eyebrows, dark mole above her plumped lips, and that chin length bob, Maria Sinclair was the poster child for age-defying maintenance. Vivian grabbed the People magazine. She could not let Maria recognize her nor see the smile on her face.

CHAPTER 17

Crisp white linens draped the tables of the otherwise drab and dimly lit interior of the Thai restaurant. An older couple sat at the window while a family of four quietly ate their meal at the far end of the restaurant near the kitchen. A gold statue of a sitting Buddha greeted patrons at the host's podium.

Clive went up to the hostess and spoke to her in Thai. The hostess nodded then led them to a table in the back corner.

"Should I call 911 and report a kidnapping?" Kate joked as she sat and placed her phone on the table.

Clive and Russ did not respond.

"What language were you speaking?" Kate said to Clive.

Clive glanced at his menu. "Don't worry Kate. We don't mean to be so secretive. We're just playing with you."

Russ picked up Kate's phone and turned it off. "Clive lived in Thailand for a year. That's how he knows Thai."

"What are you doing with my phone?" Kate reached towards Russ.

"We want your full attention for this lunch meeting." Russ returned the phone to Kate then winked.

Kate cautiously took the phone and placed it in her purse. "I didn't know this was a formal meeting." She placed her hands on the table then looked from Russ to Clive. "So boys, why are we here?"

Russ looked at Clive. "We've got a buddy who hit it big over at Google. Every year, he throws a big party for his birthday. Flies us in and pays for everything." He looked at Kate "Last year it was Vegas. This year it's San Francisco. Don't know what to expect this time around."

"But why are we at this restaurant?" Kate asked as she looked around at the modest space.

Clive tapped his index finger on the table. "Remember back in May, we told you we thought up our idea for Virtual Presence in a restaurant. How we wrote it down on the back of a napkin?"

Kate nodded her head.

Russ raised both of his arms. "This is the place."

A waiter approached and set three glasses of water on the table. He looked at everyone then in broken English asked, "May I take your order?"

"Kate? Do you know what you want?" Clive asked.

Kate shook her head. "I have no idea. Perhaps you should order for all of us."

Clive took this queue and rambled off their order.

After the waiter left, Russ leaned in closer to Kate. "We flew down here for the party."

"And it happened to be perfect timing," Clive added.

Russ placed his arm around Clive's shoulder, "We wanted to tell you in person–"

"Our product is finally done!" Clive exclaimed.

"Surprise." Clive and Russ said in unison.

Kate tried to sound enthusiastic but couldn't hide a sickening feeling in her stomach as she looked from Russ to Clive. "Really?"

"It's been a lot of hard work but I know Sander will love all the changes we've made to it." Russ took his arm away from Clive's shoulder and grabbed his glass of water.

Clive held up his index finger and bit down on his lower lip. "The analytic piece is going to blow his mind. No one has anything like it. We're going to change how people are entertained. We'll be able to track everything and use the data to better market shit to customers. It's a win, win for everyone. "

"Do you think we can show it to Sander while we're down here?" Russ asked.

The walls and ceiling of the restaurant felt like they were closing in on Kate. A couple hours ago, it seemed easy to forget about Cayenne and go after Logan. But now being here with them, she started to have second thoughts. "So it's done and ready to show Sander?"

Russ looked at Clive and they both smiled.

"Yes," Russ said.

"We'll be in the area until Monday afternoon," Russ added.

"Monday would be the perfect day for us to meet with Sander as we'll be busy with the party until then," Clive said.

Kate closed her eyes and took a deep breath. She was trying to absorb what they were saying but they were talking too fast.

"Will we need a new NDA?" Russ asked.

Kate opened her eyes.

"I went back through my notes on our meeting with Sander at the beginning of May. I swear we signed an NDA but I can't find our copy," Clive added.

Russ jumped in. "I remember Amy, telling me she'd be our connection between Sander and legal. Or is that what she tells everyone just to get them in bed?"

Kate looked wide-eyed at Russ. Amy and Russ?

"Don't act all surprised Kate," Russ said as he leaned in closer. "It was a brief fling after we met. She actually flew up to Seattle only three times. I'm surprised she hasn't returned any of the voice messages I left her this past week."

"We don't want to get Amy in trouble," Clive continued. "That's why we left you a message on Monday about the NDA."

"So what did you find out?" Russ asked.

Now the walls and ceiling of the restaurant felt like they would collapse on top of Kate. Amy had a fling with Russ? And Logan was back. She struggled to keep a straight face as she tried to dig through the debris in her mind surrounding Cayenne's NDA. Were they all somehow connected?

When she did not respond, Russ and Clive looked at each other and then at Kate.

The waiter arrived with their food.

Kate felt her face begin to flush but covered it up by grabbing a fork and taking a bite of a spicy noodle dish.

"It's hot, isn't it," Russ smiled as he looked at Kate.

Kate nodded.

"We did sign an NDA, didn't we?" Clive asked.

"And Sander's still interested in buying our product—right?" Russ added.

Kate took a sip of water and went for the quick fake. "That's great, the product is done. I'll see what I can do about setting up a meeting with Sander for Monday. But, you need to understand, we won't be able to make a move until the quiet period is over."

"When is that?" Clive asked.

"We filed with the SEC May 11, so it's over on Dec 11, one month after our stock goes public," Kate said.

"When are you launching your IPO?" Clive asked.

"We price on Tuesday. I bet that's why you haven't heard from Amy. But to be fair, you guys never told me when Virtual Presence would be finished."

"True," Russ said nodding his head.

"I see your point," Clive added. "So you'll bring the current NDA to our meeting with Sander?"

"Definitely," Kate responded with relief, as this would give her several more days to find it.

After twenty minutes, Russ looked at his wristwatch, tapped the table with his finger and looked at Clive. "We've got to get going."

They all got up from the table. Clive handed the waiter some cash and they walked out of the restaurant.

Clive pulled up in front of the entrance to Obsidian. Kate reached for the latch to open her door. Russ grabbed her shoulder. "Let us know what time we need to be here for our meeting on Monday. We're excited to see Sander."

"Excited," echoed Clive.

Before stepping out of the car, Kate looked back at Clive and Russ. "Enjoy your party."

As she closed the car door, Kate gave one last wave goodbye then headed back into Obsidian. Walking towards the elevator, she reached in her purse for her phone and felt the white envelope.

CHAPTER 18

"He's back," Vivian declared as she stormed into the kitchen and threw her purse down on the granite countertop almost hitting Nate's coffee.

"Who's back?" Nate asked as he rescued his cup and winced at the sudden movement.

"Logan!"

The color in Nate's face instantly drained.

"Maria Sinclair was at the nail salon. I heard her tell that sister of hers that Logan flew in this past weekend."

"Seriously. Really?"

Vivian looked at Nate. They stared at each other for a long while without talking. Then almost simultaneously a smile came over both of their faces.

Nate shook his head. "We've waited for this day for over twenty years.

"I know," Vivian said nodding her head.

"Why now?"

"Cross Creek?"

"Doesn't make sense."

"But it is awfully coincidental. Maybe that's why William wanted to meet."

Nate grabbed Vivian's hand and closed his eyes.

Vivian squeezed his hand.

Nate opened his eyes and radiated a renewed vigor Vivian

had not seen in years. "Logan back in town is a good thing for us. He's here for a reason. It's got to be important because he must know we'll come after him."

Nate took Vivian into his arms.

Vivian bit her lower lip and began to cry.

Tears streamed down Nate's cheeks as he kissed Vivian's forehead.

Nate and Vivian clung on to each other as the years of frustration, anger and depression came together in one long, unified emotional sob.

CHAPTER 19

Kate quietly opened the door of the stairwell onto the 10th floor of Obsidian's legal department. She cautiously looked around. Account Managers were only seen on this floor when they had a problem. She walked onto the floor and closed the door behind her. She spotted the seating area at the center of the floor and saw a magazine on the table. As she strolled by, she picked it up and pretended to be absorbed in an article from The American Lawyer. She casually walked through the floor to the row of interior offices.

Rick was sitting at his desk quietly reading something on his monitor. Although he was the same age as Brett, his receding hairline and enormous gut made him look ten years older.

"Hey Rick," Kate said as she folded up the magazine, placed it under her arm and leaned up against the doorframe.

Rick looked up and smiled. "Kate Crawford. What brings you down here?"

"I was on the floor and thought I'd stop in to say hi."

"Thanks. Good to see you."

"I bet you're busy with the IPO launch?" Kate walked into Rick's office and sat in the extra chair.

"Yes but my part is done. Now I just have to wait until we actually launch."

"Then you are free Friday night?"

Rick swiveled his chair around to face Kate. "What are you proposing?"

"I happen to have two extra tickets to the Sharks vs. Avalanche that I can't use."

A smile spread over Rick's face. "Seriously? Are they good seats?"

"They are good but they won't cost you a dime."

"Really?"

"Yes, but I wondered if you would do me a favor?" Kate leaned back and closed the door.

Rick pushed his chair back from his desk and folded his arms. "What kind of favor?"

Kate leaned in closer to Rick. "I need you to do a global search on a file."

"A file? Why don't you go to your regular contact?"

Kate smiled sheepishly. "Can you keep this just between the two of us."

Rick inched forward to the edge of his chair.

"I don't like to speak badly about anyone, but I don't think my contact looked hard enough."

"Who is it?"

"That doesn't matter. The hard copy of an important NDA is missing. The digital copy should be on your servers, but my contact doesn't have the search skills…like I've heard you do."

Rick looked at his monitor and then Kate. "An NDA? Is it for an account of yours?"

Kate nodded her head.

"Did you sign it?"

Kate raised her eyebrows. "Yes."

"That's not good. If one of your accounts signed an NDA that is now missing, we have no recourse if they stole any product ideas from us."

"Or vice versa."

Rick stared at Kate.

Kate inched closer to Rick. "I can't find my copy and I need it for a meeting with Sander on Monday. You guys keep digital master copies, correct?"

"I'm not supposed to work on anything outside my purview."

Kate took the tickets out of the white envelope and placed them on the desk in front of Rick.

"Club level center." Rick looked past Kate through the window in the door. "I'm only searching for a specific NDA?"

"That's right."

Rick eyed the tickets again. "Ok. What's the file name?"

"Cayenne," Kate said.

"Never heard of them," Rick said as he wrote the name on a Post It note. "It'll take me until Friday, but if it's there, I'll find it."

CHAPTER 20

"Now what?" Courtney asked as she turned off the TV in her small yet luxurious room at the Regent in the heart of Altamont Heights. She placed her Samsung phone on the nightstand, pushed the "answer" button and hit speaker.

"A priest by the name of Father O'Connell is back in town. This could really mess things up. We need to find out why he's back," Ruby said.

Courtney shook her head "Hmm, now a priest. That's a new one I haven't tried. Should be fun."

"Don't get any ideas. I just want to find out why he's back."

Courtney rubbed the bandage on her right arm. "You're not telling me everything."

There was a pause in the conversation. Ruby took a deep breath, "You don't need to know everything. All I need you to do is get close to the priest and figure out why he's back. He'll be at that fundraiser I told you about."

"At the Altamont Heights Country Club?"

"Yes. I don't care what it takes. I need you to get close to the priest. Be my fly on the wall and find out everything. And get that phone from Kate."

"What aren't you telling me?"

"Don't think. Just do."

"I guess I can do that. Should I consider Father O'Connell a potential problem like Rudolf?"

"Not yet."

"But I didn't really get to do anything to Rudolf. Let me do something to this priest. Tie him up, make him bleed a little–"

"I don't want to know the details of your twisted mind. If we need to go there, I'll tell you."

"Will do." Courtney stood and walked over to the closet. She opened the door to reveal eight outfits neatly spaced 2 inches apart. She grabbed the wood hanger holding a black Dior dress and draped it across her body. The plunging neckline would easily show off her voluptuous breasts. "I'll definitely be at the fundraiser."

"Have you checked Walter's iCloud account?"

"No location on the phone yet."

"Let me know as soon as you find out anything new."

CHAPTER 21

The Altamont Heights Country Club was all about money. Old money. Members of the club were the founding families of Altamont Heights, Oakview and the San Tomas Hills. From the moment you drove past the solemn stone lions in front of the tall iron gates, you were ushered into a world of exclusive privilege. Only a handful of the new moneyed, Silicon Valley elite, with the right connections could fight for the exorbitant $1 million initiation fee and $250K annual membership. All others were excluded for their lack of status or social heritage.

The tree-lined, newly-paved driveway leading to the clubhouse wound through ten of the eighteen perfectly manicured Tom Nicoll golf course holes, before reaching the club house at the top of the hill. Adjacent to the club house was an Olympic size swimming pool surrounded by chaise longue chairs with white umbrellas and ten blue-surfaced tennis courts.

The clubhouse, nicknamed "The Parthenon," was one of the finest examples of neoclassical architecture in the area. Four Doric columns flanked the front of the 50,000 square foot, 82-room mansion. It was something of a historical landmark as it once housed the patriarch of the Sinclair family, Lawrence Sinclair.

For the Din for Grins fundraiser, the clubhouse was transformed into a manse from the swing era of the late 1930s. A black Rolls-Royce Wraith and a gleaming green Packard Phaeton were parked head-to-head in front of the grand marble steps leading up to the clubhouse.

The wait staff wore cartoon pinstripe zoot suits with white handkerchiefs in the breast pocket and two-tone black and white spectator shoes. The large ballroom held fifty tables around the dance floor's gleaming parquet, each draped with crisp white linen, white napkins, gold antiqued chargers and silverware, and centered with a fall harvest floral arrangement of orange Asiatic lilies, sunflowers, burgundy daisies, solidago, and red glycerized oak leaves. A twenty-five-piece band played the music of Artie Shaw, Benny Goodman, Louis Prima, Duke Ellington, and Glenn Miller as a light undertone of voices hung in the background. Most people engaged in conversations at their tables but also surreptitiously watched the parade of wealth around them.

Louis Prima's Sing, Sing, Sing filled the room. Kate watched the scene from a table in the back corner as she finished her dessert of crème brulee. The money here was spent on a different kind of silicon--to keep the trophy wives in pristine, youthful condition. Their low cut dresses and expressionless faces revealed the true assets of the valley's privileged elite. It was all about appearances, who looked the best, most kept and had the most connections. The women discussed their designer dresses and which private schools their children were applying to while the men scrutinized the latest $100 million start-up acquisition.

Kate felt out of place in a simple black cocktail dress. Most everyone wore 1930s inspired costumes. These people paid the $2,500 a head to be here. They had the time to create an image or at least hire someone to create it for them.

Eric Crawford sat next to Kate. He kept picking at the stiff collar of his shirt and seemed uncomfortable in the rented suit. It had been some time since he had the need to dress up. Eric was a younger version of their father but his shaggy brown hair and partial goatee concealed any emotion as he stared at the party goers.

Nate looked the part of a councilman in his black tuxedo as he walked confidently from table to table talking with everyone. As he stood, he occasional stepped back to arch his back. Vivian trailed behind, occasionally engaging in conversation. For once, she blended in quite well with the crowd in a black flapper dress Kate had never seen before. Where had she gotten it on such short notice?

Kate and Eric remained in their seats assessing the guests.

"You okay?" Kate asked.

"Yeah, haven't worn a suit in a long time—we dressed pretty casual in rehab." He flashed a smile. "How'd Mom convince you to attend?"

"She called and asked. What? You don't want to be here?" Kate said.

"Hell no. I don't like being around people who are drinking. And I hate being near the Sinclairs."

"What do they have to do with anything?"

Eric ignored Kate's question. "Of course. Eagle-eyed Mom Crawford is watching my every move. I'll tell you one thing, I'm glad you're here."

"I think the bigger question is how did Dad get Mom here?"

"That's a mystery we'll never solve," Eric laughed as he pulled a pack of cigarettes from his inside breast pocket.

Kate had forgotten how funny her brother could be and started to relax.

"Look at them now." Eric pointed at their parents. "Pretending to like each other."

"What do you mean?"

"They were arguing quite loudly this morning. Brought me back to the time before Jenny–" Eric stopped himself.

"To what?" Kate questioned.

Eric leaned in towards Kate. "They used to fight all the time."

"I've rarely seen them fight."

"You were pretty young. It got bad right before Jenny died."

"What did they fight about?"

Eric looked towards his parents then back at Kate as he pulled a cigarette out of the pack. "Whatever it was, Jenny and I would just turn up the music and distract you."

A memory of dance parties in Jenny's room instantly brought Kate back to her childhood. Could they have been a distraction from her parents arguing? The only thing she remembered her parents disagreeing on was her mom spending too much time at work. But where had her mom worked before Jenny died?

"Where's Brett?" Eric asked as he tapped the cigarette on the table.

"Working late."

"Lucky man."

Kate rolled her eyes. "This isn't so bad. Look around the room. When do you ever get to see so many Silicon Valley heavyweights under one roof? I've seen Mark Zuckerberg, Dick Costolo and you can't miss Marissa Mayer in that red Oscar de la Renta gown."

"And don't forget your very own CEO Sander Walker," Eric said pointing towards the bar. "What a fraud."

Kate reared her head back. "Sander made Obsidian into what it is today. Why do you resent him so much?"

"I'm just amazed a schmuck like him actually made it."

Kate scanned the sea of people for Sander Walker. His signature rectangular glasses made him easy to spot. His short dark hair was textured perfectly in a hip style but his glasses gave him that erudite, European look. He stood confident in his black tuxedo as he spoke with a group of followers. Obsidian was about to launch its IPO and was recently listed twenty-fifth on Forbes Best Small Companies Top 100. Everyone wanted to say they knew Sander Walker.

"I don't know what you're talking about," Kate said as she noticed her manager Amy dressed in a red, beaded flapper dress standing next to Sander. "He's a self-made man. Earned some scholarships that put him through college and graduate school. He worked from the bottom up at start-ups like Netwurks, Halflife, and GrandWuld. Then landed at Obsidian two years ago. I don't see that as being a schmuck."

"Well, when I knew him, he was a pot smoking groupie of that Sinclair kid."

"Sinclair?"

"Yeah, Logan Sinclair."

Kate's skin prickled. She'd be meeting with Logan tomorrow. Had Jenny really killed herself because of him? Before she could probe further, she felt a hand on her back.

"How's it going?" Nate said as he pulled out a chair between Kate and Eric for Vivian. "We're having a great time and I love the music."

"Not really my type of music–" Eric stopped in midsentence and pointed at a table in the center of the room. "What's he doing here?"

"Who?" Nate asked.

Everyone looked at the center of the room.

"Look over there at the center table. His red hair is now white but he's got those same rosy cheeks and freckles. You can't miss him. What the fuck is Father O'Connell doing here?"

"Who's Father O'Connell?" Kate asked.

"Eric, don't use that kind of language," Vivian said as she grabbed Eric's hand, took the cigarette and broke it in two.

Nate threw darts with his eyes at Eric as he sat in the chair next to Kate. "His family runs St. James Seminary."

"When we knew him, he oversaw St. Mary's Convent and the Seminary," Vivian responded as she looked sternly at Eric.

"Father O'Connell left Oakview when you were really little," Nate said.

Eric pushed his chair back and stood abruptly. He grabbed his pack of cigarettes off the table. "I'm going to get some air."

Kate watched Eric disappear through the French doors leading out to the patio.

Benny Goodman's Putting on the Ritz began to play. Nate looked at Kate then stood. He arched his back then said to

Vivian, "Do you mind if I take our daughter out for a whirl?"

Vivian did not respond. She stared despondently in the direction of Father O'Connell's table.

CHAPTER 22

Sander stood with his hands interlocked behind his back in a small circle of followers. He knew people would flock to him at this event but this crowd had exceeded his expectations. Everyone was eager to hear what the young CEO had to say. He had finally arrived. Life was good and would only get better come Tuesday. His utopian daze was disrupted when he felt a hand on his arm and sensed the presence of someone by his side whisper, "We need to talk."

Sander casually turned around to see William Sinclair walking towards the bathrooms.

"Don't worry, there's no one in here," William said to Sander as he entered the bathroom.

Sander surveyed the six stalls that were more like individual rooms with floor-to-ceiling marble walls and dark stained louvered doors. He walked up to the sink area opposite the stalls and washed his hands. As he grabbed a cloth towel he said, "Great night. Maria really out did herself."

William placed his hands on the counter and looked at Sander in the mirror. "What are you doing with Logan?"

Sander stared at William. "What do you mean?"

William turned towards Sanders. "Why is he back? He could ruin everything."

Sander threw the towel into the wicker basket under the sink. "I don't think this is the time or place."

William jabbed his index finger into Sanders chest. "Logan says you're helping him. That Obsidian is going to buy a product he created. Is that true?"

Sander smiled as he brushed William's hand away. "You've got it all wrong."

"Do I? Then why did he confront me about this plan of his the other night? He says you're helping him. Purchasing his product will make him a legitimate success. And that I'll want to take him back." William stopped talking and stared at Sander to judge his reaction.

Sander did not respond. He knew how to play William.

William shook his head. "When we're this close, you think I'd just turn a blind eye and accept Logan back?"

Sander faced the mirror and combed back a few loose strands of hair with his fingers.

William stared in the mirror at Sander. "We're building a new era for the Sinclair name. After Obsidian goes public, our futures will be set."

"I appreciate you saying that," Sander said as he looked at William in the mirror.

"With Logan back, the Crawfords might stir up the past. That's why I'm making all nice with Nate–that cock-sucking leach."

Sander continued to stare at William. "Don't worry about Logan. That situation will take care of itself."

"Even with the Crawfords?"

"Why do you think I hired Kate? She's my security if anything goes wrong."

CHAPTER 23

Eric stepped out onto the expansive stone patio that overlooked the 18th hole. A slight chill in the air encouraged him to button up his jacket. He walked passed the crowd of party goers huddled around the outdoor bar and found a quiet area with an unoccupied stone bench facing the clubhouse. The low lights illuminating this area would keep him well hidden from others. He sat down, lit a cigarette and inhaled. Exhaling slowly, he leaned back and surveyed the ballroom alive with people dancing and having fun.

"Can I bum a smoke?"

Eric looked up but was blinded by the bright light from the bar area where the voice had come from. He held up his arm above his eyes. "Excuse me?"

"Can I have one of your cigarettes?" A woman asked as she walked over to the bench and sat down next to Eric.

"Oh yeah…sure." Eric stumbled over his words as he realized the voice was a striking brunette with a scarlet smile and plunging neckline. He patted down his suit jacket until he found the pack of cigarettes.

The long-haired brunette watched Eric intently as he handed her a cigarette. She took it between her two fingers of her right hand and slowly inserted it between her scarlet colored lips.

Eric raised the lighter to her mouth and cupped the flame

as he lit the tip of her cigarette.

The brunette took a deep inhale, flung her head back then exhaled letting the white smoke envelop both of them. "That's exactly what I needed."

CHAPTER 24

Nate took Kate by the hand then pulled her in close to his chest as they began to dance slowly.

"I didn't know you knew how to dance?" Kate smiled.

"I've always loved to dance. I just haven't done it in a while." Nate broke away from Kate then swung her to his right side and then back to his left before they came together. "Ouch."

"You okay?" Kate asked with concern.

"My back's still a little sore. Do you mind if we just keep it low key."

Kate smiled. "Of course not." She surveyed the room then asked "Have you spoken with the Sinclairs tonight?"

"Not yet?"

"Where are they?"

Nate motioned with his head to a table adjacent to the dance floor and winked. Kate had seen images of the Sinclairs in the local Haut society magazine but had never seen them in person.

Maria looked the part of a privileged wife in her navy blue flapper dress, perfectly styled blonde bob cut with beaded headband, perfect make-up, slightly tan skin, shiny white smile, and manicured red nails. William was slightly weathered for his age but played the role of the dutiful patriarch in his black tuxedo as he smiled, made conversation and surveyed the room for his next target.

"Renee here tonight?" Kate asked.

"Of course. She practically lives here during the week." Nate nodded to a table next to the dance floor.

Renee Verano sat quietly in a vintage black Versace silk pantsuit as she gazed onto the crowd with her nose in the air and hands on a black cane.

Nate moved them around to the other side of the dance floor. As Kate glanced at the bar, a glimmer of something shiny caught her eye. She turned around, looked back and saw the same sparkle.

The lights above the dance floor robotically flashed on a man leaning against the wall next to the bar. He was dressed all in black and sipped a dark colored cocktail. Something in his hand produced the glimmer whenever he tipped the glass up to his mouth. She looked over again and their eyes locked. A surge of energy rushed through Kate's body.

This man was studying Kate's every move. He never looked away. His eyes followed her across the dance floor. She tried to shake the urge not to look back but she couldn't resist. His gaze fed an intoxication feeling throughout her entire body.

The song ended.

"That was fun," Nate said as he walked Kate to the side of the dance floor. "Do you mind if I go mingle?"

Kate looked back at the location where her admirer had been standing. He was gone. "Thanks, Dad, for the dance." She gave Nate a kiss on the cheek. "I'll be fine. I'll go find Eric."

Nate walked towards a group of people huddled around a table next to the bar. Kate stood idle on the side of the dance floor, scanning the room for Eric.

The band launched into Duke Ellington's slow and melodic I Got It Bad. As the clarinet solo ended, Kate felt a hand slither in around her hip.

CHAPTER 25

Vivian followed Father O'Connell behind the black curtains draped around the stage. After all these years, she had nothing to say to him. Yet his sudden appearance was curious. He stopped, held up his hand, looked from side to side then turned around.

She held her breath and looked up at his face. Their eyes met. He appeared to be the same person she had known twenty years earlier but now with white hair and lines of time across his face, she could see he had changed. The noise from the party faded.

Father O'Connell moved his lips as if trying to say something but nothing came out.

Vivian crossed her arms and took a step back. "Why didn't you at least call? Tell me you were back."

"I couldn't Vivian." Father O'Connell wiped both hands down over his face. "It all happened so fast."

Vivian looked down at her red manicured toes peeking out from the black spaghetti strap shoes. "Why didn't you ever contact me? Didn't you care to know–"

"I do know."

Vivian's eyes began to well up with tears. "You son of a bitch." She raised her hand and pointed at him. "Occasional photos and stories provided to you by others don't tell the whole truth."

Father O'Connell looked down. "I never meant for any of this to happen. I never wanted to hurt you."

"Bullshit!" Vivian's voice became louder.

Father O'Connell looked behind Vivian to see if anyone in the ballroom could hear their conversation. As the music was still playing, he grabbed on to Vivian's arms and pulled her in close to him. He looked into her eyes. "I had no choice. I had to leave to save Kate."

"What the hell do you think you're doing?" Nate roared as he rushed at Father O'Connell. "Get away from my wife."

"Wait, Nate. Please," Father O'Connell pleaded as he released his hold of Vivian and held up his hands. "I came back because I want to help."

Nate stopped. He lowered his head then looked back at Vivian. "Help? Where were you twenty years ago? That's when we needed your help. I don't want you near my family. Just stay away." Nate took Vivian by the hand and began to walk back to the dance floor.

"It's important," Father O'Connell begged.

Vivian pulled on Nate's hand. He stopped, looked up at the ceiling, and then turned around.

"I'm here not just to save the Seminary." Father O'Connell spread open his arms. "There's more going on than any of you realize."

Nate smiled and shook his head. "I doubt that. How would a priest know anything?"

Father O'Connell stepped towards Nate. "Because Logan is back."

CHAPTER 26

Kate looked down at her side. She noticed a hand around her waist wearing a gold ring with a silver crest in the shape of an "S" on the ring finger. It twinkled from the mood lights scattered around the dance floor. Kate grabbed the hand and spun around.

She gasped. Her heart began to race. The man who had been watching her dance was standing right in front of her, holding her hand.

Before Kate could say anything, the man took Kate's right hand. "Dance with me?"

The man did not wait for an answer. They skimmed across the floor to the center. He pulled Kate's body in close to his.

Kate placed her left hand on his shoulder as her feet followed his lead to the slow beat of the song.

The singer's velvety voice sang the words, "I got it bad and that ain't good."

Kate felt the man's torso against her chest. He was lean and muscular with an inviting scent of suede, musk, and sweat.

The man looked down at Kate. His skin was slightly tan with a few wrinkles above his brow. His emerald eyes darted around Kate's face, attempting to capture her mood.

"I've seen you somewhere," the man said.

"I don't think so. I'd remember," Kate replied with a laugh.

"You dance quite well." The man boldly pulled Kate's body even closer to his.

The man released his hold of Kate's right hand. He slowly brushed his fingertips down the nape of Kate's neck, over her shoulder, and down her side. He leaned in closer and brushed his stubbly chin against her cheek.

Kate did not protest. She took a deep breath of his scent and exhaled. "Who are you?"

The man leaned back. "I've been watching you dance."

Kate tried to conceal a smile.

The man pulled his face slightly away from Kate.

"You still haven't answered my question." Kate said.

The man tilted his head in to the side and smiled. "Just listen to the music and follow my lead."

The soulful melody entranced Kate. She tried to resist the urge to follow his command but boldly allowed her body to move up against his to the rhythm of the song. She pushed out her right hip and then her left, swaying smoothly back and forth, as the man's right hand crept down to her backside. Kate felt the hair on the back of her neck stand up on end.

She threw back her head, letting her hair fan out. The man bent over and gently stroked her mane.

The song came to an end.

The man pulled Kate up and then let go. He placed his hands together in a triangle and gave Kate a slight bow. "Thank you for the dance."

Before Kate could respond, he turned around and disappeared into the crowd.

CHAPTER 27

Kate scanned the room for Eric. Their table in the back was vacant. She hadn't seen him since he abruptly took off after spotting Father O'Connell.

Walking by the bar, Kate decided to get a drink. As she waited, Kate spotted Eric outside on the terrace. He was smoking and talking with a pretty brunette. The woman was clearly flirting with Eric. She'd tilt her head back, laugh and then touch his arm. Kate got her drink and decided to investigate.

"You're not from around here are you?" Eric said to the brunette as Kate walked up.

The brunette turned towards Kate. Her blue eyes popped out of her face as her scarlet smile lured you back in.

"Kate," Eric said as he stood. "This is Courtney."

Courtney remained seated with her head lowered as she shook Kate's hand.

"Nice to meet you," Kate said as she noticed a large bandage on Courtney's right arm.

"So you're Nate Crawford's kids," Courtney said as she wiped her hand on her dress. "You must be very excited that your dad won the election."

"We helped with his campaign," Eric said as he offered his seat on the bench to Kate.

Kate smiled as she sat next to Courtney. Eric had found a friend. Kate didn't want to ruin the moment. Perhaps she should leave. Before she had a chance to do anything a phone started to ring.

Courtney reached into her purse, looked at her phone display then hit the mute button. She stood. "It was nice to meet both of you. But I've got to go."

"What? Are you going to turn into a pumpkin?" Eric joked.

"Funny, Eric. Really funny." Courtney leaned into Eric, kissed him on the cheek then turned around and quickly walked away.

Eric watched Courtney walk back into ballroom then spun around and sat next to Kate. His whole demeanor had a renewed energy Kate had never seen.

"What was that all about?" Kate asked.

Eric grinned from ear to ear as he tapped his iPhone. "She gave me her number."

"I think you're in love."

"In lust."

"Think you'll call her?"

"Maybe. Maybe not." Eric lit another cigarette, inhaled, and motioned towards the ballroom. "I saw you dancing."

Kate froze.

"Dad's a great dancer."

Kate exhaled. "I had no idea."

"He and Mom used to go out dancing quite a bit when Jenny and I were younger. That's why Mom had a flapper dress for tonight."

"I've never seen them dance."

"A lot has changed." Eric took a drag from his cigarette.

Kate looked at the ground. She wanted to ask Eric about Logan but didn't know where to begin.

"What's bothering you?" Eric asked.

Kate looked up and smiled. "When we were talking inside, at the table, you mentioned something about Sander Walker being the groupie of Logan Sinclair."

Eric threw his cigarette on the ground and stomped it out with his foot. "Logan's the kid that always got whatever he wanted. And Sander was his wingman."

"You mean Sander and Logan are friends?"

"They were quite the team back then. Double trouble if you ask me."

"How did you know Logan?"

Eric looked back at the bar and frowned.

Kate spotted their mom walking towards them.

"They both knew Jenny," Eric said.

Vivian walked up to Eric and Kate. "It's time to go. The party is winding down and your father and I are leaving."

"I can give Eric a ride home," Kate offered.

"I don't think so," Vivian said a little too sharply.

"Mom! You're being—" Kate started.

"No worries Kate," Eric interrupted. "Mom's right. I need to go home with them."

Vivian waited.

"I'll be right there Mom," Eric said.

Vivian turned around and walked slowly towards the ballroom.

Eric whispered, "Kate, there are things you need to know. Father O'Connell and that fucking Seminary are at the root of all our problems."

Kate narrowed her eyes and looked at Eric as they continued to follow Vivian.

"Are you two coming?" Vivian called out.

Eric waved at Vivian as he quickened his pace.

Kate covered her mouth as she walked passed Eric and whispered. "Can you meet me at Rodney's? Tomorrow. 9 AM."

Eric nodded his head.

Kate quickened her pace and walked past her mother into the ballroom. Upon entering, she spotted her dad talking with William and Marie Sinclair.

CHAPTER 28

Only a handful of people remained at the tables scattered around the dance floor. Weeknight events always ended before midnight. The band was packing up their instruments as Kate crossed the dance floor. Nate stood behind Maria and William Sinclair who remained seated at their table.

Nate noticed Kate walking towards them. He cut his conversation short as she approached. "William and Maria, I would like to introduce you to my youngest, Kate."

William stood and shook Kate's hand.

Kate noticed William wore an ornate gold ring with silver "S" crest on his right ring finger.

Maria remained seated, mesmerized by Kate's sudden appearance. "Kate, you're all grown up."

"Have we met?" Kate asked as she offered Maria her hand.

Maria took Kate's hand and delicately shook it.

Kate noticed the large ruby ring on Maria's right hand ring finger.

Maria smiled. "I don't think we've met but I know a lot about—"

William interrupted. "You're quite lovely my dear. It was nice to meet you. Unfortunately, we can't stay and chat. We must be going."

Maria stood but kept studying Kate.

William shook Nate's hand. "I'm glad your entire family came tonight. I look forward to working with you and the rest of the Oakview City Council."

"I welcome the opportunity," Nate said.

William nodded then coaxed Maria with his outward hand to walk towards the exit.

When the Sinclairs were out of range, Kate whispered, "Making friends with the enemy?"

"This is not the place," Nate said a little too harshly.

"Dad. I was teasing." Kate protested as she felt her cheeks getting hot.

Nate forced a smiled and waved at someone behind Kate. "Let's talk about it later. For now, I'll walk you out to your car."

CHAPTER 29
Thursday

Father O'Connell's chin slowly lowered and touched his chest. He immediately bobbed his head up, opened his eyes wide and surveyed his tight quarters. He was seated in the inner confines of a smooth, intricately carved dark mahogany confessional. Only the morning light shining down through the blue and red stained glass window above the altar illuminated the sanctuary. He sat in a chair with his knees barely grazing the door. Lattice grids covered dark screens on either side of the boxed chamber to view the penitent compartments.

He had stayed later than he wanted for the Din for Grins fundraiser. He was not used to the time difference or the demands the elders had placed on him since his return. Father O'Connell had been assigned the morning penitent for the students.

He looked through the lattice screen but did not see anyone. He must have fallen asleep. Had he seen all of the students before they left on the retreat? Father O'Connell had not been invited. He had been ordered to stay behind and mind the Seminary.

Father O'Connell leaned back in the chair, closed his eyes, and took a deep breath.

The confessional shook.

Father O'Connell leaned forward, pushed back the lattice grid in front of the dark screen to see the outline of a hooded figure kneeling. He raised his right hand and greeted the student with the sign of the cross.

The student responded in a low, raspy voice, "Bless me Father for I have sinned. It has been…like never since my last confession!"

Father O'Connell sat up, startled by this abnormal greeting.

"Is the Lord Almighty the only other entity besides yourself who knows what you did back then?" The hooded figure said in a slightly higher voice.

Father O'Connell remained still but opened his eyes wide. Was this a student? "Excuse me?"

"What did you do before you took off for Italy? Boys? It's always boys. Were you sent away because you did some nasty things to some boys?"

"My child, who are you?" Father O'Connell questioned as he tried unsuccessfully to sneak a peek at his subject. Was he addressing a man or woman?

"What did you do to them? Did you film them? Was it a video of you and some of the local boys having an orgy? I bet you're into that kinky kind of shit. I'm into the kinky stuff myself. Or I should say I've learned to enjoy it."

Father O'Connell held his breath as he realized he was talking with a woman.

"I like to tie men up then shave them down to their smooth skin. Gives me a better view of the damage I'm about to inflict. I start with hot wax to tease them into thinking they know what's going to happen. I ease them into the pain with leather and penetrating love bites. And then when they least expect it, I show them who is in control of their life."

Father O'Connell sat speechless not knowing what to do or say.

"But that's just me. That's what I like. And I've never been caught…except. I bet you messed up? I bet you got caught. That's why the Seminary sent you away, all those years ago, to cover up your sins."

Father O'Connell rubbed his hands together and muttered, "What are you talking about? You don't belong here." He began to stand.

"Sit down old man! I've got a gun pointed at you. Don't even think of trying anything."

Father O'Connell sat down as instructed.

"No one's going to help you. They all left on that bus. I watched and waited for each and every one of them to visit you, sniveling about their transgressions, before coming in. There's no one here to help you."

"What is it that you want?"

"The truth."

"The truth?"

"What are you doing back in Oakview? You've been in Italy for what, twenty years? Why come back now?"

No response.

The hooded figure held up a black-gloved hand holding a gun. It's silver metal gleamed in the dim light.

Father O'Connell replied in a slightly quivering voice, "I've come back to save the Seminary from destruction."

"That Cross Creek project?"

"Yes."

The gun was retracted. "Do you know who Walter Rudolf is?"

"Walter Rudolf?"

"That Oakview councilman who died the other night?"

"I'm sorry. I've only just returned this past week. I don't know any of the council people."

"You don't know what was on his phone? Perhaps a video of you fucking some choir boy?"

"Phone? Video? What are you talking about?" Father O'Connell slumped back in his chair.

The penitent compartment shook as the stranger stood.

"If I hear you told anyone about our conversation...I'll put you in the creek like that councilman."

Father O'Connell did not respond.

The figure sat back down. "What do you know about the Sinclairs and the Crawfords?"

Father O'Connell grabbed his rosary and rubbed it between his fingers. "What is there to know?"

"There's something you're not telling me."

"You have no idea what you're talking about? Who sent you here?"

"I'm asking the questions."

Father O'Connell leaned forward. "I have come back to seek forgiveness for the misdeeds of my life. I'm back to make amends and save this institution. Let me help you my child. Let me help you find forgiveness and become one with God. God will forgive all that you have done."

"God? When was there ever a God to protect me from my father? I'm a fallen angel sent to clean up his messes. I'm a healer of the deranged men who prey on the innocent."

Father O'Connell held his breath not wanting to utter another word.

"You better not be bullshitting me."

"I'm not," Father O'Connell pleaded as he placed his elbows on his knees and buried his face in his hands. "I don't know a Walter Rudolf. I don't know anything about a phone and I damn well don't know anything about a video."

Father O'Connell waited for a response.

Nothing.

He slowly raised his head and edged forward on the chair. He looked through the lattice screen. The dark hooded figure was gone.

CHAPTER 30

"Do you believe Patrick?" Vivian asked Nate as they sat in the small breakfast nook of their kitchen eating cereal.

Nate put down his cup of coffee and leaned back in his chair. "We need to be very careful. Patrick said Logan was back but we don't have any proof."

"I think we have our confirmation from what I overheard Maria say at the salon."

"Patrick has nothing to gain from lying about Logan meeting with Obsidian," Nate said as he picked up four ibuprofen pills and threw them in his mouth.

"At least Patrick is trying to make amends. He didn't have to tell us."

Nate gritted his teeth then took a gulp of coffee. "So now all is forgiven?"

"I didn't say that."

Nate ignored Vivian's comment. "Do you think Kate could get involved or hurt somehow?"

"Are you ready to tell Kate?"

Nate took Vivian's hand in his. "If Logan is back, we need to tell Kate everything."

CHAPTER 31

Rodney's Coffee House was located in the Verano Shopping Plaza. The Spanish Style architecture blended in well with the surrounding neighborhood but the roof was beginning to show its age with a scattering of broken tiles. The independent roasting house with its expansive outdoor patio had become a gathering spot for the residents of Oakview and Altamont Heights. Eric was already camped out in the crowded brick patio at a corner table under a heat lamp. He had a coffee in one hand and a copy of the San Jose Daily spread out on the table. He combed his fingers through his damp hair then adjusted his sunglasses. Kate couldn't tell if he saw her.

"Morning," Kate waved as she approached her brother.

Eric raised his head. "Hey there."

Kate put her hand on Eric's shoulder. "I need some caffeine. You want anything?"

"No, thanks." Eric continued to read the paper.

Kate headed inside and returned with a latte. As she sat down, she watched Eric reading the paper. He appeared serious yet oblivious to the world around him. She had to lighten the mood. "You thinking about calling that girl? What was her name?"

Eric looked up at Kate then sat back in his chair. "Courtney. I don't know. I still need to work on myself."

"Maybe a new friend is what you need," Kate suggested as she took a sip of her latte.

Eric folded the newspaper in half and let out a sigh. "I've spent too many years punishing myself. I think maybe I'm ready to move on. Still, I need closure on a few open questions."

Kate sat up in her chair.

Eric took off his sunglasses and placed them on top of the newspaper. "The drugs. The alcohol. I totally blamed myself for what happened to Jenny. I ran away from the mess at home and there's no excuse. It doesn't change anything now and I couldn't have changed what happened back then."

"Is that why you left?"

"Partially. But there's more to it." Eric raised both arms and looked around the patio. "This shopping center was the start of everything. "

"The start of what?"

Eric stared intently at Kate. He grabbed the arms of his chair and pulled closer to the table. "You don't know anything—do you?"

Kate shook her head as she tried to understand what Eric was saying.

"How much do you know about what happened the night Jenny died?"

"Mom and Dad said Jenny killed herself over a boyfriend. And they think Logan Sinclair was involved."

"Killed herself?" Eric put down his coffee and looked across the street towards the Altamont Heights neighborhood. "I've been back with Mom and Dad for three weeks and have come to realize they've been hiding the truth from you for years."

"What do you mean?"

"Do you remember Jenny's best friend Carolyn?"

Kate closed her eyes and tried to remember. Parts of her childhood were completely blank. Then again, she had only been five years old when Jenny died.

"Carolyn Walker?" Eric repeated.

Kate opened her eyes and shook her head.

"You know her older brother."

Kate was completely confused.

"Carolyn's older brother is your schmuck of a CEO Sander Walker."

Kate cocked her head to one side and opened her mouth to say something but couldn't find the words.

"Our moms used to work together."

"Where?"

"At the Seminary. That's how they became friends. Carolyn and Jenny were always together, so Sander was at our house a lot. Dropping off or picking up Carolyn. I can't explain it but I got a weird vibe from him. He'd always linger a little too long. And the way he looked at Jenny gave me the creeps."

Kate took a sip of her latte. Her mind began to spin into overdrive as she thought about Fortunato. Why had Sander personally assigned that account to her? "How does Logan fit into all of this?"

"A couple months before Jenny died, Sander started showing up with him."

"Logan?"

"Yep. He really was a piece of work. Especially the week before Jenny died."

"What'd he do?"

"He started calling every night around 5 PM asking to speak with Jenny. She never spoke to him. But I did. That's how I ended up at the Convent."

Kate felt numb. She put down her latte, crossed her arms and leaned back in the chair. "How did Logan get you there?"

"Drugs."

Kate's mouth became dry. She couldn't move. All she could do was focus on Eric.

"Logan told me he'd just scored a shitload of weed. He was going to unload it that night at a gathering…a gathering at the Convent."

"The Convent?"

"Yeah. It was still standing back then and had become the party place ever since they had shut it down."

"You were into drugs?"

"Don't sound so surprised."

Kate back peddled, "I didn't mean–"

"Don't worry about it." Eric placed his arms on the table. "Back then, I was just dabbling. I thought it'd be cool to tell my friends I had bought some weed."

"Where were Mom and Dad?"

Eric shook his head and rolled his eyes. "Out."

"Where was I?"

Eric looked at the coffee shop then sat back in his chair. He grabbed his sunglasses and put them on. "With me."

Kate's heart skipped a beat as she blocked out the peripheral noise of the people around them. "What do you mean?"

"I was taking care of you that night. I thought we'd only be gone for 30 minutes. I took Dad's car and drove us over there."

Kate closed her eyes and kneaded her brow trying to remember. "You can't be serious."

"I'd taken the car out before without Mom and Dad knowing. I thought it would be no big deal."

Kate opened her eyes wider as it began to sink in that she had been a part of that night. "How did Jenny end up there?"

"I think Carolyn told her what was going on."

"How'd Carolyn know?"

"I guess from Sander? I don't recall. The point is that Jenny wanted to stop me. So she left Carolyn's house and rode her bike over to the Convent."

"And you took me with you?" Kate shook her head in disbelief. "What happened when we got there?"

Eric leaned in closer to Kate. "I left you in the car. Logan and Sander were there with three other guys and a girl."

"Did you know any of them?"

"No. They were all a couple years older except the girl was Jenny's age."

"Was Jenny able to stop you?"

"I had already bought the weed when she showed up. That's when I did something really stupid." Eric picked up his coffee and guzzled down the remaining contents. "Logan convinced me to try this other stuff, some white powder. I didn't want it but everyone pressured me into it. And that's when things got kind of fuzzy."

"Fuzzy?"

"I got completely wasted. Jenny was there one moment and then…I don't know." Eric folded his arms. "All I know is that I heard her scream."

"You saw what happened?"

"No. I remember running. Running towards the scream. And then I found her."

Kate raised her right hand up in front of her mouth and gasped.

"She was lying on the steps of the main entrance. Eyes open to the sky." Eric's voice started to tremble as tears ran down his cheeks. "She looked so peaceful."

"Was she alive?"

Eric wiped his nose on his shirtsleeve. "There was so much blood. It kept filling in the cracks of the cement steps. I got up…started walking, walking away." Eric shook his head. "I left her. I left her all alone."

Kate looked around the patio. No one was listening to their conversation.

Eric took a deep breath and wiped the tears away from his cheeks with his fingers. "Jenny never would've come to the Convent if I hadn't decided to do something as stupid as buy some weed. I'm such a jackass."

Kate reached towards Eric and took his hand in hers. "What happened with the police?"

Eric shrugged his shoulders, "They said it was suicide. Jenny killed herself over a boyfriend. That's bullshit."

Leaning back in her chair, Kate mumbled, "Jenny didn't kill herself?"

CHAPTER 32

Courtney looked down at her manicurist. She was slowly and delicately applying the Chick Flick Cherry to her toenails, careful not to let any of the syrupy red polish touch Courtney's skin. This woman took pride in her work. And so did Courtney. "Don't forget the top coat!"

The manicurist looked up and smiled.

The skull and cross bone silver bedazzled Samsung phone vibrated, "Ruby. I'm here," Courtney snapped.

"Did you see Father O'Connell? Ruby asked.

Courtney looked around the nail salon. Four other customers were seated across from her on the other side of the room. Her manicurist barely spoke English and the chatter from the other stations provided just enough coverage for her conversation. Courtney responded in a slight whisper. "I saw him at the fundraiser but paid him a visit this morning."

"You did what?"

"I went to confession."

"Did anyone see you?"

Courtney shook her head and smirked, "Of course not."

"What did he say?"

"Doesn't know anything about Walter Rudolf. Didn't even know who the guy was."

"He could've been lying."

"Not with a gun pointed at his head."

Silence.

Courtney scanned the salon. "You did say to do whatever it takes to get him to talk. I just rattled his cage."

No response.

"He's back in Oakview to save the Seminary from that Cross Creek project."

"Good God, why?" Ruby inadvertently uttered.

"Something about repenting for sins he's committed. Does the video on Walter's phone have anything to do with the priest?"

"That doesn't concern you. Where's the phone?"

"I don't have it, but I'm getting to Kate…through her brother."

"No more bodies. I just need Walter's phone and to know if anyone has seen the video."

"Don't worry. I'll be careful."

"I trust you will. Or I'll have to call your daddy."

The call ended.

CHAPTER 33

Eric shook his head, "No way. Jenny didn't kill herself."

"Was there ever an investigation into Jenny's death?"

"Logan took off for Europe so the police never got to question him. And Sander wasn't talking. No one was talking."

"That's why you think Sander and Logan were responsible?"

"If Jenny threw herself from the tower, why did she land face up? She also had a welt on her cheek. It looked like a small half circle. Someone had to have put it there."

"Someone hit her?"

"Exactly."

"Did you tell the police?"

"Of course but they ignored me. Said I wasn't a credible witness because I was wasted."

"What about the welt on Jenny's face?"

"Police said it must have been there for a couple days. They didn't have forensics like we do today." Eric leaned forward and grabbed a pack of cigarettes from his pant pocket. "Jenny didn't commit suicide. I think Logan killed her."

Kate sat back in her chair. She couldn't move. Her entire life flashed before her eyes. Why had her parents lied to her all these years? She could only think of one thing to ask Eric. "Why?"

Eric did not respond. He took a cigarette out from the pack and began to tap it on the table.

"There has to be a reason. Why do you think Logan killed her?"

"I don't want to even think about it."

"Was Jenny trying to defend herself?"

"Probably. But we'll never know."

"And Logan's conveniently been gone this whole time."

"Yep. Stinks to me." Eric said as he put the cigarette in between his fingers and rolled in back and forth.

Fortunato loomed in the back of Kate's mind. She was meeting Logan that morning. Was it just a coincidence? "What about Sander?"

"He claimed he was never at the Convent. And those jackass friends of his remained silent. I bet the Sinclairs paid them off."

"Did the Seminary see or hear anything?"

"You'd think since it was in their own backyard? But no, the police couldn't question the head of the Seminary because Father O'Connell left town."

"Who exactly is Father O'Connell?"

Eric sat back in his chair and crossed his arms. "Mom used to work for him. Helped manage their books. They got to be pretty good friends."

"Why did he leave after Jenny died?"

"Supposedly took a sabbatical."

Kate tried to absorb her past but found it hard to believe. She began to get upset. Why had she been led to believe Jenny killed herself? "Why didn't Mom and Dad ever say anything to me?"

Eric shook his head. "To protect you. That's probably why they sent you to the all-girls school. They didn't want you to be around boys."

Kate was irritated with Sander. He was her CEO. She felt violated. He had to know she was Jenny's younger sister. And there had to be a reason he personally assigned Fortunato to her. Kate looked around her surroundings and realized Eric had never explained his first comment when they started their conversation. "How does all of this relate to Verano Shopping Center?"

Eric took the cigarette and put it in his mouth.

"You can't smoke that here," Kate said.

Eric got up from the table and walked over to the parking lot. He lit the cigarette, took a couple puffs then dropped it on the ground and stamped it out. He returned to the table and sat down. "Sorry about that."

"No problem."

"Months before Jenny died, Dad was in negotiations to buy this property. He didn't have the capital so Renee Verano somehow got involved."

"Is that how they first met?"

"Yep. After Jenny died, Renee asked Dad to come work for her and develop the shopping center. No one believed me about Jenny, Dad was consumed by this new project and spent all of his time with Renee. And Mom became the ice queen. I couldn't take it. It was the perfect opportunity to disappear." Eric took off his sunglasses and looked intently at Kate, squeezing her hand. "I'm just sorry I left you. I should have stayed. I'm so sorry, Kate."

Kate tried to smile but was consumed by emotion. She patted Eric's hand as a tear fell down her cheek. "You're here now."

For several minutes, Kate and Eric stopped the world around then and just stared at each other.

Eric took a deep breath and exhaled. "The one good thing Dad did in all of this was find me. I get a second chance. I get to prove once and for all that Logan and Sander were responsible for Jenny's death."

"How are you going to do that?"

Eric released his hold of Kate's hand. "I don't exactly know. Dad's asked me to help him do some research on Cross Creek."

Kate closed her eyes as the reality of the situation began to sink in. What kind of game was Sander playing? Why had he wanted her to come in contact with Logan? The NDA for Cayenne could not have been misplaced. It had been obliterated for a reason.

"Dad wants me to find information on the lease—why the Sinclairs leased the land to the Seminary. He thinks it somehow relates to Cross Creek. I was going to start at the main library in San Jose. Perhaps I'll find something there."

"Really?" Kate opened her eyes wide and sat up as she remembered her conversation with Jessica.

"What's gotten into you?"

"We've been thinking the same thing."

"We have?"

Kate leaned forward on the table. "On Monday, Sander assigned a new account to me, Fortunato. My friend Jessica Knight is a reporter up in Seattle. I asked her to dig into the Sinclairs."

"Why?"

"Logan Sinclair is the head of Fortunato."

Eric slumped back in his chair.

"It got me thinking about Jenny. Did she really commit suicide because of Logan? I asked Jessica to dig into the Sinclairs, find anything about their real estate deals around the time of Jenny's death. The San Jose Daily hasn't digitized their archives earlier than 1990 but the library has microfiche."

Eric remained quiet.

"Now we can broaden our search to include Sander. There's got to be some connection that links everything back to Jenny's death."

A loud beep came from Kate's phone. "Excuse me." Kate looked through here purse. Her phone display read 10 AM. There was a message from her calendar app. "Shit!"

"What?"

One hour until her meeting with Fortunato. Kate bit her lower lip as she stood. "I'm meeting with Logan."

"What the fuck!" Eric gritted through his teeth.

"I don't know if I can do it..." Kate's voice faded as she placed her hand on the table for support.

Eric's face turned red as the veins in his neck tensed. "I don't like this at all. Sounds too convenient if you ask me."

Kate hesitated. Should she tell Eric about Cayenne?

Eric stood and walked over to Kate. "I'm not losing another sister."

Kate could not contain her emotions. "Walk with me."

Eric left his belongings at the table as they walked out of the patio over to Kate's car.

Kate rummaged through her purse for sunglasses.

"If you ask me, you're playing with fire." Eric said.

Kate's throat began to tighten as she tried to swallow. She found her sunglasses. As she raised them to her face, she fumbled them onto the paved ground.

Eric retrieved the sunglasses as he led Kate over to her green Mini Cooper. When they got to the car, he wrapped her into his arms. Kate placed her head on his chest. "Why would Logan kill her?"

Eric hugged Kate closer. "I don't know Kate. I wish I knew."

Kate was exhausted. She couldn't imagine ever going back to Obsidian. How could she face both Sander and Logan after everything Eric had told her? What kind of game were they playing? But then she thought about Cayenne. How had they become the innocent victims in this perverse game? A perverse game dreamed up by the same people who may have killed Jenny? Kate fought back her tears as she looked up at Eric.

"I don't understand what's going on," Eric said looking down at Kate.

"Neither do I," Kate responded.

Eric brushed the wisps of hair stuck on Kate's check away from her face. "This is happening for a reason. I can't explain it but now thinking about it, you've got to go to that meeting. Find out why Logan's back."

Kate nodded her head.

"It's not like you'll be alone with him."

Kate took a step back as she blotted her eyes with her fingers. "It's just a lot to take in at once."

"Does he know who you are? Have you ever spoken to him?"

"No." Kate stammered.

Eric placed both his hands on Kate's shoulders. "This is huge Kate. This could be the break we've been waiting for. You need to meet Logan. Find out why he's back."

Kate closed her eyes and took a deep breath. She opened her eyes and looked up at Eric. "I guess I have nothing to lose."

Eric smiled. "That'a girl!"

A chill went down Kate's spine. Eric's smile was exactly the same as Jenny's; a single undulation that ended by curling up on the right side.

CHAPTER 34

Kate entered her office and closed the door. She slowly sat down in her chair. How could she walk into the most important meeting of her career and pretend she wasn't rattled. She needed to collect herself. Had Logan really killed Jenny?

Logan and Hashim would be here soon. She took her phone and used the camera to look at herself. Her eyes were still red from crying. How could she meet Logan without thinking about Jenny?

Kate opened a desk drawer and took out a small bottle of eye drops. She titled her head back and squeezed the bottle. As she blinked, she glanced over at the file cabinet and saw the silver iPhone she had found down in the creek. Was it charged?

A beep came from Kate's phone. She looked at the display and saw a text message from Jessica with an attached photo.

Kate clicked the attachment. A very grainy, pixilated black and white image appeared on her display. She zoomed in and then out. It was not what she expected. She began to relax.

The image was of a scrawny kid with glasses. He had tried to smile, but the camera caught him in between takes, which made for an awkward pose. He looked weak. Not the monster she had envisioned.

The office phone rang. Kate looked at the display: Lobby.

Kate stood alone in the elevator holding a plastic manila envelope, watching the florescence green numbers above the doors count down as her body temperature slowly rose. Rubbing her hands down the side of her skirt wiped away the excess moisture but could not calm her anxious heart. Kate closed her eyes and took a deep breath. As she exhaled the elevator doors opened.

Walking out into the lobby, Kate immediately noticed two men. A middle-eastern man with thick dark hair with a computer satchel slung around his torso was talking with the receptionist. Another man dressed completely in black, stood in the far corner studying a digital art display.

"Hashim?" Kate offered her hand to the middle-eastern man.

"Kate Crawford?" Hashim responded with a British accent as he shook her hand.

"Great to finally meet you," Kate said.

"Likewise Kate. I know you're going to be impressed with Mirage."

"I hope so. Where's Mr. Sinclair?"

"Oh yes." Hashim surveyed the lobby. His gaze fell on the man dressed in black studying the digital art. Hashim waved and called out, "Logan...Logan."

The man did not turn around.

"Sorry. When he's concentrating, it's hard to pull him away. I'll get him."

Kate followed Hashim.

"I must apologize ahead of time," Hashim whispered under his breath. "I'm afraid Logan does not know your name. He doesn't care for the details. He's mostly interested in Sander Walker's presence at the meeting."

"I can understand," Kate said with relief. Logan was not expecting to meet Jenny Crawford's little sister.

Hashim walked up to Logan. Without turning around, Logan said, "I often wonder how man can create such unusual images in his mind and translate them into media for the rest of the world to see." Logan leaned over the display. "This artist is quite talented. I should buy it." He turned around and faced them.

Kate's mouth fell open. Her chest tightened. Her cheeks instantly flushed as she broke out in a cold sweat. Logan was her dance partner from the Din for Grins fundraiser.

"I'd like you to meet the account manager responsible for setting up our meeting today, Kate Crawford," Hashim said.

Logan's smile evaporated.

Kate offered her hand as she squeaked out, "Logan Sinclair. Nice to meet you."

Logan did not take Kate's hand. Instead he turned to Hashim and curtly asked, "Is this some kind of joke?"

"I'm sorry. I don't understand," Hashim replied as he looked from Kate to Logan.

Logan looked around the lobby then turned to Hashim, "Give us a moment." He motioned with his hand for Kate to walk with him to the other corner of the lobby. "May I speak with you—alone?"

Kate looked at Hashim and then nodded. Her gut told her to stay put, but she had no other choice. Logan paced back and forth. "I can't explain this anomaly, of you and I meeting, like this, at Obsidian. What do you have to do with this meeting?"

"Sander assigned Fortunato to me. You're my account."

Logan stood perfectly still as his eyes circled the lobby. He finally stopped on Kate and now looked at her with fire in his eyes. "I'm not playing games here. You and your family better not interfere with my business at Obsidian."

Before Kate could respond, Logan hastily turned around and walked back to Hashim.

Kate walked over to security to retrieve their visitor badges. With her back turned to Logan, she closed her eyes. *Breathe.*

Logan impatiently looked at Kate then the elevators. "What are we waiting for? Let's get upstairs. I want to see Sander."

CHAPTER 35

The elevator doors opened on the fourteenth floor. Logan pushed past Kate with Hashim in tow. The ride up had been deceptively quiet. Kate had remained silent resisting the urge to ask Logan questions about Jenny. Logan ignored Kate, as if she disgusted him. Sensing something was off, Hashim did not utter a word.

Kate quickened her stride and pointed Logan in the direction of the Lava conference room. For once she was relieved to see Amy's severe bob and Prada suit waiting for them.

"Logan, this is my manager, Amy Bourdon," Kate said as they walked into a large rectangular room with floor-to-ceiling windows overlooking the San Thomas Hills and an oval conference table with ten chairs.

"Director of Strategic Accounts," Amy corrected Kate as she shook Logan's hand.

"Nice to meet you," Logan smiled flirtatiously as he shook Amy's hand longer than normal.

Amy's tight lips slowly relaxed into a wide smile.

"And this is Hashim." Kate interrupted disgusted by Logan's sudden change in demeanor. "He's the lead engineer on the Mirage product."

Amy reluctantly released her hand from Logan and shook Hashim's hand.

"I'd like to thank Kate for being able to put together this meeting on such short notice," Logan turned towards Amy. "It tells me a lot about the caliber of your people."

"Kate is one of our rising stars. I had no doubt she could do it," Amy forced a smile. "Let's sit while we wait for Sander."

As they all sat in the chairs, the dull thud of heavy footsteps on the carpet came from outside the conference room. Everyone stopped talking and looked towards the doorway.

Sander Walker marched in, looked at everyone and commanded the room. "I'm here. Let's get started."

Kate walked up to Sander and offered her hand. "Sander. Thank you for taking the time to meet with us. We–"

"Yes. Kate Crawford." Sander shook Kate's hand while looking behind her. "Logan Sinclair. It's been awhile."

Kate moved to the side.

"It has," Logan replied as he stood and shook Sander's hand. "And now you're the CEO of Obsidian. Who knew."

"I knew," Sander responded.

Kate looked at Amy then Hashim. What were Logan and Sander talking about?

"Thank you for assigning Kate Crawford to us as our account manager," Logan offered sarcastically.

Sander pursed his lips but did not reply.

Sensing an awkward confrontation, Kate tried to take charge. "Sander, this is Hashim Abbasi. He is the lead engineer for the Mirage product."

Sander turned towards Hashim and shook his hand.

"Okay, then. Let's get started," Sander said making eye contact with Logan and then Amy. "Have we signed an NDA?"

Kate stood and walked over to Sander. From the plastic manila envelope, she produced three sheets of paper. She spread them on the table and handed Logan a pen.

"What's this?" Logan asked as he took the pen.

"Standard non-disclosure agreement," Amy said as she leaned in towards Logan and pointed at the document. "We need to protect your product. Whatever you show us today is to remain confidential."

Kate added. "We can't copy your product idea."

Logan looked up at Sander, "Well that's not likely to happen...is it?"

Sander laughed.

Logan signed the papers then handed the pen back to Kate. Kate looked at Sander.

"What?" Sander said coldly.

"Don't you want to sign it?" Kate asked.

Sander looked at Amy and then Kate. "You're the account manager. You sign it."

Kate held the pen just above the paper but hesitated. She had signed the NDA for Cayenne. But now it was missing. What would this mean if her name was also attached to this NDA? Kate felt the world around her pressing in. Everyone was watching. She couldn't falter now. Kate pressed the ink on the paper and signed her name.

Sander smiled. "Good. Now let's see this demo."

As everyone sat down at the conference table, Hashim opened his laptop and connected it to a cable for the 65-inch flat screen TV mounted on the wall.

Sander took a seat next to Hashim then looked back at Logan. "What's the product called?

"Mirage," Logan replied.

"Quite appropriate," Sander snickered.

The room fell silent.

Kate looked over at Amy.

Amy sat next to Logan expressionless.

Hashim launched into the demo.

CHAPTER 36

Amy closed the door to her office, walked past Kate and sat down at her desk. She did not make eye contact. Instead, she taped on her tablet and began to read something.

Kate could not contain herself. Her entire face became red. "That, that product, Mirage—"

Amy held up her hand. "I know you have a lot of questions."

"It's exactly the same as Cayenne's. Does Sander really want to buy Mirage?"

"The products are slightly different."

Kate bit her lip, straining to hold back what she really thought.

"You haven't seen Cayenne's product since August, right?"

Clive and Russ didn't mention new features over lunch except for the analytics component. Kate knew Amy was right.

"So you really don't know what they have right now?"

Kate remained quiet for a moment and looked down at her hands, carefully composing her next sentence. "Sander just told Logan Sinclair that Mirage is a perfect fit for Obsidian's product lineup. But it's too similar to Cayenne's product. Based on the product we previewed in August, I see no difference between Cayenne's Virtual Presence and Mirage. The features and User Interface are way too similar. And they both have an analytics component. How do we know Fortunato didn't steal Cayenne's product?"

Amy turned around. "Hold on. Let's not start making accusations."

"Only you, Sander and I were in the meeting in August."

"Cayenne could have shown the product to someone outside of Obsidian."

"Not possible. Cayenne wants Obsidian to buy their product. Now after seeing the Mirage demo, I'm concerned that Cayenne's NDA is missing."

Amy became still as she stared at Kate. "Missing? What do you mean?"

"It was in my file cabinet and on the server one day and gone the next. If we don't have that NDA, Cayenne is hosed."

Amy turned and looked outside her office window. "Sander wants Mirage. We need to deliver it to him."

Kate looked at Amy with disbelief. Why didn't she care about the NDA? Or was it because Amy's name wasn't on it. Kate alone would be held accountable for any wrong doing.

"Do we have more than a verbal agreement with Cayenne?"

Amy saw Sander give Russ and Clive the go ahead—they had tweaked the analytic component based on his specs. Kate nodded her head as she felt her face become redder in frustration.

"A handshake isn't legally binding." Amy walked over to Kate and sat on the edge of the desk. "Just do your job. After the IPO, we will all be in a better situation, including you."

Unnerved by the direction the conversation was taking, Kate impulsively blurted out, "How well do you know Sander?"

Amy's face turned bright red. She carefully pulled down the sides of her orange and blue Emillo Pucci print blouse and walked back to her chair to sit down. "We're done here."

Kate slowly stood then made her way to the door, deliberately trampling the rug as she went.

As she opened the door, Amy snapped, "We have dinner with Logan and Hashim in two hours. You have until then to adopt a new attitude."

CHAPTER 37

Standing in front of the Divine Science Community Center in Altamont Heights, Eric took one last drag from his cigarette. He threw it on the ground and snuffed it out with his right foot. He glanced around him. Most everyone was either smoking cigarettes or drinking coffee or both. Past habits were written all over their bodies. The wrinkles, welts, sores, discolored skin and decayed teeth all told a story. Eric felt lucky his body had recovered from the damage he'd inflicted on it.

People began filing into the main entrance of the center. Eric followed the signs for Narcotics Anonymous.

Roughly thirty souls filled the room. Eric sat in the back and observed. These people were of all ages and cultural backgrounds, as drugs do not discriminate. Eric watched and listened to the heartbreaking stories of those seeking redemption. He had yet to share his story with this group.

Restless and distracted by the morning's conversation with Kate, Eric's attention locked on the entrance as the door slowly opened. Courtney, the raven-haired woman from the fundraiser, snuck in.

Eric sat up in his chair. Courtney was not the typical addict. She seemed fresh, new, and uncomplicated. He made eye contact with her. She smiled and walked towards him.

"Courtney," Eric whispered.

"Eric?" Courtney said softly as she sat down next to him and rubbed hand sanitizer on her palms.

"Good memory."

When the meeting ended, Eric and Courtney remained seated as the room emptied.

"Nice surprise seeing you here." Eric said.

"When I met you the other night, I realized it was time for me to check in. It's been almost a month," Courtney said.

"That's why I've never seen you here. I've only been coming for the last three weeks."

Courtney smiled and slightly touched Eric's shoulder as she leaned back and stretched her arm over the back of the chair.

"We didn't get to talk much about this the other night. How are you doing?" Eric said as he leaned forward in his chair.

"I take it day by day." Courtney looked down at the floor.

"How long has it been for you?"

"Just over two years." Courtney looked up and made eye contact with Eric.

"You seem good."

"I take it one day at a time. There's no cure." Courtney slowly moved her arm from the back of the chair to her knee.

"You seem to be doing much better than all of us. I mean look at you. You're so much more put together." Eric leaned in closer to Courtney. "You really have your life together. I hope to be there some day."

"That is so not true." Courtney lightly touched Eric's arm. "What about you? How long?"

"6 months, 3 weeks, and 4 days."

"You do take this seriously."

"I have no choice. I have someone to live for…"

"Your sister? The one I met at the party? What's her name?"

"Kate."

Courtney took Eric's hand in hers. "What got you here?"

"It's a long story."

"I've got all the time you need."

Eric relaxed and sat back in the chair. "You really want to hear this?"

"Absolutely." Courtney smiled.

Eric looked down at his hand, intertwined with Courtney's hand. He glanced around the room. "It all started with the death of my twin sister."

CHAPTER 38

Nate found himself once again at the Oakview police department. The lobby had changed quite a bit since that morning twenty years ago. Larger windows brought in more light to the newly painted waiting area. The furniture was new too, but it was just as uncomfortable as the old.

An average looking forty-something man trying to appear younger in jeans, a white button down shirt, and a navy blue blazer walked into the lobby. "Nate Crawford?" the man said as he offered his hand.

Nate stood and shook his hand.

"Detective Bob Harris."

"Nice to meet you," Nate said.

"I hear congratulations are in order for our future councilman."

Nate coughed. "Thank you."

"What's your interest in the Rudolf death."

Nate looked around the room. "Are you working the case?"

"I was assigned to it."

"Was?" Nate asked.

The detective motioned for Nate to sit down in the corner of the lobby for more privacy. "Yes. The medical examiner determined Walter died in the car crash by accidental drowning. We found no signs of foul play. The body's being released tomorrow."

"That quickly?"

"Walter's wife wanted to keep things quick and quiet. What's your interest?"

Nate shook his head. "Walter's wife called me the night he died."

The detective took out a note pad and began to jot down some notes. "Were you friendly with her?"

"I've never met her."

"Why did she call?"

"She was looking for Walter and wondering if I had spoken to him."

"Were you expecting him?"

Nate frowned. "No. This is exactly what the officer asked me the night of the accident."

"So what happened that got you thinking?"

"I didn't tell the officer something."

"Why not?"

"I've been here before–"

"Yes. I know. Your daughter Jenny. I was just starting out on the force when that happened."

"Then you know I lived down here. No one would give me the time of day. Everyone said the same thing, that Jenny killed herself. Committed suicide. But I know that isn't true."

Nate stopped himself and took a deep breath. "I've had a couple days to think about the night Walter died. When Elizabeth called, she was asking some really personal questions which seemed odd."

Detective Harris leaned back on the couch. "How so?"

"She asked whether Walter and I had ever spoken about the Cross Creek project."

"Wasn't that the main point of contention between the two of you?"

"True. But we never discussed it. Walter failed to show up for the debate on Monday. My point is Elizabeth asked if Walter had ever spoken to me about the death of my daughter."

"Well, that is public information."

"Yes, but doesn't it seem odd she would ask me these questions while she's trying to locate her husband?"

"I see your point but why would a phone call relate to Walter's car accident?"

Nate rolled his eyes. "Just like last time."

"Excuse me?"

"I'm going to be installed on the Oakview City Council in less than a month. Can you at least look into it? Ask Elizabeth what she meant?"

Detective Harris closed his note pad and stood. "We finished walking the accident site this morning. There was no sign of foul play. Walter simply lost control of the car and crashed. It is unfortunate the creek was full of water and he drowned. I don't want to drag Elizabeth back down here to ask her more questions."

Nate bit his lower lip. "You won't just call her and ask?"

"She's already been through enough. I won't do it."

Nate nodded his head, stood and offered his hand. "Thank you for your time."

Detective Harris shook Nate's hand. "Sorry I couldn't be of any more help."

Nate turned around and walked out of the building. He pulled out his phone and looked through his contact list. He selected Renee Verano's number and sent the call.

After four rings, a hoarse voice answered, "How'd it go?"

"Just as I thought." Nate reached his car, unlocked it and got in. "What's the address for the Rudolf's house?"

CHAPTER 39

The afternoon light slowly disappeared behind the San Thomas Hills as Nate drove his Silver Toyota Prius onto the crushed pea gravel driveway of the Rudolf property. An older black Lexus sedan covered in a thin grimy film was parked at the foot of the slate steps leading up to the white column entrance of the house.

Nate cut the engine. He looked at the house and noticed a light was on in one of the front rooms. He got out of the car. Walking towards the front door, Nate felt the crunch of the gravel under his feet. As he reached for the large, distressed ring knocker, the front door slowly opened.

"What do YOU want?" a woman said from within the house.

"Elizabeth? Is that you? It's—"

"I know who you are. What do you want?"

"Do you have a moment? I need to talk with you. It's important."

"I have nothing to say to you." Elizabeth started to close the door.

Nate lunged forward shoving his foot just inside the opening. "Why did you ask me about my daughter's death?"

The door stopped moving.

"I want to help," Nate offered.

"Just go away. I can't do this. They'll know we've talked."

"Who will know? What are you talking about?"

The door opened a crack more. Nate stepped back and saw Elizabeth in full view. He had seen photos of her in society magazines but she was hardly recognizable. No make-up could hide those red swollen eyes and dark circles. Her white bathrobe was soiled with a mustard stain on the collar and smeared black mascara on both sleeves.

"Elizabeth. I'm sorry about Walter. I really am. I know you've been through a lot these last couple days. When you called, why'd you ask me about my daughter, Jenny?"

Elizabeth clung to the door and looked outside behind Nate. "I don't know you and I don't know your daughter."

"But why would you ask me that question?"

"Find Walter's phone. It'll answer all your questions." Elizabeth slammed the door shut.

CHAPTER 40

Courtney leaned against the headboard of the bed in her hotel room with Walter's laptop on her thighs. She had been checking his iCloud account but the phone could not be located. To keep herself busy she was doing a search on the Crawfords.

When Eric told Courtney about Jenny, she realized the video on Walter's phone was more valuable to her than she first thought. She had blindly entered this partnership with Ruby to save her own ass. But if she found the phone, she could perhaps blackmail Ruby.

Her Samsung phone began to vibrate. Courtney looked at the display, Ruby. Quelle surprise. "I'm here."

"Have you found the phone?"

"No. Next question."

"What about the brother?"

"I had a long chat with him at his NA meeting this afternoon"

"What? You didn't do anything stupid?"

Courtney looked around the neatly kept hotel room and sighed. No tie me up, tie me down today. "No. But he told me his whole life story."

"Did he mention any names?"

"What names? Does this relate to the video on Walter's phone?

"I'm not asking for your input. Does he know anything about Walter's phone? Does his sister have it?"

"I couldn't just ask. He was so vulnerable and cute, it would look too obvious."

"Push him more. The IPO launch has got to go smoothly." Ruby stopped herself.

What IPO launch? Courtney was intrigued. An IPO meant money. Was that what Walter's wife had mentioned? What was the name of the company? This situation was getting more interesting by the minute. Maybe she wouldn't need her daddy's money after all. "I'm meeting up with Eric tomorrow for dinner."

"Good. Call me when you know more."

The phone call ended.

Courtney adjusted the pillows behind her head and woke up Walter's computer. Eric and blackmail money. What more could a girl ask for?

CHAPTER 41

Amy and Kate walked outside the main entrance of Obsidian and headed down 4th Street towards the main business district of downtown Altamont Heights.

"Have you adjusted your attitude?" Amy asked.

Kate felt her face turn red as she watched Amy turn and continue to walk ahead. She wanted to die right there on the sidewalk but decided not to give Amy the satisfaction.

When Kate caught up to her, Amy asked, "Are we confirmed at St. Anthony's Alley?"

"Yes. I hear they have a new chef. I hope the food is good."

"I'm sure it will be fine."

"Amy, what am I supposed to tell Cayenne about meeting with Sander on Monday?"

Amy shook her head. "Let me think about it. I'll figure something out by then." Amy stopped mid stride then turned towards Kate. "In your research on Fortunato, have you found out anything about Logan Sinclair?"

Kate thought about her conversation with Eric. She knew better than to trust Amy. "There's not much out there on him. All I know is that he's originally from Oakview but he's been living in Italy for the past twenty years."

"Is he married?"

Kate felt sick. Amy had fallen for Logan's tricks. "No idea."

Amy smiled. "I got a good vibe from him when we met."

"I think we need to be careful since Sander and Logan have a history."

"They do? How do you know?"

"Umm…" Kate tried to stall. She stared straight ahead and kept walking.

"What makes you think that?"

Kate's eyes lit up. She remembered something that was said during the meeting. "When Sander and Logan shook hands, Sander mentioned they hadn't seen each other in a long time."

"Really? I missed that."

Kate knew more about Logan than Amy. She stood taller and more confident as they made their way towards the restaurant.

CHAPTER 42

St. Anthony's Alley was located off the main business strip of Alma Ave, down an obscure street, housed in an old wooden building. The entrance had a thick metal door with a carved bust of a male angel hovering above the mantle.

Kate opened the door and motioned for Amy to enter.

"We have a reservation under Crawford," Amy said to the short blonde hostess as they entered the restaurant.

Kate rolled her eyes as Amy tried to highjack her dinner.

"Ah yes. We've already seated half of your party." The hostess came around the podium. "Follow me."

With its distressed wood paneling, dim lights and deep purple tapestry, the restaurant resembled the inside of a wine barrel. It was divided into three rooms that formed a U. The hostess led Kate and Amy through the entire crowded restaurant to a table by a window facing the street. Only Hashim was seated at the table.

Hashim stood and leaned over to shake Kate and Amy's hands.

"Is Logan here?" Amy asked as she sat across from Hashim.

"He stepped out to take a call," Hashim said.

Logan walked up to the table. He was wearing a black cashmere sweater and dark denim jeans.

Amy immediately perked up.

"Sorry. Problem at my hotel. Something about an uninvited guest," Logan announced arrogantly to the table.

Amy stood, completely ignoring Logan's comment. "No worries."

Logan leaned in and gave Amy a kiss on each cheek.

Kate didn't allow Logan the same opportunity. She stood and offered her hand. "Thanks for meeting with us tonight."

A grin spread over Logan's face.

Kate was not going to play by his rules.

Logan shook Kate's hand and muttered, "Looks can be deceiving."

Kate did not take the bait. "We're glad to have you on board."

Amy glared at Kate then focused on Logan. "We thought dinner would be a good opportunity for you to get to know us and ask questions about Obsidian. Establishing a partnership can be complicated."

"Are you complicated or just this process?" Logan joked.

Amy threw back her head and let out a laugh.

Kate was disgusted. She had never seen Amy flirt with anyone. As she sat down next to Hashim, the waiter approached.

Before anyone had time to look at their menus or hear the specials, Logan took charge. "Portaci due bottiglie di Barolo piu bella la tua," Logan commanded in Italian as he ordered the wine.

The waiter nodded that he understood.

Logan continued to speak Italian in ordering food for the entire table. When the waiter left, Logan smugly commented, "It's family style. It's the least I could do for all of you."

Amy nodded her head in agreement as she moved her chair closer to Logan.

Kate sat back wondering what else Logan had up his sleeve.

"I assume since Obsidian's launching the IPO next week, we won't be able to do much work together for another month," Logan said as their wine glasses were delivered to the table.

After the wine was poured, Kate tried to regain control of the table by countering, "That's not true. Hashim can work with our engineers to ensure Mirage works flawlessly with our products."

Amy interrupted. "This won't interfere with the quiet period. The key is not to draw any attention to yourself or the fact that Obsidian is working directly with you." Amy looked to Hashim and then Kate. "Kate can set up an office in our building for you. That way you can get help when you need it."

Hashim nodded and smiled at Kate.

Kate tried to relax. She was relieved to find one ally at the table.

Logan nodded his head. "Good...good. I guess this means I shouldn't break out the Champagne glasses and tell my family just yet."

Amy raised her eyebrows as she looked at Kate then Logan. "Why would you want to do that?"

Logan placed his elbows on the table and threaded his fingers together. He released his hands then started to twist the gold ring on his right hand. This was the same ring Kate had noticed the night of the fundraiser.

"I've worked so hard to get to this point. I deserve some recognition." Logan slowly stretched his arms up over his head and smiled. "Telling one or two people won't matter, will it?"

Kate was stunned. Logan could disrupt the IPO if he talked. "We need to treat this entire transaction with the strictest confidence," she said.

"Let's not jump ahead of ourselves," Amy interjected. She turned to Logan and smiled. "Sander has given you a verbal, but since we haven't discussed the specifics of any agreement or signed a contract we should consider these talks informal and confidential."

Logan sat back in his chair and considered Amy's words. He looked over at Kate, his eyes sparkled. "How long do you think it will take Hashim to integrate Mirage with your suite of products?"

Kate furrowed her brow. What was Logan doing? Condescending one moment and charming the next. "It all depends on how well your code will integrate with ours." Kate turned to Hashim. "If I can speak for Hashim, he won't know until he sits down with our engineers."

"That's right, Kate," Hashim added warmly.

"That gives us a little over seven weeks to get it done," Logan said.

"Excuse me?" Amy sounded surprised.

"Sander wants the product ready to go by the beginning of the year," Logan said nonchalantly.

Amy looked at Kate. "I hadn't heard that. Kate?"

Kate gnashed her teeth. Amy always put her in an awkward position when she didn't know the answer to a question. But this time Kate had an answer. "Seems like a logical plan given our IPO launch, the holiday schedule, and the trade shows at the beginning of the year. Sander probably wants to announce at CES in Las Vegas."

Logan nodded in agreement then took a sip of water. He turned to Hashim. "If you're here on site for the next month, don't you think we can meet this date?"

Hashim looked at Kate and shrugged his shoulders. "With Kate's guidance, I'm sure I can."

"Kate was never part of the plan," Logan grunted as the waiter arrived with the first course.

CHAPTER 43

When the foursome had finished dinner, Hashim excused himself to use the restroom. Kate had hardly touched her plate. She couldn't stomach the conversation. Logan's plate was wiped clean. Amy had only touched the salad as she was more interested in talking with Logan.

Amy's Samsung phone vibrated. She looked at the display. "Excuse me, I need to take this call."

Kate watched Amy disappear into the bar. She reluctantly turned her attention back to the table.

Logan stared at Kate, tapping his right ring finger on the wine-stained tablecloth.

Kate fidgeted in her seat. Her instinct was to excuse herself and run away, but her resolve to know more about Jenny glued her to her seat. She needed to make a connection, to gain his confidence. "Can I ask you a personal question?"

Logan leaned in closer. "I am intrigued. Please."

Kate pointed at Logan's hand. "What's the significance of your ring?"

Logan stopped tapping his finger. He sat back and took a sip of water. "Why must there be a significance?"

"I met your mother and father at the fundraiser–"

"You met my father?"

"They were hard to miss. Though you seemed to mysteriously appear and disappear."

"Oh yes. The fundraiser."

"Your father was wearing the same ring you have. Is there a family significance?"

Logan looked at Kate. He bit his lower lip, looked down at his hand then turned the ring from side to side.

When Logan did not respond, Kate offered softly, "I don't mean to pry, I just thought it was interesting."

Logan looked up at Kate. He stared intently into her eyes, waiting for her to blink.

Kate began to feel anxious. Logan was rattling her confidence.

"How long have you lived in Oakview?" Logan finally asked.

"My entire life."

A slight grin appeared on Logan's face as he turned his ring. "I just thought your parents would want a fresh start somewhere else, after what happened."

Kate frowned and looked out the window of the restaurant. She wasn't sure she could play Logan's game. "What did happen?"

Logan did not respond.

Kate turned towards Logan. "Twenty years ago. June 18. My sister, Jenny, died. I have no idea what actually happened."

Logan smirked then looked at his ring. "I'm sorry about your sister."

Kate furrowed her brow. Logan knew how Jenny died. She was sure of it. "You knew Jenny. That's what Eric told me."

Logan stopped twisting his ring. He folded his legs then arms as he continued to stare at Kate. "How is your brother? Well?"

"You and Sander were both there the night Jenny died. What happened?"

Logan refused to blink. Instead he grabbed Kate's hand and squeezed it gently. "You tell me, you pretty little bitch."

Kate froze. Had Logan just called her a bitch but also made a pass at her? She felt flushed. Her breathing increased and her body got warmer. She felt like she was going to pass out.

Logan let go of Kate's hand.

Hashim walked back to the table and sat down. "What did I miss?" Hashim asked.

Logan never took his eyes off of Kate. "We were just talking about my ring."

Hashim looked at Kate. "He hasn't told you anything has he?"

Kate shook her head and took a sip of water as she tried to regain her composure.

"I think some girl gave it to him," Hashim said as he winked at Kate.

Kate looked at Logan and took a deep breath. "I bet it's a family heirloom. His father wears a similar ring. I think the "S" stands for Sinclair."

"That's the best explanation I've ever heard," Hashim smiled.

Logan scowled and looked out the window. "It's just a family tradition that each male Sinclair child receives a signet ring on his eighteenth birthday."

Amy returned to the table and sat down. "Sorry, that took a lot longer than I anticipated,"

"No worries." Logan draped his arm around the back of Amy's chair.

The waiter placed the check on the center of the table.

Logan reached for it, but Amy snapped, "Kate, get that."

As Kate reached for the check, her fingertips brushed Logan's hand.

Logan smiled.

Kate flinched.

Without looking at the bill, Kate fumbled in her purse for her wallet as she gave the waiter her credit card. As soon as she paid, she stood to leave.

Amy glared at her.

Logan stood to pull out Amy's chair. "Amy, can I talk to you for a second?"

"Sure," Amy said a little too eagerly as they both walked several feet away from the others into the bar area of the restaurant.

Kate wanted to run.

Hashim turned to Kate. "Thank you for dinner. And thank you for giving us a chance."

"You're welcome," Kate said heading for the door, hoping to sprint back to Obsidian.

Hashim managed to keep pace. "You don't know how much you've helped us today by setting up that meeting with Sander."

"When did you start working on Mirage?" Kate asked, slightly irritated.

"Logan hired me at the beginning of June. For a couple weeks, I tinkered with an older version of the product, if you can call it that. It was more ideas for features."

Kate stopped walking and faced Hashim. "June? How did you develop Mirage in five months?" Kate asked as she fished in her purse for her phone.

"I didn't, that would have been impossible. If it hadn't been for the chunk of code Logan gave me in late June, I would never have gotten Mirage to where it is today. Especially the analytics."

Kate pulled her hand out of her purse and stared at Hashim. She tried to digest what he was telling her but started to feel lightheaded as she had earlier in the day.

Logan and Amy caught up to Kate and Hashim as they all exited the restaurant.

"Thank you for dinner," Logan said to Amy and Kate.

"Yes, thank you again," Hashim said.

"I think we are all squared away with the next steps….the plans for integration," Amy said as she winked at Logan. "Hashim, we look forward to seeing you on site next week."

As Amy and Hashim were shaking hands, Logan boldly leaned in towards Kate, kissed her cheek, then grabbed her arm and whispered slowly, "Pretty little bitch is turning me on with her detective work." He leaned back, smiled then turned around and walked off towards the adjacent parking lot with Hashim trailing behind.

Kate stood motionless in a haze of confusion. What had Logan just said? She looked over at Amy for support.

Amy was seductively biting down on her lower lip watching Logan walk away.

Kate almost threw up. She ran down the street back towards Obsidian.

"Kate? Kate, wait for me," Amy called out.

Kate had no plans to stop. She couldn't let Amy see the tears streaming down her face. What kind of monster was she dealing with? How had she gotten involved with this mess? She had no one to blame but herself.

CHAPTER 44

"Where are you?" Brett asked with concern as he stood and looked outside his office window onto the evening lights of downtown Altamont Heights.

"I'm in my car, down in the garage." Kate said as she anxiously tapped the steering wheel of her green Mini Cooper.

"Kate? What's going on?"

Kate stared into the dark shadows of the dimly lit Bank of Bay building underground garage. "I'm on sub level 3. Hurry."

She tossed the phone into the center console then grabbed the sun visor. She pulled it down then opened the mirror. The initial glare of the light blinded her. She looked at her reflection. Puffy red eyes and dark streaks of mascara lined her cheeks. She felt around the glove compartment for a pack of tissue. She blotted her face then closed the mirror. Kate leaned back against the seat. *Breathe!* She tried to relax but the soft buzz of the florescent lights in the garage made her anxious.

A soft knock from the passenger window made Kate jump.

Brett. She unlocked the doors.

Brett got in the car.

Kate rushed to give him a hug. He was warm, smelled of a beer and Chinese food. The rhythmic beating of his heart had a calming affect but it couldn't keep pace with her own. She pulled away.

Brett held onto her hand. "What's going on?"

"I don't even know where to begin," Kate said resisting the urge to cry.

Noticing the tears welling up in her eyes, Brett squeezed Kate's hand. "Just spit it out."

Kate shook her head and closed her eyes, "I can't do it. I can't keep pretending I don't know. He's too much!"

"Who?"

"Logan," Kate said as she opened her eyes.

Brett stared at Kate without responding.

"He's such a manipulator. I can't stand it anymore."

Brett placed his other hand around Kate's shoulder. "I don't get it. What's wrong with him?"

"One minute he is charming and the next he's psycho. He even called me a bitch. But now I think it was his sick way of coming on to me?"

Brett sat up. "Hold on. You need to explain."

"Remember I told you that my sister committed suicide over a boy?"

Brett nodded his head.

"That boy supposedly was Logan."

Brett leaned in towards Kate with a quizzical look on his face. "Kate. Stop. I'm confused. Last we spoke, you were bringing Logan in to meet with Sander. How is Logan connected to your sister's death?"

"I met Eric for coffee this morning. He said Logan and Sander were friends back in high school. They were at the Convent the night Jenny died. It's a long story but Eric was there and thinks Logan killed Jenny."

Brett narrowed his eyes. "Wait. You believe him?"

"After meeting Logan today and then dinner, our conversation, and he called me a bitch. He knows what happened to Jenny."

"Back up. You're not making sense."

Kate ran her hands down over her face then cupped her chin. Her eyes enlarged as a thought came into her mind.

"The NDA. It's missing for a reason."

"The NDA for Cayenne?

"Yes!"

"But if Sander doesn't want to buy Cayenne's product, does the NDA even matter?"

Kate held her breath as she looked over at Brett. "You know about that?"

Brett rubbed his hands together and avoided making eye contact.

Kate fell back against her seat as she let out a sigh. "How much do you know?"

"Just what you told me the other day. How Sander assigned a new account to you, headed up by Logan Sinclair."

"But I didn't know Sander wanted to buy Logan's product until today."

Brett remained silent.

Kate leaned in closer to Brett. "When did you find out?"

"Kate, there are things about my job we can't talk about. Let's just say I've known for a couple days."

Kate frowned. "But Sander didn't see the demo until today."

"Did you talk with Rick about the NDA?"

"He's looking for it. Said he'd get back to me by tomorrow."

"So is the NDA for Cayenne really necessary at this point?"

Kate rolled her eyes as she gripped the steering wheel with both hands. "Of course it is."

"For who?"

"Cayenne."

"But you work for Obsidian."

Kate was confused by Brett's words. Could she really turn a blind eye to Cayenne? That wouldn't be ethical especially if Russ and Clive found out. They'd sue Obsidian and she would be to blame. What was Brett not telling her? "Did Sander tell you he wanted to buy Mirage?"

Brett remained silent and avoided looking directly at Kate.

"If he did, it's important. There's something going on.

141

With the NDA missing, Cayenne's going to get screwed and if they try and fight it, I'll be the scapegoat."

Brett leaned forward and placed his head in between his knees. He took a deep breath.

"I know you get fed confidential information but this is different. Sander might be bringing you in on something illegal."

Brett turned his head to the side and looked at Kate. "What makes you so sure Sander is even involved with the missing NDA?"

"Only Amy, Sander and I were in the meeting back in May with Cayenne."

"What about Amy?"

Kate looked up at the ceiling of the car. How could she be so blind? Russ had said he had a fling with Amy. That's why she didn't care the NDA was missing. She already knew. Kate closed her eyes. *Breathe!*

Brett rubbed Kate's shoulder. "I don't know what's going on but I think you need to be careful."

"Of what?" Kate said as she looked directly at Brett. "Finding out the truth?"

"Sander is the CEO of Obsidian. He has a lot of powerful connections in the Valley and from the sounds of it, so do the Sinclairs. If Sander and Logan have kept a secret about your sister's death for this long, there's no telling what they'll do to keep it that way, especially with the IPO on Tuesday. Assuming everything goes as planned, they are both going to make a shitload of money."

Kate shook her head. "I don't care. Logan basically told me to stop digging. He even called me a bitch. That alone proves he has something to hide. I'm done playing the victim. The truth has to come out. We need to make Sander and Logan accountable for their actions. They've been out there living. I never got to know my sister. You can't possibly understand how that feels–"

Brett squeezed Kate's hand. "You're right. I don't know what it feels like. I didn't mean to upset you. I just want you to be careful. There's a lot at stake for both of us, especially our careers and stock options. But how does all this relate to your sister?"

"All I know is that my sister is dead. My parents told me she committed suicide over a boyfriend. Now Eric says Logan killed her. Whatever happened back then is the reason Logan is working a deal with Sander and the NDA is missing."

Brett nodded his head. "Why don't you just ask your parents?"

Kate thought about Brett's words before responding. "There has got to be a reason they told me Jenny killed herself. They will freak out if they know I've seen Logan. I need to have some hard evidence before I can say anything."

"And where are you going to find your evidence?"

"The library."

"You're kidding!"

"No. Eric and I are going to head down to the San Jose Library to look up some old newspaper articles on microfiche. He's researching the Seminary and Cross Creek. I'll dig into the Sinclairs. We're bound to find something from back then that connects everything today."

Brett leaned in and gave Kate a kiss on the check. "I don't like where this is going but I can't keep you from looking into it. Just be careful. Don't tell anyone what you're doing. There's a lot at stake...for everyone."

"I'll be careful."

"Do you have to spend any more time with Logan?"

"God, I hope not."

Brett puffed up his chest as he stretched his arms the width of the small interior then rested his left arm around Kate's shoulder. "Good. I don't want you anywhere near that creep."

CHAPTER 45

"Come here, you bitch!" The door to Room 856 slammed open against the wall. Logan pushed Amy inside the dark room as he forced his tongue into her mouth. He shut the door with his left foot, then slammed Amy against the back as he turned the dead bold. He grabbed her right thigh and lifted her leg up around his waist.

As Logan pulled Amy across the room, he reached for a switch on the wall. The gas fireplace in front of the bed came to life and produced a soft orange glow over the room. Logan pushed Amy on the bed then stood perfectly still. He wanted to give Amy the chance to fully comprehend what was about to happen.

Sander had warned Amy about Logan. How he was a player. But when they met at Obsidian earlier that day, Amy couldn't help herself. There was a mutual attraction. When the dinner meeting at St. Anthony's Alley ended and Logan whispered in her ear to meet him at The Prestige for a drink, she couldn't resist. Why not become friendly with Logan. It could only help her rise at Obsidian.

Half way through their first drink, Logan had touched Amy's thigh. At the start of their second, his fingers lightly brushed a strand of hair away from her face. By the third drink, Logan's unblinking eyes had penetrated Amy's soul to a point of surrender. But their encounter at the hotel bar had been too brief. Logan already had plans for them.

The elevator ride up to the 8th floor had been a frenzied session of hands groping body parts. There was no passionate caressing or kissing as she had been lead to expect back at the bar. And then he had called her a bitch. Logan was on a mission.

Now looking around the room, Amy wondered how she had fallen for his charm. The room was luxurious and well-appointed with a desk, wardrobe, and four-poster bed, but the sheets on the bed were disheveled and slept in and take out containers and empty bottles littered every surface. Maid service hadn't made up the room in quite a while. A set of metal handcuffs was locked on the post on each side of the bed frame. The dangling cuffs were open and without padding. Logan had obviously planned ahead or was Amy not the first? Was it too late to escape?

Without speaking, Logan unzipped his pants. He slightly lowered his boxer shorts. He was already hard. He walked up to Amy and thrust her head into his groin forcing himself inside her mouth. He closed his eyes as he rhythmically massaged the back of Amy's head.

After several minutes, Logan pushed Amy back onto the bed, and pulled her up to the center with her arms above her head. The orange glow of fire on Logan's face revealed a demented, crocked smile and eyes intently ablaze.

Logan held Amy's arms together with one hand as his ran his other down the length of her clothed body. A creepy smile came over his face as he let out a slight gurgle. He grabbed Amy's right arm and crudely rolled her over on to her stomach then pulled her hand up to the post. He clenched the cuff down around her wrist. Before Amy could react, he pulled her other arm up to the other post and closed the cuff.

"You like it this way?" Amy tried to question him seductively.

"Gives my imagination free reign." Logan pressed his body on top of Amy's back then fondled her covered breasts from behind.

Amy strained her neck to look back at Logan but he pushed her head down. She had wanted to be with him but didn't expect him to be this aggressive. Logan was now in complete control.

"How do you plan on taking off my clothes?" Amy said trying to make light of the situation.

Logan smiled. "That's the fun part." He grabbed the back of Amy's hair and pulled her body up. With his right hand, he grabbed her blouse, cut an edge at the neckline with his teeth, than forcefully tore the blouse off her body.

"What the hell?" Amy blurted out surprised and panicked. Not playing the victim, she quickly added, "That's an Emillo Pucci."

Logan ran his fingers down Amy's naked back. "I don't give a fuck who designed it."

"Did you have to destroy it?"

"Enough talking!" Logan sneered as he slowly twisted the Emilo Pucci blouse into a knot then forcefully used it to gag Amy's mouth, tying the sleeves around her head.

Amy tried to talk but it was useless. She had willingly entered Logan's hotel room and now she had to play by his rules.

Logan pulled off Amy's shoes and threw them on the ground. He easily unbuttoned and unzipped her slacks then slid them off her body. Amy was left with only her black bra and panties protecting her body.

Amy closed her eyes and took a deep breath. She suddenly felt a cold hard object jabbed into her back.

Logan was massaging Amy's back with his Colt 45. The M1911A1 was a rather large, heavy pistol that had a reputation for its raw stopping power. He ran the metal piece down the length of her body and then up to her bra strap. He placed the gun under the strap then jerked it up. The strap easily broke free and snapped back on Amy's skin leaving a red mark. Her breasts were now exposed. Logan lustfully leered at the situation as he slowly placed the gun on the nightstand.

Amy gulped the last bit of saliva in her mouth when she saw the gun next to her. She closed her eyes.

A metal belt buckle clanked against the bed frame as Logan ripped it from his pants. He folded it in half and snapped the leather together.

Amy winced. She had never felt so intimately vulnerable and threatened by anyone at the same time. The sound of leather slapping against something smooth caused Amy to open her eyes. What was Logan doing?

And then Logan was behind her, straddling Amy from behind. Before she had time to react, he wrapped the belt around her neck, pulling her head up.

Logan whispered in Amy's ear, "Tonight, you're my bitch. And you'll do exactly as I say."

CHAPTER 46
Friday

Grey clouds blanketed the sky and a heavy fog hung over the San Thomas hills like a white blanket as Kate looked out her office window. She couldn't concentrate on work. She was uncomfortable being around Sander and Logan, much less working with them. Hashim had inadvertently told her Logan stole Cayenne's product and Rick Moore hadn't called about the missing NDA. Her job and stock options were on the line and maybe even her life. But she couldn't shake the feeling that Russ and Clive were getting screwed. Kate was not going to let Logan and Sander destroy another life. She had to act quickly.

Kate spun around to face her laptop and desktop computer. She noticed the silver iPhone on the file cabinet. It should be charged by now. She walked over to the file cabinet and grabbed it. As she placed her thumb over the power button the office door opened.

"We need to talk," Amy said as she shut the door and slowly sat down in the chair opposite Kate.

"Are you okay?" Kate said as she set the iPhone back down on the file cabinet and returned to her chair. Amy was wearing a baggy black turtleneck sweater with black leggings. Her hair was pulled back in a low ponytail and she was wearing very little makeup. This was not Amy's typical polished self.

"Yes. I'm fine," Amy responded a little too abruptly.

"What's up?"

"Yesterday. You mentioned Sander and Logan are friends. What do you know about their relationship?"

"Umm," Kate hesitated. Amy was all business yesterday and didn't care. What had changed? "I think they went to the same high school."

"They've been friends since high school?"

"Yes."

Amy clenched the sides of the chair with both hands. Kate noticed red marks on her wrists.

"I need to know everything about Logan…if we're going to be working with him."

"I'm sure he wants to know everything about you too," Kate joked.

Amy did not respond. All the color drained out of her face as she sat back in the chair.

Kate paused. Amy was falling apart before her eyes. She stood to offer help as her office phone rang. "Are you okay?"

"I'm fine. You should get that."

Kate looked down at the display, "Rick Moore" showed up on the screen. Kate slowly picked up the receiver, "Hello?"

"Kate, it's Rick."

"Yes," Kate desperately wanted to talk with Rick but not with Amy in the same room.

"I wanted to get back to you about the NDA for Cayenne."

"Yes," Kate repeated as she sank back into her desk chair. With Amy staring her down, she could feel her body temperature rising as beads of sweat started to form on her forehead.

"I found a folder for Cayenne but it's completely empty. There's no NDA. It must have been deleted."

"How do you know?"

"On this particular server, the only time we create a folder is when an NDA is signed for a new account. Someone deleted the NDA but forgot to delete the folder."

Kate looked at Amy then back at the office phone, "Who would have access?"

"That all depends. Sander. He has universal access but then again, your manager may have been given permissions."

"Thanks. I appreciate the help."

"Sure thing, Kate. And thanks for the tickets. I can't wait for the game tonight."

Kate ended the call and tried to look composed. Her mind was reeling.

Amy smirked. "What was that all about?"

"Just want to make sure the NDA we signed yesterday with Fortunato made it to legal's servers."

Amy looked over at Kate's computer monitor. "Do you have access to Sander's calendar?"

"Ah no." Kate half smiled.

"Of course not." Amy slowly stood and walked over to Kate's laptop. "Do you mind?"

Kate pushed back her chair and let Amy access her keyboard. As Amy leaned over and began to type, Kate noticed a red mark on her neck peeking out from her turtleneck. Concealer had been caked on the bruise but Kate could still see the mark.

"Looks like 10AM Monday is the only time available. I'm going to book it for Cayenne." Amy finished typing then walked back towards the chair.

"You mean Fortunato is not a done deal? Won't Sander object?" Kate asked.

Amy smiled as she slowly reached for the door. "Let's just say, I'm interested to know why Sander wants to buy Fortunato over Cayenne. Especially after last night. I want to force the issue."

Kate hesitated. This was not like Amy. She was asking the questions Kate wanted answered. Was Amy now helping her?

Amy opened the door. Before she exited the office, she said, "Kate, be careful. Logan is not to be toyed with."

"Okay."

After Amy shut the door behind her, Kate sat staring at

her monitor. What had just happened? Was Amy helping her? What had changed overnight? Why would Amy warn her about Sander? Could Cayenne still be in the game? Kate picked up her phone and sent a text to Clive:

Monday

10 AM

Confirm?

As she sent the message, Kate saw a text from Jessica:

wayd 4 lnch?

Kate looked at the clock on her display. 12:35 PM. She accessed her calendar. No afternoon meetings. She replied:

nothng

While waiting for a response, Kate gathered her hair from behind, wrapped it around her thumb and twisted it up into cone shape. She grabbed a black clip from her desk drawer and secured her hair in place.

Jessica responded:

@ sfo

Kate replied:

wtf?

Jessica responded:

pickin nu wedin local. hlp me

Kate replied:

werja want to meet?

Jessica responded:

1 pm st james seminary

Kate grabbed her purse and bolted out of her office.

CHAPTER 47

Nate walked into the Altamont Heights Country Club members lounge. The mahogany-boxed, coffered ceiling and dark, raised-wood paneled walls solemnly offset the warmly lit Tiffany lamps, scattered around the side tables among the dark leather chairs. The room was silent except for the occasional cough and rustle of newspapers. Nate easily spotted Renee Verano wearing a buttercup Chanel pantsuit. She looked ancient. A thick layer of makeup plastered the deep dry ravines of her face. Her dyed red hair was up in a poodle style cut, which was too young for her age but, considering it had been out of style for fifty years, most appropriate. Her wrinkled fingers glistened from her diamond, ruby and emerald rings as they slowly slid across the iPad display.

Renee was sitting alone in a brown leather lounge chair by the cracking fireplace. A cup of tea, still hot from a pour was on the side table next to a pile of magazine and books. She wore large brown bifocal glasses hung on the edge of her nose as she read from her red, bedazzled iPad.

"I still can't believe you know how to use one of those," Nate said as he pointed at the iPad. He stood over Renee and waited for her to respond.

Renee slowly looked up from her iPad and smiled. "And good morning to you, Nate Crawford."

Nate blushed, "Yes, good morning Renee."

"I'm old but I'm not dead. The iPad and iPhone allow me to keep up with the company." Renee squinted at Nate as her eyes adjusted. "All from the comfort of this here chair."

Looking around the room, Nate sat down on the footrest in front of Renee, leaned in and whispered, "I saw Elizabeth."

Renee looked up and concentrated on Nate.

"What did she say?"

"We need to find Walter's phone."

"Phone?" Renee placed her iPad on the side table next to her tea cup.

"She said it would explain everything."

"How?"

"Probably a photo or video, something to do with the Sinclairs."

Renee grabbed onto Nate's arm. "This phone could be what we've been waiting for all these years."

"That's what I'm thinking." Nate patted Renee's hand then stood as he arched his back. "But how do we find the phone? Elizabeth doesn't have it."

"Do you know if the police found it?"

Nate slowly paced as he massaged his lower back with both hands. "They searched the whole accident site yesterday. If they found anything incriminating, they wouldn't have closed the case."

"Maybe Walter uploaded whatever it is onto his computer."

"I thought about that but there's no way Elizabeth is going to talk to me again."

Renee shifted her body in the chair. "Why?"

"She was scared." Nate leaned in closer and whispered. "She barely opened the door. She said she couldn't talk because they'd know."

"Stinks of the Sinclairs." Renee slowly reached for her cup of tea. "They got to her."

"Do we assume they had something to do with Walter's death?"

"Definitely. Now that Elizabeth said something it's got the

Sinclairs written all over it." Renee's hand shook as she picked up the teacup. Nate reached over and helped her steady it with both hands. She nodded in appreciation as she took a sip and returned the cup to the saucer.

"Maybe we should concentrate on something else like Logan."

"Logan Sinclair?" Renee questioned.

"Vivian was at Bella Salon and thinks she overheard Maria Sinclair say that Logan is back in town."

"After all these years? Why would Logan come back?"

Nate shook his head.

"Logan is a huge liability for William."

"I agree." Nate sat down on the arm of the chair and leaned in closer to Renee. "Father O'Connell is back."

Renee looked up at Nate.

"He also confirmed that Logan is in town."

Renee grabbed Nate's hand. "I saw him at the fundraiser. He was talking with Vivian."

Nate looked at the yellow flames of the fire. "He's back to save the Seminary from the Cross Creek project."

"But Patrick wouldn't just come back to save the Seminary."

"Don't even go there." Nate clenched his fists, stood and walked over to the fireplace. He placed his arm on the mantle and looked back at Renee.

Renee looked around the room then whispered, "You can't keep that a secret forever."

Nate ignored Renee's comment and began to pace. "I think he's following Logan. Patrick thinks Logan is back to sell a product to Obsidian."

Renee furrowed her brow. "A product? That means Logan must be in contact with Sander. This is not good. What about Kate?"

Nate closed his eyes for a moment and then opened them, staring at Renee with intensity. "I don't want her any where near Logan."

"We will keep Kate safe."

"I hope so."

CHAPTER 48

The sun broke through the gray clouds and reflected off the puddles of water pocketing the asphalt road leading up to St. James Seminary. The road began at Paseo Grande, perpendicular to Verano Shopping Center, and snaked along a grove of oak trees that paralleled Sinclair Shopping Center and the creek. The route eventually bisected the land being considered for the Cross Creek project. Eucalyptus, oak, pine and redwood trees grew roadside and ended at the Seminary's weathered red brick fence.

The fence stood five feet tall and paralleled the road until it met up with an old weathered iron gate. The gate opened to a driveway, which tunneled through low hanging tree branches, winding back and forth twice before coming to a clearing. At the end of the road stood the rectangular three-story Seminary brick building with white limestone trim.

Kate pulled her car into the parking lot. She spotted Jessica, sitting on the enormous limestone steps leading up to the main doors at the center of the building. Kate cut the ignition and sat in the car looking at the Seminary.

A cement walkway led away from the parking lot, through a circular boxwood garden with four enormous palm trees on either side, up to the steps. The front stairs opened up to an enormous limestone slab of a stoop and two large wooden doors beneath an ornate white sandstone archway. At least this section of the Seminary was relatively well kept compared to the back of the property. Kate shivered. There were dark shadows and corners everywhere. What if her attacker still lurked?

Jessica stood and waved.

Breathe. Kate took a deep breath and looked around the property. Today she would be with several people. She would be fine. Kate got out of her car and walked over to Jessica. The tall leggy, long-haired brunette towered over Kate.

Jessica stooped to give Kate a hug.

"Love the hair," Jessica said as she stepped back and pointed at Kate's head. "Didn't recognize you."

Kate smiled and felt the back of her head. "I know. I rarely wear it up. But tell me…what's going on?

"It's a long story. Ms. Walker wanted me to check out the chapel."

"Ms. Walker?"

"She's the organist at Holy Trinity. I called her the other day to ask about her availability to play at my wedding in June and she told me that Holy Trinity is going through a major renovation and the organ won't be available in June."

"Walker, Walker, why does that sound familiar?"

"Her son is Sander Walker, your boss. Kind of cute that the CEO of Obsidian has a mom who plays the organ."

Kate felt light headed. What had Eric said? Carolyn's mom had known their mother through work? "Why didn't anyone say anything to you about the remodel?"

"We questioned Kent's father but he was no help. Then we spoke with great grandmother, NaNa. She said the church had been planning this remodel for over a year. She called Father di Luca who said he would marry us at another local church."

"Sorry, Jessica. This is too amazing. So what's the connection with the Seminary?"

"Every church in town is already booked, so Ms. Walker suggested we try St. James Seminary. She knows a priest and pulled some strings for us."

"How?"

"Ms. Walker used to play the organ here."

Kate froze. Should she tell Jessica what Eric had told her?

The sound of a car approaching interrupted their conversation. A light blue Cadillac emerged from the tunnel of trees. Jessica waved at the car as it came to stop in the parking lot.

"That must be Ms. Walker." Jessica tugged on Kate's sleeve and started down the steps. "By the way, I dug up some shit you need to see."

"Wait. What?" Kate asked.

Jessica kept walking towards the Cadillac but called out, "Let's talk about it after our tour."

Kate did not follow. Instead, she looked back at the Seminary and thought about her brother's words from the other night. Could the Seminary be the root of all their problems?

CHAPTER 49

A short woman with curly brown hair and circular, rimmed glasses stepped out of the car. She waved to Jessica and reached back inside for a purse before closing the door.

"Ms. Walker?" Jessica asked.

"Yes, dear," Ms. Walker replied as she walked up the stone steps to the Seminary.

"I'm Jessica," Jessica said offering her hand. "Thank you for meeting us here today."

Ms. Walker shook Jessica's hand then held onto her arm as she looked up at the Seminary building. "I'm glad I could help my dear. It's been a while since I was last here."

Jessica led them over to Kate. "This is my friend Kate Crawford."

Ms. Walker froze at the mention of Kate's name.

"Kate's my maid of honor. I asked her to come help me with my decision," Jessica said.

Kate offered Ms. Walker her hand.

Ms. Walker did not take Kate's hand. Instead, she raised her eyebrows. "The Crawford girl? That was twenty years ago."

Kate felt a chill run down her spine. She looked at Jessica then Ms. Walker. "Yes, that was my sister Jenny. I'm Kate, her younger sister."

Ms. Walker looked at the Seminary then the ground.

Jessica began to walk to the front doors of the seminary. "I know your time is precious Ms. Walker. Shall we go inside and look at the church?"

As they walked towards the large wooden doors, Kate's phone vibrated. She looked at the display, Brett. Kate tapped Jessica on the shoulder. "I need to take this."

"We'll see you inside," Jessica said as she walked into the seminary.

As the doors closed, Kate answered her phone.

"Hey Brett."

"How are you doing?"

Kate looked at the tall palm trees swaying in the light breeze. "Better. Thanks for being there for me last night."

"Of course."

"What's up?"

"I just stopped by your office but you weren't there. I wanted to make sure you're doing ok."

Kate smiled. "In a strange way, I think things are better...because of Amy."

"You're kidding?"

"No. She's being really cool. And I think she may actually be helping me."

"Hold on, Kate."

As Brett cut out, Kate stood on the steps and enjoyed the afternoon sun.

"Sorry, Kate. I've got to take this other call. Let's talk later."

"No worries. Bye." Kate ended the call. At the same time, she received a text from Clive:

Confirmed!

Kate returned the phone to her purse. She looked back at the garden then she realized she was alone. She quickly turned around and walked into the Seminary.

CHAPTER 50

Entering the foyer of the Seminary, Kate glanced down at the burgundy carpet with gold inlay. She had the distinct impression she had been here before, playing with her dolls on this rug. Looking around she did not recognize anything else, but decided to investigate.

The interior was clean and plain with high ceilings, beige walls, white baseboards and crown molding. A grand staircase with oak paneling and detailed carvings anchored the back of the foyer. On either side of the front door were two identically-sized, rectangular sitting rooms. Victoria style furniture adorned both rooms but appeared more for decoration than use from the layer of dust on the surfaces. The room on the right had an empty fireplace with a painting of a priest above the mantel.

The man was blond and wore the traditional white clerical collar and black cassock. He was standing in front of the circular garden at the base of the Seminary. The palm trees behind him looked newly planted. Kate walked into the room past the couch and coffee table to take a closer look.

At the bottom of the picture frame, a small black plaque with gilded letters read, Father Edward O'Connell 1850-1931.

"That was my great uncle," a voice said from behind Kate.

Kate immediately turned around and stumbled into the coffee table. She looked up and was surprised to see the priest from the fundraiser. He was dressed in a black clerical suite and shirt with a white collar. She instantly felt her face flush.

"I'm sorry, my dear. I didn't mean to startle you," Father O'Connell said.

Kate regained her footing and took a step closer to Father O'Connell. She looked down at his hands then up into his face. For someone who was close to her dad's age, he still looked young. His milky light skin with a sprinkling of freckles showed little signs of sun damage. He was quite stocky and tall; a good four inches taller than Brett who was six feet. But his hands caught her attention. They were enormous and by the texture of the skin quite weathered from perhaps a lifetime of manual labor.

"Edward O'Connell founded St. James Seminary back in 1910. My mother was Edward's niece. I am Father O'Connell."

Kate stared at Father O'Connell, searching for something to say. She finally blurted out, "This place has quite a history."

Father O'Connell smiled. "Are you lost, my child?"

"No. Well, yes, I guess I am. I'm here with Ms. Walker. But I got tied up with a call and she went ahead into the church."

"The chapel," Father O'Connell corrected Kate.

"Yes, the chapel. This is a beautiful building. From the outside, I didn't know what to expect."

"Yes, it is a large building. The second and third floors have dormitory rooms," Father O'Connell said as he led Kate back into the foyer and pointed at the grand staircase.

Kate walked to the railing and looked up the three-story stairwell to see a large octagonal skylight atop the roof that brought in natural light.

"The hallway to your left leads to classrooms," Father O'Connell pointed out.

Kate saw six interior doors. At the end of the hallway was an exterior door with a window to the outside.

"In the middle of the building is our inner courtyard with gardens and a fountain. You access it from this door over here," Father O'Connell said motioning to a side door next to the stairwell.

"Is the chapel down that hallway?" Kate asked motioning to her right. She could feel her hair slowly start to unravel from the French twist. Her nerves were unraveling too.

"Yes, it is. Let me take you."

At the end of the hallway were two large oak doors framed by two columns rising to an arch. Within the oak arch was a carved image of Christ standing with his arms outstretched and a halo above his head.

They began to walk toward the doors of the chapel.

"We normally do not allow visitors to see the chapel," Father O'Connell said. "Ms. Walker used to work here so I agreed to let her test the organ and show you the chapel."

"She's not showing it to me," Kate said as she grabbed the clip from her hair and let her locks fall down around her shoulders.

Father O'Connell stopped at the oak doors and took a long look at Kate. "Excuse me, child? You're not here to view the chapel?"

"My friend Jessica Knight is looking at the chapel, not me. I'm Kate Crawford. I think you know my parents, Nate and Vivian?"

Father O'Connell took a step back as he continued to stare at Kate. "What are you doing here?"

"I told you. I'm here with my friend Jessica."

Reaching for the latch on the door, Father O'Connell redirected his arms towards Kate's face and gently touched her cheek with his hand. "I…I didn't expect to meet you like this."

Kate pulled away, surprised by Father O'Connell's intimate touch.

Father O'Connell quickly lowered his hand to his side.

"Should we go in and join the others?" Kate stammered as she pulled on the handle of the Chapel door.

CHAPTER 51

Mahogany paneling and coffered lattice wrapped the entire chapel, echoing the ancient churches of Europe. Kate stepped onto the burgundy carpet and looked up the wide aisle to the altar. Three rows of pews faced the aisle on each side and flanked the entire length of the carpet. The oak pews were worn smooth from years of diligent service. The afternoon sun filtered through the stained-glass windows of the clerestory above the altar, bathing the entire chapel in an ethereal glow.

Ms. Walker walked up to the group.

"Patrick. Thank you for seeing us today," Ms. Walker said as she gave Father O'Connell a hug.

"I'm glad I could be of service," Father O'Connell said.

Kate looked towards the altar with its smooth white marble surface and large silver cross vertically positioned on a burgundy runner. As Jessica and Ms. Walker walked towards the altar, Kate sat down on the pew in the front row.

She noticed a swirling "S" design carved into the side of the pews, the same design on Logan's ring. Father O'Connell sat down next to Kate.

"This is an amazing space," Kate said, trying to recover from her earlier awkwardness.

"It's quite an architectural wonder," Father O'Connell replied.

"Where is the organ?" Kate asked.

Father O'Connell pointed back to the large oak doors they had just entered. "Look above."

Large cylindrical vertical pipes of varying sizes encased an image of Jesus with the apostles; rays of light emanated from his halo.

"That balcony was originally used by our nuns from St. Mary's. We had to remodel it a bit, but the organ just fits," Father O'Connell said.

"What would the nuns do up there?" Kate asked.

"Sing. They'd stand on the balcony and sing. It was a beautiful sight to behold. Their voices were so comforting."

"Where was the organ originally?"

"We acquired that organ up there back in the 1960s." Father O'Connell turned to face the altar and pointed at the arched door in the corner. "We used to have a small organ in that location. When we removed it, we did some remodeling and put a door out to a small inner courtyard. It's very peaceful. I go out there almost every night."

Kate leaned in closer to Father O'Connell. "I hear you just got back from living in Italy."

Father O'Connell took a deep breath. "Yes, I was on an extended sabbatical."

"What brought you back here?"

Father O'Connell shook his head. "The Cross Creek project. Our lease on all this land expires next year."

"Expires?" Kate never knew it wasn't a lifetime lease.

Father O'Connell looked up to the arch above the door where the bust of Christ looked down on them. "Uncle Edward didn't have enough money to buy the land. Lawrence Sinclair stepped in and offered this parcel to him. My uncle was humbled by their gracious gesture. And I think the Sinclairs benefited by a rise in social status."

"Then why do the Sinclairs want to take back the land and tear down the Seminary? Why don't they just sell it to the Seminary?"

Father O'Connell looked down the hallway past Kate. "There's a history with our families. Regardless of Lawrence

Sinclair's original wishes, I don't think the family ever intended the Seminary to stay here forever. I'm hoping to change their minds."

"You know my father has been elected to the Oakview City Council. I bet he'd be an ally for you on this whole Cross Creek deal."

"Oh, I don't know if your father would want to help me." Father O'Connell stood and began to walk towards Ms. Walker and Jessica.

"I really think you should talk with my dad," Kate called out.

Father O'Connell looked back and smiled. "I may just do that."

CHAPTER 52

Father O'Connell opened the large mahogany doors to the entrance of the Seminary. He escorted Kate, Jessica and Ms. Walker outside into the afternoon light where a light breeze had kicked up. Although Jessica had not said anything, Kate knew her decision had already been made. The Seminary. The location, its beauty, and uniqueness all screamed Jessica.

"This place is truly amazing," Jessica said beaming to Father O'Connell.

"I'm glad you like it, my dear," Father O'Connell responded.

"I'd be honored to have my wedding here," Jessica said as she took out her iPhone and scrolled through to the calendar application. She turned to Father O'Connell, "Can I ask you a question about the date I have in mind and how many people the chapel can accommodate?"

"That's my cue," Ms. Walker said with a smile. "Unfortunately, I need to leave."

"Of course. How rude of me." Jessica leaned over and gave Ms. Walker a hug. "Thank you so much for arranging this meeting. You don't know how much it means to me."

"You're welcome, dear." Ms. Walker gave Father O'Connell a hug, nodded at Kate then made her way down the steps.

As Jessica and Father O'Connell discussed the details of

the wedding, Kate watched Ms. Walker walk towards her blue Cadillac. She saw an opportunity. Kate ran down the steps calling out, "Ms. Walker, Ms. Walker."

Ms. Walker reluctantly stopped and turned around. "Yes dear?"

"You know my sister, what happened to her?"

"Yes, I remember that day. We all remember that day."

"Is there any way I can talk with your daughter about what happened?"

Ms. Walker looked back at the Seminar then at Kate. "Carolyn is married now and lives in Denver. She has a new life. Those memories are very painful for her."

"I understand, but perhaps I could call her? I have reason to believe Jenny didn't kill herself. Since Sander and Logan were there—"

Ms. Walker narrowed her eyes. "Don't go looking for trouble." She turned around and started back towards her car. "The only person who can really answer these questions is your mother. Ask her."

Jessica walked up to the women. "Ms. Walker. I can't thank you enough. I can't wait to get married here."

Ms. Walker smiled as she opened her car door. "I'm glad I could help." She waved at Father O'Connell as he closed the Seminary door, then got in her car and drove away.

Jessica turned to Kate. "What's going on?"

"You have no idea."

CHAPTER 53

Kate walked over to her green mini cooper. She reached down to grab the car door handle then stopped.

"What's wrong with you?" Jessica probed as she lightly touched Kate's shoulder.

Kate flinched.

"Talk to me," Jessica said as she held on to Kate's shoulder. "Is this because of the attack? I can tell you're upset."

Kate looked at her reflection in the car window, her hair was all tangled and she had dark circles under her eyes. She turned around and leaned up against the car. "I don't even know where to begin."

"Just start talking."

"It all relates to the Seminary."

"I'm confused."

Kate dug in her purse for her phone. She looked at the display, 2 PM. "Do you have time?"

"As much as you need."

"You weren't wrong about Jenny."

"What do you mean?"

"Eric told me Jenny never had a boyfriend. She hated guys like Logan. I think Logan Sinclair killed her to hide something."

Jessica took a step back as she stared at Kate. "And the Sinclairs covered it up by sending Logan abroad."

Kate looked at the ground and kicked at a small pebble. "My mom used to work here with Ms. Walker."

"Seriously?"

"Ms. Walker's daughter, Carolyn, and Jenny were best friends."

"That I did not know."

"Eric told me that Sander and Logan were friends. They both knew Jenny and were both at the Convent the night she died."

Jessica's mouth fell open as her eyes began to turn the wheels in her mind. "Now you've got my attention."

"What creeps me out is that I've worked at Obsidian for over two years with Sander knowing who I am. And now he's gone and assigned Logan's–" Kate stopped herself.

"Logan's what?" Jessica asked as she leaned in closer to Kate.

Kate took a deep breath. "I shouldn't tell you. It's confidential."

Jessica grabbed onto Kate's forearm. "Listen. If you're in real trouble, you'll need someone to corroborate your story. Now, give."

Kate looked at the tall palm trees swaying effortlessly in the light wind. Their shadows cast four long pillars against the brick of the Seminary building.

"Just talk in generalities. I'll figure it out," Jessica said.

Kate squinted. "Sander assigned Fortunato to me."

"Fortunato is the company headed up by a Logan Sinclair. A Logan Sinclair who is friends with Sander. And they were both at the Convent the night Jenny died?"

Kate nodded her head.

Jessica put her arm around Kate's shoulder as they both leaned against the car. "Do you have any proof to connect Logan and Sander to Jenny's death besides a strong hunch?"

Kate shook her head. "That's what I was trying to get out of Ms. Walker. I asked her if I could talk with her daughter.

Supposedly, Carolyn told Jenny something that got her to the convent that night."

"Did Ms. Walker tell you anything?"

"She told me I need to speak with my mom. My mom can answer my questions."

"Questions about what?"

"I don't know. And that's why I'm thinking everything comes back to the Seminary and this damn Cross Creek project. It's where my mom met Ms. Walker and Jenny met Carolyn, Sander and then Logan. It's all related."

"But if Logan has been gone for twenty years, why would he come back now?"

"Logan has something Obsidian wants."

Jessica put her hand up to her mouth and gasped. "Sander is going to buy Fortunato's product? This doesn't feel right."

Kate's phone beeped. She dug through her purse then looked down at the display, a text from Amy.

wer r u?

Kate pointed at her phone. "And this whole Cayenne crap —"

"Amy? The raging bitch? What are you talking about?"

"Oh, Jessica." Kate turned around then started to open the door to her car. "There's too much going on…I can't even tell you."

Kate's phone beeped again. She paused to look at the display, another message from Amy:

need 2 talk, Cayenne. find me ASAP

"I've got to go."

"Let me help you."

Kate slowly returned the phone to her purse. "The stuff going on with Logan is confidential. If anyone found out, it could blow our IPO next week." Kate grabbed the handle of the car door and pulled back.

"Stop!" Jessica pushed the door shut and grabbed Kate's arms. "I get that you can't tell me everything but I think I've come across something that can help."

Kate stood still waiting to hear what Jessica had to say.

"I did some digging…on Sander. It turns out your CEO

has been under investigation for questionable practices at two of his previous firms — Halflife and GrandWuld. Corporate espionage, stealing product ideas…that sort of thing. But he's always managed to evade an indictment."

"No doubt, the long arm of Sinclair Enterprises." Kate slumped against her car and mumbled. "Now everything makes sense."

"I'm guessing since the other companies failed, Sander needs Obsidian to be a winner."

Kate shook her head. Sander accused of stealing product ideas? The NDA for Cayenne hadn't just disappeared. It was destroyed on purpose.

"Wait." Jessica stood tall and faced Kate. "Was the attack yesterday related to any of this?"

Kate looked at the ground then turned around to face Jessica. She glanced at the Seminary. "I…I don't know."

"Walter Rudolf dies on Tuesday. You're attacked on Wednesday. Logan's back in town and he's working on something with the CEO of Obsidian, who also happened to be at the Convent the night Jenny died. A CEO who needs this IPO to save his reputation and, no doubt, his butt. You've got to do something."

"Really, Jessica? If anything, this proves we are all powerless against the Sinclairs."

"Kate, listen. I've seen this happen all too often in my line of work. You are in danger. You need to get a handle on this and take charge. Stop blindly questioning people like Sander's mom. You need a strategy and you need allies. Your life depends on it."

Kate thought about Logan. How he had called her a bitch. They were playing her for a fool. Now she was mad. She grabbed Jessica's hand and squeezed it, "You're right. I've got to stop being the victim. Stand up for myself. I just need to find that one thing that connects it all together."

Jessica released her hold of Kate. "That'a girl! I don't leave until tomorrow night. Let's take 10 minutes now to strategize. Figure out your next move."

Kate smiled. "Thanks, Jess."

CHAPTER 54

"Did you get my text messages?" Amy demanded when she saw Kate walking into her office.

"Yes," Kate replied as she shut the door and took a seat. "I was out for lunch. I came here as soon as I could."

"Did you hear from Cayenne?"

"We're all set for Monday at 10 AM."

"Good. Things are going to be a little crazy with the IPO launch. After Sander meets with Cayenne, he'll be heading out to New York to ring the opening bell at NASDAQ on Tuesday morning."

This was something Jessica and Kate had not planned on. "Wow. When was that announced?" Kate asked.

"It hasn't. We'll leak it to the press on Monday."

"What about Fortunato? What do I do with them?"

"Business as usual. Sander hasn't signed any legal documents. Just keep Hashim and Logan occupied until we know what Sander wants to do. Sander may not know until after he gets back from New York."

Maybe buying Mirage wasn't a done deal? This would give Kate more time. "Will do," Kate said as she began to stand.

"Have you been able to dig up anything on Logan?"

Kate paused as she thought about Logan and his connection to her sister's death. Jessica had told her not to trust anyone with this information, especially Amy. "No, not yet."

"If you do, definitely contact me. Even if it's over the weekend."

"Okay."

As Kate exited the office, Amy called out, "Be sure Hashim attends any meeting you have with Logan."

"Of course." Kate lied as she closed the door and walked back to her office. Jessica and Kate had decided the only way to uncover the truth about Jenny's death was to get close to Logan.

It was 3:30 PM.

CHAPTER 55

Kate returned to her office and shut the door. She pulled her phone out of her purse and sent Brett a text:

u arnd

She waited five minutes. No response.

Sander had attended UC Berkeley but Kate wanted to learn more about how he became the CEO of Obsidian.

She woke up her computer then Googled Sander Walker. On the first search page, Kate found information she had already known. On the second page, she discovered something new. Sander had attended undergrad and grad at Berkeley on a full scholarship, the Sinclair Family Trust scholarship established in 1929 in memory of Lawrence Sinclair.

After Sander received his BS in Business, he went on to the Haas School of Business on a different Sinclair scholarship. Kate paused. The Sinclair family was keeping Sander quiet. How could she prove it?

Kate's phone beeped, a message from Logan:

dinner 2nite?

What did he want? Kate had uncovered too many unsavory facts about Logan to feel comfortable being alone with him, especially after he had called her a bitch, Amy's warning and Brett's concerns. But she wanted to know the truth about her sister. Kate responded:

u and Hashim?

Two minutes passed before Logan responded:

y

Kate hesitated. She looked at the clock on her phone. 4 PM. Every impulse in her body told her to reply NO. But Hashim would be there. Perhaps he could provide more insight about the development of Mirage. Something could prove Logan stole Cayenne's product idea. She responded:

tym

Logan responded:

7 Triad

Kate responded:

k cu @ 7

CHAPTER 56

"Are you free tonight?" Courtney was sitting in her black jeep holding her Samsung phone up to her ear. She was parked on a tree-lined street, across from an apartment complex. The street lights had just come on.

"Sure. What do you have in mind?" Eric eagerly asked.

"Let's meet at the Regent Hotel. I hear they have a great steak house." Courtney sat up when she realized a door to a downstairs unit of the apartment complex had opened. "Meet me there around 6:30 PM."

"I look forward to seeing you."

"Me, too. Sorry, but I have to go. Got to finish up some work."

"Ok. Bye."

"Bye." Courtney ended the call abruptly as she watched Kate Crawford exit her apartment. She had her dog in tow as they walked through the dimly lit courtyard.

Courtney grabbed a black baseball cap from the passenger seat and wrapped her long dark hair up inside as she placed it on her head. She pushed the brim low over her forehead then slowly slipped on her black leather gloves. Although it was getting dark, she decided to wear sunglasses since Kate had met her up close at the fundraiser. When Kate and her dog were out of sight, Courtney grabbed a clipboard and a small black bag and quickly walked across the street.

The two story, "L" shaped apartment complex was surrounded by sycamore and oak tress. Kate's apartment was at the foot of the "L" and closest to the street. A small courtyard framed by boxwood with a crape myrtle at its center provided just enough cover for a solicitor to go unnoticed.

Courtney walked up to Kate's door and knocked. She looked around the complex but did not notice any nosy neighbors. Having examined the door two days prior, she knew what to bring. Courtney placed the black bag on her clipboard then unzipped it.

She took out a gleaming silver lock pick gun with three picking needles. It had come in handy over the last five years especially in gaining access to information on her father's money. The dumb-ass, technophobe kept all his documents in a locked closet in his den.

Courtney jammed the gun into the keyhole, jimmied it around, and then pulled the trigger. When she heard the click of the pin tumblers falling into place, Courtney turned the doorknob and entered the apartment. She quickly closed the door behind her, removed a small black flashlight from the bag and surveyed the small quarters.

There appeared to be a living room, kitchen, bedroom and, she assumed, a bathroom at the back. By now Kate knew what was on Walter's phone, so she had to do a thorough search in a short amount of time without tossing the place.

She set her clipboard and bag on the coffee table then dashed over to the couch and lifted up all the cushions. Nothing. She placed the cushions back down then looked under the couch. Nothing. She looked through the magazines on the coffee table. Nothing.

In the kitchen, there were only four overhead cabinets, two lower cabinets, and four drawers. She scoured everything but only found the usual kitchen paraphernalia.

Next, she walked into a small bathroom. Nothing but a pedestal sink, shower stall, and medium sized, double-hung window over the toilet. She opened the medicine cabinet. There weren't even any interesting drugs inside. How did this girl survive in such a small cramped space? She continued into the bedroom. It was sparsely decorated with only a bed, nightstand, chest of six drawers with some family photos on top and a closet. Courtney began in the closet.

She pushed back the rack of clothes and felt each outfit. Nothing. A shelf above the rack held eight boxes. She ran back into the kitchen and grabbed the chair from the small dinette. Each box contained summer clothes or shoes. She found three more boxes on the floor of the closet with a layer of dust on top. She shook her head as she opened them. Lots of useless stuff: high school and college papers, yearbooks, high school memorabilia, two scrapbooks, trophies and award ribbons. No iPhone. Nada.

The double bed was a simple metal bed frame with a standard box spring and mattress. She lifted up the mattress and looked between it and the box spring. Nothing. She pulled back the sheets and pillow and felt everywhere. Nothing. She made up the sheets then looked under the bed. Nothing but dust balls, an ugly brown rug and hair from that dog.

The dresser was the last place to look. Courtney opened each drawer and carelessly felt through all the clothes. Nothing. The last drawer she checked was the lower right one. It contained sweaters. She felt them all and was in the process of closing the drawer when she felt something move in the back. She took out the sweaters and found a brown box the size of a small margarine container. She placed it on top of the dresser then put the sweaters back in and closed the drawer.

Courtney held the flashlight in her mouth by clenching down on it with her teeth then aimed it at the box. It had been worn smooth. She slowly placed her hands around the sides of the box then pushed the top open with her thumbs. Black velvet lined the box and something inside sparkled. She reached in and pulled out a silver necklace with rhinestone letters attached to it. She lay it down on the dresser and saw the letters formed the word Jenny. Why would Kate have a necklace with the name Jenny on it. Then Courtney remembered that Kate's dead sister was named Jenny.

As she stared at the necklace, Courtney heard the sound of

a dog barking. She ran into the living room and looked out the window. Kate was walking back toward the apartment with her dog. Courtney couldn't go out the front door. She quickly looked around. She grabbed her clipboard and bag from the kitchen and ran into the bedroom. She grabbed the chair and put it back in the kitchen. And then she saw the bathroom. Courtney ran inside and shut the door.

CHAPTER 57

Kate slowly pushed open the door to her apartment. It was unlocked. Had she forgotten to lock it? She pulled Dillon in close as she looked behind her. A familiar black jeep was parked across the street, but she couldn't remember where she had seen it. She turned back to the front door of her apartment.

"You go in first." Kate released Dillon from his leash and let him into the apartment. She waited. All she could hear was Dillon's nails clicking on the hardwood floors and then the sound of him lapping up water.

She cautiously walked into the apartment, turned on the lights and looked around. Nothing seemed to be disturbed. She walked through the living room into the kitchen. Everything was in its place. She noticed the bathroom door was closed.

"Come here." Kate placed Dillon in between her legs as she turned the door knob.

Dillon raced into the small bathroom, sniffed the toilet then turned around and came back out. Kate noticed the shower curtain was pulled shut. She cautiously walked in and held her breath as she yanked back the curtain. Nothing. Kate glanced over at the window above the toilet. It was open just a little bit. She pushed it down and secured the latch.

Kate peeked into her bedroom from the doorway.

Everything appeared normal. She walked in and opened the closet. Nothing. She crouched down and looked under the bed. Nothing. She sat on the bed. Dillon came over and nuzzled his head up into her hands. As Kate was massaging his neck, she noticed the small wooden box on top of the dresser. Jenny's necklace was spread out next to it. Though, she often brought out the necklace to study it, she had no recollection of taking it out today.

She walked back into the living room and turned the deadbolt on the door. Jessica had told her to be careful but her mind must be playing tricks on her. Kate chalked it up to being on edge since the attack. She took one last look out the window and noticed the black jeep across the street was gone. She had no time to think. She had to get ready for dinner.

CHAPTER 58

A brisk gust of wind filtered through the main entrance of Triad back to the bar and snapped at Kate's bare legs causing her to sit up and look around. A young hipster couple walked in and waved to friends. Kate returned to her glass of wine, annoyed. Triad was a new "see-and-be-seen" restaurant in Altamont Heights featuring Italian-Asian-American fusion cuisine. It was 7:30 PM. Logan and Hashim were half an hour late.

"Want another?" the bartender asked.

"No thanks." Kate let out a deep sigh. "Can you bring me a glass of water?"

"Waiting for someone?"

"Yes. They were supposed to be here thirty minutes ago. And they're not answering their phones."

Kate savored a last sip of her Tobin James Zinfandel and set it down on the bar.

The bartender brought over a glass of water.

Kate took a sip and caught her reflection in the mirror behind the bar. Her make-up was too sparse and her hair had not been styled. She blushed at the sight of the sales tag sticking out behind the neckline of her new dress. She discreetly yanked the tag and put it in her purse. *Breathe.* She was anxious about having dinner with Logan but hoped to glean more information from Hashim about their product development.

The dim amber lights of the restaurant made it hard to recognize anyone, but Kate stood out against the ebony and chocolate decor with her strawberry blonde hair and form fitting, emerald sweater scoop-neck dress. She closed her eyes and cocked her head to one side to stretch her neck. She'd wait five more minutes and then head home.

The stench of alcohol filled Kate's nose as she felt heavy breathing inches from her right ear. "Sorry I'm late. There's no excuse."

Kate did not move. She opened her eyes and saw Logan in the mirror. He was standing behind her. His hair was a mess. She turned and immediately noticed his black button-down shirt was wrinkled and one tail hung out of his belted pants. Logan was alone.

Grabbing the back of Kate's chair, Logan squeezed his body in between Kate and the person seated next to her.

"How are you?" Logan asked as he teetered back and forth.

"Where's Hashim?" Kate asked trying to contain her panic. *Breathe.*

"Something came up. He won't be joining us. Let's get our table. I'm starving."

Kate felt the adrenalin surge. Amy had specifically instructed her to include Hashim in any meeting with Logan. What seemed to Kate as a micromanaging power play at the time now felt incredibly prudent. She flashed to the bruise on Amy's neck. Should she run?

"After you." Logan licked his lips then cleared a narrow path with his body away from the bar.

Kate hastily grabbed her purse and rummaged through it for some cash. Her hands were slightly shaking.

Logan put his hand on hers. "I've got it." He waved at the bartender with his other hand. "Put hers on my tab."

The bartender nodded.

Slightly stunned, Kate mumbled, "Thank you."

"It was the least I could do since you had to wait for so

long." Before Kate could react, Logan grabbed her hand and pulled her away from the bar towards the hostess podium.

The hostess smiled at Logan. "Your date finally arrived?"

"I'm not his date," Kate protested as she yanked her hand away from Logan's grasp.

The hostess looked from Kate to Logan. "I'm sorry, Sir, I just thought, because you were here—"

"Do you still have a table?" Logan interrupted.

The hostess looked down at the computer and touched the screen. "Yes. The one you requested. Follow me."

Kate realized Logan had been there the entire time. What game was he playing? Now she felt stupid for trying to confront Logan on her own. At least she felt some comfort being in a crowd.

After they were seated and had ordered their food, Kate focused their conversation on Logan. "Things seem to be going well for you."

"Yes, yes they do," Logan responded.

The waiter brought a glass of water for Kate then set a Vodka tonic with a wedge of lime in front of Logan.

"Why aren't you drinking with me?" Logan protested as he took the lime and squeezed the juice into his drink.

"I'd rather keep a clear head when I'm working."

Logan wiped his fingers on his napkin then took a long sip of his drink. "Who says we're working tonight?"

Kate tried to stay on track. "I thought you guys had stood me up."

Logan looked down at his glass and smiled. "Oh that. I was over in the lounge the entire time."

Kate looked at the lounge then back at Logan. "Why didn't you come over?"

"I wanted to watch you," Logan smiled as he took a sip of his drink.

Kate narrowed her eyes. The urge to run was overwhelming, but she stayed put.

Logan looked down at his glass and jiggled the ice. He leaned back in his chair, smiled and pointed a finger at Kate. "You're a clever girl. Very smart." He took another sip of his drink. "Brains and beauty, a deadly combination. Just like your sister."

Kate did not react; she didn't want to give Logan the satisfaction. She forced a smile and changed the subject. "How do you feel about Obsidian buying your product?"

Logan dramatically rolled his eyes and let out a sigh. "Your life is much more interesting than mine, Kate. But if you must know, I've worked really hard on Mirage. I'm finally getting what I deserve."

"What's that?"

"Recognition…that I can be a success."

"You're a Sinclair, what do you have to prove?"

The waiter interrupted the conversation by delivering their food; a porter house steak with a maitake mushroom demi-glace topped with a drizzle of rosemary pesto for Logan and a wild striped bass in a bed of cannellini beans and celtuce for Kate.

Logan immediately grabbed the steak knife and drove it into the meat. He carelessly hacked off a large portion then sloppily divided it into quarters. He poked his fork at one of the pieces and missed, making a loud clank on the plate.

Kate could not concentrate on her own meal with Logan self-destructing in front of her.

When Logan finally secured the meat on his fork, he raised it then took a moment to stare at Kate before plunging the piece into his mouth. He turned towards the entrance of the restaurant and as he chewed said, "I always knew I'd have to come back here someday, to reclaim my proper place."

"From Sander?" Kate braced herself for Logan's reaction.

Logan picked up his drink, tipped the glass back and slurped the last of its clear liquid down his throat. He spotted the waiter across the room and pointed at his glass. "You are blunt, aren't you?"

"What do you care about me anyway? I'm your pretty little bitch. You and your deranged family, you don't even think I matter."

Logan pointed his fork at Kate. "You know…you and I could've been family."

The waiter brought another Vodka tonic and left.

Kate put down her fork. "What do you know about my family?"

"That you have an older brother."

"Yes, Eric. He's ten years older than me. But you already knew that since you're the one who got him hooked on drugs in high school."

"Sure, without my help he would have been a perfect angel." Logan took a swig of his drink and held it between both hands, pondering the crowded restaurant. "Why did your parents wait so long to have another child? Ten years seems odd."

"I don't think so. I was a welcomed surprise."

"Really? A surprise...yes. But welcomed?"

Kate frowned. Logan was getting too personal. She had to change the subject.

CHAPTER 59

Eric closed his eyes and relaxed his head into the soft pillow of the deluxe King size bed. Courtney kissed his chest and ventured down his abdomen under the sheets.

It had been a long time since he had been with a woman. At least this time he would actually remember the encounter. Courtney and Eric had spent the previous afternoon discussing their lives and steps towards recovery. When she called this afternoon and suggested dinner at the Regent, Eric had no idea she had also reserved a hotel room.

His sponsor had told him to go slow when it came to relationships. Courtney made it impossible. With her blue eyes, long dark hair and devilish smile, it was hard to say "No" especially with what she was expertly performing that very moment.

Courtney emerged from under the sheets, wiped her mouth with her hand and took a breath of air.

Eric caressed her face and stroked her locks as his hand made its way down her arm. He stopped on the bandage. "What happened?"

"Oh that…nothing."

He stared at her with longing in his eyes for more. "I know I should take it slowly, but you…"

Courtney planted her lips on Eric's mouth. She hadn't planned to take it this far, but she couldn't resist. She straddled his naked pelvis and slowly let him enter her. She was now in control of the situation.

Eric cupped her breasts with both hands as he pulled her towards his lips, closed his eyes and kissed her erect nipples.

Using her breasts as a distraction, Courtney reached over the side of the bed to the space between the mattress and the box spring. She felt the smooth, polished stacked leather grip of her Little Fin. Fin had been by her side ever since an accident had turned into a hobby.

She grabbed the knife. Courtney didn't know if she felt more aroused riding Eric or handling Fin. She began to fantasize about the other men she had manipulated. The expressions on their faces, right when they were about to come, she'd hold the knife up, let them realize what was about to happen, and then plunge the sharp edge down into their heart, and twist it around.

Courtney tightened her grip on the knife as she became wetter thinking of the possibilities. And then she heard her Samsung phone beep. What the fuck? She lost her concentration. Why had she agreed to help Ruby? Damn it! She had made one mistake in Cabo. She didn't shut the curtains. The damn curtains. She had to help Ruby find Walter's phone or her trust fund would be gone and she'd end up in prison. She'd lose everything. Eric wasn't worth losing her trust fund over.

She pushed the knife back between the box spring and mattress. For now, Eric would get a free ride.

CHAPTER 60

Kate sat up in the chair trying to regain her composure. *Breathe*, dammit! *Breathe*. Don't let Logan control you. Change the subject. "Did you develop a product for Obsidian because you knew Sander owed you?"

Logan looked down at his right hand and began to fidget with his ring, his jaw clenched. "Why did your dad run for Oakview City Council?"

"To stop your parents' Cross Creek project." Kate paused to gauge Logan's reaction.

Logan sipped his drink but did not respond.

"Do you feel uncomfortable working with me because of the conflict between our parents?"

"Why would I feel uncomfortable? That's my father's gig, not mine. I don't let what my father does influence my life. He cut me off a long time ago."

"Cut you off?"

"I don't want to talk about it." Logan reached in his pant pocket and brought out his vibrating Samsung phone. He looked at the display. "Excuse me. This is so rude but I must take this call." Logan stood and stumbled towards the front entrance of the restaurant.

Kate forced herself to take another bite of the sea bass then a sip of water. From the mirror behind the bar, she could see Logan. He was outside the restaurant pacing back and forth. He looked angry. Kate wondered who was on the other end of the line. More people entered the restaurant and blocked Kate's view of Logan.

Logan returned with a fresh Vodka tonic. He placed the drink and his phone on the table then grabbed his chair and moved it right next to Kate.

"Thought I'd save the waiter a trip," Logan slurred his words as he sat down and placed his arm on the back of Kate's chair.

"Why'd you really ask me here tonight?"

Logan rubbed his chin with his hand then lifted his drink and took another sip. "To spite my father."

Kate raised her eyebrows.

Logan toasted his glass to the air, spilling Vodka down the front of his shirt. He ignored the moisture then slowly took a sip. He let the ice sink back into the glass before setting it down on the table. "It all started with afternoon drinks with my parents. It was supposed to be a quick visit. My father doesn't like to spend much time with me. But Mother insisted. She thinks we can work it out. Get me written back into the family will. It's all part of the plan." Logan took another deep sip then licked his lips. "I told him about meeting you. That I thought we had a connection and he lost it."

"Is that why you asked me here tonight?"

Logan smiled, showing his perfectly straight teeth. "Our dance."

"Seriously? Why'd you call me a bitch the other night?"

Logan ignored Kate's comment. "Didn't you feel a connection?"

"I have a boyfriend."

Logan grabbed Kate's hand. "I know you felt something when we danced."

Logan was completely intoxicated. Kate was ready with a counterpunch. "That was before I knew who you were."

Logan frowned. "Ouch."

Kate pulled her hand away from Logan's grasp. "Sorry, but it's the truth. You knew my sister and you killed her."

The waiter approached. Logan sat back in his chair and

looked up at the waiter as he took away their plates. He then picked up his drink and stirred the contents with his index finger. "You get right to the point."

"I've heard my brother's side of the story, why don't you tell me yours."

Logan placed his finger in his mouth then sucked off the excess vodka. "How'd you get the job at Obsidian?"

"You're changing the subject."

"Am I? Just go with me on this. Everything will become crystal clear."

Kate slowly nodded her head.

"You went to college right? What was your degree?"

"History. Why's that important?"

"How does a history major become an account manager at Obsidian? Did you ever work in high tech before this job?"

"No. But I got my start with the Inside Sales department. Within a couple months, I was recruited into the strategic accounts group."

"But how did you get that first job?"

Kate thought back to the spring before she graduated from college. The only work experience she had was waitressing at the Blue Mango in La Jolla. How had she gotten an interview with Obsidian? "My mom told me Obsidian was looking for new hires. I submitted my resume, interviewed and started that August."

"How did your mother get the tip?"

Kate ignored Logan's comment. "My manager is a fellow alum from UC San Diego. I guess that could have helped me get hired."

"Don't be so naive."

"What are you implying?"

"You and I...Our mothers always help us out of everything."

"What are you talking about?"

"Your mother called Laura Walker and demanded that you get an interview at Obsidian."

Kate shook her head. "What do you mean?"

"Sander."

Kate considered Logan's words but was still confused. "Why would Sander want to help me?"

Logan beamed a deliriously drunk, soaked smile. "Regret, remorse…whatever the fuck you want to call it. A weak moment of noblesse oblige." Logan smirked, proud to insult Kate and Sander in the same breath.

Kate studied Logan's face. Small beads of perspiration lingered just above his brow while his cheeks and part of his neck had turned flush red. His pupils were the most disturbing as they were larger than normal and totally transfixed on Kate. She lowered her head, looked up at Logan and asked one last time, "What do you know about my sister's death?"

Logan took a last gulp of his drink then licked his lips. "Enough. You tried this at dinner last night and you got nowhere. It is quite tiresome, Kate. And boring."

"I remember. You called me a bitch."

Logan smiled as he looked down at the ice in the empty glass.

"Sander was there and you were there. What happened?"

Logan closed his eyes and wrinkled his nose. He rubbed his hands over his brow wiping off the excess moisture. "Sander wouldn't know how to wipe his ass even if you showed him. He's hopeless." Logan opened his eyes and stared up at the ceiling. "I don't know why they chose him for CEO…well I do—but can't everyone see he's a fraud? He's a poor substitute for a son."

Kate sat back in her chair, not wanting to interrupt Logan's diatribe.

"His products!" Logan tried to take a last swig of his drink but realized it was empty. He slammed the glass down on the table. "He didn't create any of those products. He's not an engineer. He buys everything he needs. He bought two products that helped Obsidian become relevant with social media. And mine will take it to the next level. Perfectly positioned for the IPO."

Kate glanced around at the other tables, but no one was paying attention to their conversation. "And you'll make a lot of money."

"I don't care about the money. It's what I'm owed."

"Owed?"

"Sander owes me BIG! I was the one who had to leave. I was the one who lost everything. He gained a father he never had; a father who has provided him with everything. Everything that's rightfully mine."

"My brother says he went to the Convent that night to buy some weed from you."

Logan bit his lower lip and looked off towards the bar.

"Why not tell me what really happened. Clear your conscious."

"You tell me."

Kate froze. The sadistic look on Logan's face made her skin crawl. He had mentioned this same thing the previous night.

"Don't you remember?" Logan leaned in closer to Kate, put his arm around her shoulder then whispered in her ear. "You were there."

Kate felt the wind knocked out of her. Had she really seen what had happened to Jenny?

Logan's phone lit up. He looked at the display then immediately pushed back his chair and stood. He bent down and grabbed his phone just as Kate turned to look up at him. Their lips touched.

Kate leaned back slightly startled.

Logan did not move. "Sorry. I need to go. I'll pay the bill up front."

Before Kate could respond, Logan stood and walked towards the exit.

CHAPTER 61

Kate slowly turned the key in the lock of her front door as she walked into her apartment. She was dazed from dinner. Dillon startled her as he skirted past out the door. Too tired to run after him, Kate watched Dillon from the doorway as he relieved himself on a tree in the courtyard.

As she waited, Kate sent Brett a text:

cn u tlk

No response.

Dillon returned. Kate closed and locked the door then walked over to the coach and collapsed.

She sent a text to Eric.

u arnd

No response.

She needed to talk with someone about her dinner with Logan. Jessica.

u up?

Within a couple minutes Jessica responded:

call u n 15

Eric said he had brought Kate to the Convent when he went to meet Logan. But had she actually seen what happened to Jenny? How could she not remember something so awful? She glanced at her laptop on the coffee table.

Kate typed in the URL for Sinclair Enterprises. They were a private company with multiple real estate holdings, the list of their projects dating back to the 1950s. Cross Creek was at the top of the list. The project preceding it had been completed over four years earlier. Searching the real estate section of the San Jose Daily, Kate found several articles about the Sinclairs selling off their properties. Kate had always thought the Sinclairs had an enormous empire of real estate holdings. According to an article from a year ago, the only property they still owned outright was the one they had leased to the Seminary.

She searched further, mining the site for newspaper articles from the last decade. She found several articles about the Sinclairs from the dot.com era. Sinclair Enterprises had invested in numerous companies and had been given pre-IPO stock.

Three of the start-ups had been big names in Silicon Valley. Netwurks, Halflife, and GrandWuld were all companies Sander Walker had worked for over a twelve-year period. All the companies had imploded in the aftermath of the dot.com bubble bursting. There was a brief mention of Sander Walker under investigation while Chief Operations Officer at GrandWuld, but it was inconclusive and dismissive of the probe.

Then Kate found an article about Sander coming on board at Obsidian two years ago. Obsidian had been around for nearly five years. It was a stable company based solely on its photo manipulation software developed by the founder Don Sutter. When Sander came on as CEO, he took Obsidian to the next level and Don took a back seat in all decision making. With an infusion of investment capital, Sander was able to purchase two social products that turned Obsidian into a multimedia powerhouse.

The phrase, "infusion of investment capital" caught Kate's attention. Who was investing in Obsidian? She changed her search criteria and found a link to the Wall Street Journal's Money and Investing Update website. She found a snapshot of all the investors in Obsidian at the time Sander became CEO. The original founder and head of engineering, Don Sutter, owned 10 million shares or about 40% of the company. Bravo Equity Partners, a venture capital firm out of Delaware owned 2.5 million shares or about 10% of company. An investment fund, Dubai Industries, owned 7.5 million shares or 30% of company.

Sinclair Enterprises owned 3.75 million shares of Obsidian stock. Back then their investment accounted for 15% of the company. Employees held the remaining 1.25 million shares or 5% of Obsidian. She selected the "current financial report" link.

Obsidian was still scheduled to price on Tuesday with an anticipated stock price of between $20 and $25 per share. Kate opened her calculator application. If they still held 3.75 million shares, the Sinclairs investment could be valued at over $75 million.

Kate's phone beeped. A text message from Brett:

u ok?

Meetn with board

Kate desperately wanted to tell Brett about her dinner with Logan but now had second thoughts. What if he was with Sander? Kate responded:

em fine

wantd say goodnt

Brett responded:

thx

meet @ Rodneys

2moro 10 AM?

Kate responded:

y

Kate returned her attention to her search results. She was disgusted to know that she was essentially working for the Sinclairs and helping them make money. Why would her mother, who hated the Sinclairs, put her in this position? Who was Laura Walker anyways? Kate typed in the words Laura Walker, Organ, St. James Seminary.

The results were uninspiring: Sander Walker. Yes. Holy Trinity contact info. Yes. All obvious.

As Kate dug into the third page of her search, a web site dedicated to the historical preservation of Oakview appeared.

There was mention of a dormitory at St. Mary's Convent. Laura Walker was listed as the head of the dormitory between, 1975-83. Was Laura a nun?

She enhanced her search: Laura Walker, Oakview, marriage. Nothing. Kate went back to the search results on Laura Walker. She found an article from two years before in the local Haute magazine. It was an interview with Sander Walker. Kate scanned the article. Sander rambled on about his education as years of sacrifice and made reference to his mother. A quote caught her attention.

"Growing up with a single mom was difficult. But she did whatever it took to help us get to where we are today."

This quote was so Sander. He had told Kate back in May to "do whatever it takes" to get Cayenne's product ready.

Kate's phone rang.

She looked at the display. Jessica.

"Hi," Kate anxiously answered.

"Hey there," Jessica responded

"Thanks for calling."

"Would have done it sooner but I was helping NaNa get into bed?"

"NaNa?"

"Kent's great grandmother. His parents are out for the night so I'm filling in."

"That's right. I forgot."

"I was telling NaNa about you. How your dad just won the election. We got to talking about the Cross Creek project and she mentioned Renee Verano."

"Renee Verano?"

"Yeah. I guess NaNa knew Renee back in the day. She said there's a story behind that woman."

"And?"

"The old broad fell asleep before she told me anything. Don't you worry, I'll talk with her in the morning and see what I can get out of her."

Kate looked around her small apartment as she hesitated to continue their conversation.

"You wanted to talk. What's up?" Jessica probed.

Kate closed her laptop and sat back on the couch. "I had dinner with Logan."

"What? Why?"

"After I saw you, I got a text from him. Said he and his lead engineer wanted to meet. I assumed it was a business dinner and thought I could get more intel out of them."

"Let me guess. Logan showed up alone?"

"Yep. And he was already drunk. He had a fight with his dad and had been drinking all afternoon."

"Why did he want to meet?"

"He told me to spite his father, but I think he wants to get close to me because I'm Jenny's sister."

"That's sick and twisted."

Kate spread her fingers wide over her thighs. "No, the sick and twisted part is when I asked him to tell me what happened to Jenny and he said I should remember."

"You were there...at the Convent...that night?"

"Apparently. But I have no memory."

"Oh, honey, I'm sorry. This must be very difficult for you."

"It is, but in a weird way the information has helped motivate me further in finding out exactly why Logan is back and how his reappearance relates to Cross Creek and Jenny's death."

"You think there is a connection?"

Kate grabbed her laptop off the coffee table and opened it. "I started doing some searches on-line. Did you know the Sinclairs invested in Obsidian two years ago when Sander became CEO. They're going to make a ton of money on the IPO. That's how they're going to pay for the Cross Creek project."

"You should come work for me," Jessica joked.

"I also did some research on Laura Walker."

"Why'd you do that?"

"Logan told me my mom and Laura Walker helped me get the job at Obsidian."

"Impossible. How would he know that?"

"It gets even better, did you know Laura Walker ran the Convent dormitory back in the 1970's."

"The organist, Laura Walker?"

"Yep. Sander and his sister were raised by a single mom."

"Was Laura Walker a nun with two kids?"

"It doesn't say she was a nun. She ran the dormitory until the Convent shut down in 1983 after the earthquake."

"The earthquake is a bogus story, why did it really shut down?"

"I don't know. But I think the closing down of the Convent somehow relates to Jenny's death."

"But that was five years before Jenny died."

"Doesn't hurt to look. Eric and I are going to the library tomorrow to do some research on anything related to the Sinclairs. I'll let you know what we find."

Jessica did not respond.

Kate closed her laptop and set it on the couch next to her. "Cat got your tongue?"

"No...just got me thinking. Your parents should be able to fill in some of the gaps."

"We're having dinner tomorrow. So I plan on telling them about Logan being back–"

"And that you're working with him."

"Definitely."

"Kate... There might be a lot at stake. Be careful. Really careful. I think you're being set up. Don't tell anyone else what you're doing."

"Don't worry, I won't."

"I'm serious. I don't fly back to Seattle until tomorrow evening. Call me if you want to talk before that dinner."

"I will, Jess. Thanks for always being there for me."

"Anytime."

CHAPTER 62
Saturday

A white mist enveloped the parking lot as Kate maneuvered her car into a spot at Verano Shopping Plaza. She spotted Brett pacing on the patio in front of Rodney's. He stopped, put his iPhone in his pocket and leaned up against a light post. Kate could tell from his wet hair that he had showered but his eyes were still heavy from lack of sleep.

"Sorry I couldn't call you last night. I was right in the middle of meeting with Sander and the board." Brett greeted Kate with a hug and quick kiss on the lips.

"You look exhausted. Is everything okay?" Kate stroked the hair at the back of his neck.

Brett smiled. "Let's just say it's been a tough week. I definitely need a double this morning. Why don't you get a table and I'll get our coffee.

Kate found a table in the patio area, under a heat lamp. She sat down just as her phone beeped. It was a text message from Eric:

sry. didn't c this 'til jst now
had a l8 nite w Courtney
Kate responded:
gal frm d fundraiser
Eric responded:
y

wats so impt?
Kate responded:
tel u @ lib
c u at 11?
Eric responded:
y
c u

Brett returned with their coffee. He sat down, took a sip then leaned back in the chair. "It's nice to take a break from the chaos and just relax with you."

Kate leaned in closer to Brett and grabbed his hand. They sat for a couple minutes without saying a word.

"When you sent me a text last night, did you need something?" Brett asked.

Kate had gone over this conversation in her head a hundred times. There was no easy way around it. "I had dinner with Logan."

Brett sat up. "What the fuck? Why?"

"Don't worry. Nothing happened."

"But after the other night?"

"I thought it was a business dinner that included his engineer, Hashim."

"And Hashim didn't show up? You should have called me."

"I was in a crowded restaurant. And since I was there, I thought I'd try to get more information out of him about this deal with Obsidian."

"And?"

Kate knew Brett wouldn't talk about anything that could hurt his career but given everything that had happened, she had to ask. "First I need to ask you something and if you can't tell me, I understand."

Brett frowned.

"Who are the primary investors in Obsidian?"

"You mean the underwriters?"

"No. Private investors?"

"There are several. But that's all public information."

"I know. I saw that Sinclair Enterprises is one of the

investors. I also discovered that every company Sander ever worked for had Sinclair Enterprises as an investor. None of those companies went public. All of them folded. And the Sinclairs lost their investment."

Brett looked towards the parking lot.

"I read last night that the Sinclairs own 15% of Obsidian stock. What are the restrictions on their stock? Do they have to wait a certain amount of time before they can cash out?" How much money did they invest in Obsidian?"

Brett rubbed his eyes. "And good morning to you. That's a lot of questions this early in the morning."

"I think this all relates to their Cross Creek project and Jenny's death."

Brett put down his coffee. "How?"

"Sinclair Enterprises has been a major player in real estate development over the last thirty years. They are not a public company. And they haven't developed any projects in the last four years. My gut tells me they're hurting financially."

"That's not the image they portray."

"Exactly. So what if it's all been a façade. They've bet their future on Sander and Obsidian. The IPO is going to make them a lot of money, money that can fund their Cross Creek project."

Brett leaned in closer to Kate. "Now I'm getting concerned with how much you're looking into all of this."

Kate furrowed her brows. "But what if all of this relates back to the Sinclair's covering up my sister's death?"

Brett shook his head. "I don't see the connection."

"The Sinclairs have been investing in Sander. They gave him their scholarships to college and graduate school. Every company Sander's worked for they've invested in. I think they used their connections and what money they had to land him at Obsidian."

Brett rubbed his chin. "Interesting theory."

"It's as if Sander has become their son. Logan's returned to take back what he missed out on...what he's owed. "

Several bars of the Imperial March played from Brett's

phone. He shook his head, looked at the display and frowned. "What's so important now?"

"Sander?"

"How'd you know?"

"Ringtone?"

"Sorry. I've got to take this."

"No worries."

Brett stood and walked away from the patio and began to pace on the sidewalk.

Kate took a sip of her latte and tried to relax. She felt the sun breaking through the mist and warming her face. She closed her eyes and for a second soaked in the moment. She opened her eyes and watched Brett pace. She loved the intensity in his face when he was making a point. He stopped talking, looked over at Kate then ended the call.

Kate looked at the clock on her phone. 10:20 AM.

Brett came back to the table with a look of annoyance. "I've got to head back into work."

"Seriously?"

"I can't talk about it."

Kate raised her left eyebrow. "What's going on?"

"Nothing to worry about. I've just got to get through Tuesday."

"I'm sorry. I hope I didn't do anything–"

"You didn't. Just be careful with what you're doing. There's a lot riding on our IPO. I'd hate for you to do something that could jeopardize your career. Can't you look into all your family stuff after our IPO launch?"

Kate stared straight through Brett. She chose her response carefully. "Don't worry. I'm just researching. I haven't found anything concrete. I'll let you know if I do."

"Good." Brett bent down and kissed Kate on the cheek.

As he turned and began to walk away, Kate called out, "Will I see you tonight?"

Brett stopped and turned around. "You tell me. Don't you have that family dinner thing?"

"Yeah. But I'll be done by nine or ten."

Brett mimicked himself air texting. "I'll be at Obsidian."

Kate frowned but then blew Brett a kiss of understanding as he turned around and walked off towards his car.

CHAPTER 63

Kate and Eric found their way up to the 5th floor of San Jose's Martin Luther King Jr. Public Library and walked through the rows of shelved books.

"Why didn't you call me?" Eric said in a low voice.

"We were in a restaurant. Logan wouldn't do anything with all those people around." Kate stopped in front of Eric. "I think I gained his confidence."

"Didn't you say he was drunk? He probably won't remember anything."

"But the things he told me couldn't have been made up. They only help us."

Eric looked past Kate at the entrance to a room at the end of the row of books. "I think we're here."

The California Room housed a collection of newspapers, books, maps, photos and microfiche as the original historical records for Santa Clara County. Thousands of items were crammed into the tightly stacked racks, occupying most of the room.

"Where do we even begin?" Eric said to Kate as they entered the room.

"I want to find any articles about Jenny's death. Then I'll look into why the Convent shut down. Both of these will be in newspapers from the 1980s. I think I need to start in the microfiche section."

"I'm going to narrow my search to anything on the Sinclair's land lease with the Seminary." Eric walked up to the first rack to look at its contents.

The two parted ways and went to opposite ends of the room.

Kate located the microfiche catalog for the San Jose Daily in several large metal filing cabinets. She easily found the category of newspaper articles of 1970-1986. She pulled all the films for 1986 and 1983 then headed over to the large microfiche reader. She hadn't used one of these devices since elementary school and it looked pretty much the same. The enormous display reminded her of the old tube TVs. She turned on the device then placed the film for 1986 in the glass tray.

When she came to the month of June, Kate read through each article until one title caught her attention: Oakview Girl Death a Suicide. She looked around the room for Eric but could not find him. She began to read:

Panic and disbelief spread through the quiet Bay Area neighborhood of Oakview on the evening of June 18 when the body of 15-year old Jenny Crawford was found at the vacant Convent of St. Mary's on the grounds of St. James Seminary.

Around 7:00 p.m. Oakview police received an anonymous phone call to investigate the grounds for a body. According to police officer Douglas Marshall, the girl's body was discovered at 7:20 PM face down in front of the entrance to the Convent.

Again Kate looked around the room for Eric. He had not mentioned anything about an anonymous phone call. Hadn't the police picked him up on the service road and that's how they discovered Jenny's body? And wasn't Jenny found lying on her back, face up. Could Eric have been wrong about his recollection of what happened? With Eric no where in sight, she decided to keep reading.

In working with St. James Seminary, authorities determined foul play was not the cause of the girl's death. The San Clara County medical examiner's office backed up this finding when they ruled the girl died from a blunt head trauma as a result of jumping from the clock tower. This is the first suicide on St. James Seminary property that is leased from Sinclair Enterprises. The Sinclair family could not be reached for comment.

Teachers, relatives, friends and family struggle to make sense of the girl's death even as some question whether Jenny—a girl with a radiant smile and love for life—would take her own life.

Sources familiar with the investigation speculate that a recent breakup with a boyfriend could have caused the girl to end her life.

Jenny Crawford is survived by her parents, Nate and Vivian Crawford, twin brother Eric, and younger sister, Kate.

A memorial service is being planned at Holy Trinity for Tuesday June 27.

Once again, there was the mention of a boyfriend. Could Jenny have been dating Logan or Sander without her parent's knowledge? Logan kept calling Jenny the week before she died. What did he want? Kate looked around for Eric and noticed an elderly woman enter the room. She hit the print button.

Kate exchanged the film for the one from 1983. This was the year the Convent closed down. She searched through the articles until she came to the month of July. There she found an article titled, Convent of the St. Mary Closes its Doors.

The Convent of the St. Mary sustained significant damage from the recent Coalinga earthquake. Upon inspection, the building was deemed unsafe and the facilities were immediately vacated and classes suspended indefinitely. Between 1911 and 1982, the Convent was a Catholic school for girls from leading Peninsula families. Sister Grace Riley was the first head of the Convent. She was also the cousin of the O'Connell family that built the Seminary and Convent.

Kate hit the print button. As she leaned back in the chair, she felt a hand on her back.

CHAPTER 64

"Where's Eric?" Vivian asked Nate as she walked into the den.

Nate looked up from the computer. "What?"

Vivian rolled her eyes as she took a sip of hot tea from the cup in her hands. "Eric is not here. Where'd he go?"

"He took the train down to San Jose to go to the library."

"Did Kate go with him?"

Nate pushed the chair away from his desk, then crossed his arms and leaned back. "I don't think so. He's doing research for me on Cross Creek?"

"What if he tells Kate—"

Nate held up his hand and motioned for Vivian to come closer.

Vivian reluctantly walked up to Nate.

Nate took Vivian's hands in his and squeezed. "Let's not go there. I think it's better we just tell Kate about Logan. She needs to know the truth if he's back in town."

"If Patrick is correct and Logan is working with Sander on something that involves Obsidian, Kate should know. Let's tell her everything tonight."

"I just hope we're not too late."

CHAPTER 65

The muscles in Kate's back tensed as she quickly turned and looked over her shoulder.

"It's just me," Eric said as he held up his hands.

"You scared me," Kate said with relief.

"Sorry." Eric took a seat next to Kate and placed several sheets of paper and a dark green book next to the microfiche reader. "Did you find anything?"

"Yes. Look at these." Kate handed two pieces of paper to Eric.

Eric read the article about Jenny's death then shook his head. "That's not right. That's not how it happened."

"Are you sure?"

Eric frowned. "I was wasted but I'll never forget Jenny's face. I found her face up."

"Could Jenny have been dating Sander?" Kate blurted out.

Eric coughed. "No way. I would've known if she was seeing him."

"Are you sure?"

Eric leaned in closer to Kate. "Jenny may have had a crush on someone but definitely nothing serious, and not Logan or Sander." He scratched his head and smiled. "Sander was always someone they made fun of. He looks a lot different today than he did back then."

"What about Logan?"

"Jenny never said anything about Logan. She only saw him a handful of times. And it was always when Sander dropped Carolyn at our house."

"Didn't Jenny sometimes go to Carolyn's house? Couldn't Logan have seen her there?"

"It's possible. I don't want to even think about it. There was no way she would have let him touch her."

"What about the way Logan was acting towards me last night. He was being really weird, kept saying we had a connection…a connection that probably reminds him of Jenny. What if they had been dating?"

Eric shook his head. "You had to know her. Jenny was good. She wouldn't have fallen for his tricks. If anything, she would've fought him off."

Kate looked down at the newspaper article in Eric's hand about Jenny's death. "She may have tried but failed."

Eric stared at the paper and nodded his head.

"Did you find anything?"

Eric reached for the sheets of paper he had placed next to the microfiche reader. "I did find some stuff."

"From what time period?"

"I went all the way back to the beginning, when the Seminary was built. There was a great article in the San Jose Daily from 1912."

Eric and Kate turned around to the table behind them. Eric placed a photocopy of the newspaper article in front of them. Kate read aloud, "St. James Seminary and the Convent of the St. Mary."

"This article talks about the establishment of the Seminary and the Convent." Eric pointed at the article. "Back in 1910, the Sinclair family leased the land to Edward O'Connell for 99 years."

"Does it say why?"

"No. Just that the O'Connell family raised money from other Oakview families to build the facilities. The Convent opened its doors in 1911 while the Seminary followed in 1912."

"Was that the Convent?" Kate pointed at the black and

white photo in the lower right corner of the page. The photo was of a two-story austere brick structure with windows evenly spaced. The main entrance contained a portico with a semi circular driveway.

"Yes." Eric pointed at the steps leading up to entrance. "That's where I found Jenny."

Kate looked at Eric to judge his reaction.

"Don't worry. I can handle this."

Kate thought about the height at which Jenny fell. "I don't know if I can. This is all new to me."

Eric grabbed Kate's hand and squeezed it. "We don't have to do this."

Kate looked at Eric. After everything she had uncovered this week, it was too late to turn back. "We have to keep digging."

Eric placed his hand on Kate's shoulder. "Did you find out when the Convent closed?"

"1983." Kate handed Eric the photocopy of the newspaper article she had found. "The building was deemed unsafe after the Coalinga Earthquake."

"That earthquake didn't do any damage up here."

"And if there was that much damage, why didn't they tear it down that year?"

"Probably because it cost a lot of money. That was one thing Dad was able to pressure the City into doing after Jenny died."

"Tear down the Convent?"

"Yep."

Kate sat back and pursed her lips. "If the Seminary was built around the same time as the Convent, with the same materials, why didn't it sustain the same type of damage?"

"Good point."

Eric placed another piece of paper in front of Kate then stood. He walked back to the microfiche reader and returned with the dark green book.

"What's the book?"

"It's a history of prominent families from the Peninsula. It was written back in the '70s." Eric opened the book and flipped to a photo of two young men standing next to a redwood tree. "Did you know the Sinclair empire was built by two brothers—Lawrence and Rupert Sinclair?"

"Lawrence? Yeah. I read about him but I didn't know he had a brother?"

"Yep." Eric pointed at the photo of the two men. "They were from Pittsburg, Pennsylvania; came out to California at the end of the Gold Rush and dabbled in mining; got involved with investing in the Virginia Consolidated Mine of Nevada and made a shit load of money. They moved to San Francisco around the turn of the century and built homes on Nob Hill and Pacific Heights."

"Isn't the Nob Hill home now a hotel?"

"Yes. The other was destroyed in the 1906 earthquake."

"Why did they come down to Altamont Heights?"

Eric placed his index finger on the top right corner of the page, flipped it then pointed at a map on the next page. "It says they bought 7000 acres south of Oakview on the San Thomas Creek for a cattle ranch." He looked up at Kate. "I never thought about it but the creek does snake around quite a bit. That's why part of their land is in Oakview. The rest eventually became Altamont Heights where Sinclair Shopping Center sits." Eric pointed at the map. "The ten acres that fall in Oakview was the land leased to St. James Seminary."

"Why didn't the Sinclairs ever have a house in Oakview?"

"Doesn't say. Rupert lived on the ranch but never married. Lawrence and his wife built a home in the hills of what is now Altamont Heights."

"The Parthenon."

"Exactly. And this is something I never knew." Eric flipped the page. He pointed at a photo of the clubhouse. "The Altamont Heights Country Club was established in the 1950s. Investors were looking for a location and the Sinclairs wanted in on the membership. They came to some compromise. The Sinclairs were granted lifetime membership because they donated the house and the land."

"Why don't we hear more about the brother, Rupert?"

"Because Rupert died in 1910." Eric picked up the book.

He flipped through the pages until he came to a photo of a tall man standing in front of a wood fence behind which were two large oak trees. "It mentions something about an accidental shooting. There's nothing in the newspapers from that time except his obituary."

Kate grabbed the book out of Eric's hands and studied the photo.

"What?" Eric asked.

"I have seen Rupert's name before. On a head stone in the back corner of St. James Seminary."

"There's a graveyard back there? That's creepy."

Kate put the book down on the table. "If I hadn't walked into the headstone, I would've never seen it."

"When where you out there?"

Kate closed her eyes and took a deep breath. "Earlier in the week. When I was attacked."

Eric placed his hand on Kate's shoulder. "Why were you out there?"

Kate opened her eyes. "I don't know. I was out for a run. I was curious. With all this talk about the Cross Creek project I just wanted to check it out. I didn't know someone was going to attack me."

"Of course not." Eric lifted his hand off Kate's shoulder and pointed at the image of Edward. "Why would a Sinclair be buried in some lonely graveyard? There's got to be some family plot at a prominent graveyard in Altamont Heights. What did the headstone say?"

"That's the weird part. It had his name, date of death and then something to the effect of, 'an Eye for an Eye and now all is right.' Does that make sense to you?"

"No."

"So how does the Seminary play into all of this since Rupert is buried in their backyard?"

Eric closed the book and moved it to the side of the table. He pointed at the piece of paper that had been underneath it. "This article may explain things."

"What's it say?"

"The O'Connell family came to America at the tail end of

the potato famine with five children and two nieces. They must have been quite religious."

"Why?"

"One of the sons, Edward, became a priest and two of the nieces became nuns."

Kate thought back to her visit to the Seminary and the painting of Edward in the parlor. "Edward was the one who founded the Seminary."

"You're right. After he became a priest he tried unsuccessfully for years to raise funds to establish a Seminary here on the Peninsula."

Kate remembered what Father O'Connell had told her about the lease. "I bet the Sinclairs leased the land to Edward thinking this gesture would gain them some brownie points with the Oakview elite."

Eric smiled. "Good point. Do you know who built the Seminary?"

"The Sinclairs?"

"Yep. That was their first foray into the construction business. They leased the land to Edward and built the Convent and the Seminary the year Rupert died, 1910."

"With the carving on his headstone, an accidental death seems farfetched."

"I'm saving the best for last."

"You found something even better?"

Eric slid the piece of paper to the side to reveal one last photocopy. "Did you know the Sinclairs were involved in a scandal?"

CHAPTER 66

Courtney sat at a round table just outside the California Room reading a magazine. She wore her hair rolled up inside a baseball cap. With her black sweatpants, hoody, and running shoes, she looked like all the other college students scattered around the library.

Kate was inside the California room, sitting at a table. Eric was seated next to her. Both of their backs were turned towards Courtney.

Courtney strained her neck to see what they were doing. They were reading some papers set out in front of them, clearly a research project. Courtney remembered her own research. How she wanted to dig into the Crawford's and the Sinclair's pasts, but needed access to newspaper articles that had not been digitized. Could this room house the microfiche? How fortuitous.

She slowly stood and walked towards the California Room. Eric and Kate had not moved. She walked past the entrance and down the hall to view the room from another angle. She stopped and peered in the window. There were racks and racks of material, categorized by year.

"Do you need some help?" A voice from behind Courtney asked.

Courtney turned around.

An older women with gray hair wearing a San Jose Library ID badge stood in front of her.

Courtney looked down at the badge. "Barbara. Yes, I was just admiring the California Room. What type of material does it contain?"

"It contains a substantial archive of books, maps, files, and newspapers on California politics, education, local business, and historical events mostly preserved on microfiche." The woman gestured towards the door. "Perhaps there is something I can help you find?"

Courtney looked back in the room at Eric and Kate. "I'm going to get some lunch but when I come back, I'll find you."

CHAPTER 67

Kate grabbed the photocopy off the table. "A scandal?"

Eric smiled. "I found it in the San Jose Daily from 1928."

Kate read aloud the title of the article, "Sinclair Family Name Blemished by Paternity Suit. Oh my God." She looked at Eric. "You've got to be kidding."

"When Lawrence died in 1928, he left his real estate holdings and over $30 million in the bank to be divided between his wife, Amanda, and their only son, Stewart. A couple weeks after his death, a lawyer for a Regan Gallagher petitioned the Superior Court of Santa Clara asking for a daughter's share of Lawrence Sinclair's fortune."

"This is crazy."

"It gets better. The courtroom battle was to take place two years later at the Altamont Heights court house. This Regan Gallagher and ten other witnesses were ready to testify that she was indeed the love child of a woman from the Convent of St. Mary's who died during childbirth."

"A nun or someone who worked there?"

"Doesn't say. The trial never got off the ground as the Sinclair attorney petitioned the judge to stop the trial and find in favor of the family."

Kate put down the photocopy on the table. "And the judge did it?"

Eric pointed at the photocopy. "The judge forced the jury to produce a verdict without hearing all the evidence."

"That's not ethical or legal."

"Not at all. Regan Gallagher was legally disavowed as having any relation to Lawrence Sinclair."

Kate held up her finger to her lips as she looked around the library. "So if the Sinclair's were doing shit like that back then, what are they capable of today?"

"Or when Jenny died?

Kate focused on Eric. "What about Cross Creek? What have the Sinclairs been doing secretly behind the scenes to make sure that project happens? And how will Dad's role on the Oakview City Council play into all of this?"

"Do you know how many projects Renee Verano and Dad have worked on over the years?"

"I haven't really kept a tab. How is that relevant?"

"I wasn't around back then but yesterday I looked into it. I went to the building department yesterday."

"You're taking this seriously," Kate said sincerely.

Eric lowered his head then looked up at Kate. "About two weeks ago, I started asking myself, why would Dad want to run for city council? Do you remember 55 University Ave in Altamont Heights? And 389 West California Street in Oakview?"

"Of course. Those were some abandoned buildings Dad turned into low-income housing. I think I was eight or nine when he finished the University Ave project."

"Exactly. I discovered Dad did at least one of those projects a year."

"What's your point?"

"After I left town, Dad changed the types of projects he took on; commercial to nonprofit."

"The first project I remember was the Verano Shopping Plaza but that was all for profit. And then 55 University Ave in Altamont Heights. Yes, that was low income housing."

Eric stretched out his right leg, dug into his front pant pocket and took out a folded piece of paper. "I quickly looked into a couple other projects."

Kate took the paper and unfolded it. "What is it?"

"I found a newspaper article from April 1988 that confirms what I found at the building department."

"The West California project?" Kate read the article then turned to Eric. "It says that Verano Industries took that project out from under the Sinclairs."

"At first I thought Dad was able to negotiate a better deal."

"True, but the Sinclairs were going to build high-priced condos. That would have brought in a lot of money. Why would Verano Industries not do the same? Why would they go the route of affordable housing?"

Eric pointed at the piece of paper. "Since I've been gone, Dad's never built any high-priced condos or commercial real estate. He used to when I was little. And Verano Industries still does."

Kate shrugged her shoulders. "Jenny dying probably made him rethink his priorities."

"But why would all of the projects he worked on after Jenny's death involve taking property away from the Sinclairs?"

"Do you think Dad did this to get back at the Sinclairs because he thought they covered up Jenny's death?"

"But Renee Verano would have to be in on it. What would she gain?"

Kate sat back in her chair. "Last night, I did some research on the Sinclair's. Their company is private. They don't have public information about their finances. But over the past ten years, they've sold off all their buildings throughout the Bay Area."

"Why would they do that?"

"To cover some bad investments in several high tech start-ups."

"Why would they invest in start ups?

Kate shook her head. "Sander."

"Sander?"

"He was working at each one of the start ups they invested in. And get this, they made their largest investment two years ago with Obsidian."

"Didn't Sander come on board as CEO two years ago?"

"Exactly."

Eric stood and started to pace. "So if Obsidian has a strong IPO, they'll make a lot of money?"

"And they can use that money to fund their Cross Creek project. The last property they still own."

"Unless Dad and the other city council members vote it down."

"If Walter had won the election, then the Cross Creek project was a sure thing."

"Convenient for Renee that he died in a car accident."

"We need to talk with Mom and Dad about all of this."

Kate's phone beeped indicating a new text. She dug through her purse and looked at the display. "A text from Jessica."

we nd 2 meet now!

Kate replied:

Where are you?

Jessica responded:

NaNa house

Kate replied:

?

Jessica responded:

She hs a tale bout Renee Verano…

"What's up?" Eric asked.

Kate pointed at her phone. "Jessica's fiancé, Kent, has a great grandmother who supposedly knew Renee Verano back in the day. She's got some story to tell."

"A story about Renee?"

Another text came in from Jessica:

and a Regan Gallagher

CHAPTER 68

Kate navigated her green mini cooper through the oldest section of Oakview with its tree-lined streets, manicured lawns and picture-perfect Craftsman, Spanish, and Colonial style homes. Kent's great grandmother, Mildred Roberts, lived in a house at the end of Fair Oaks Boulevard in a large, decrepit three-story Victorian.

The light blue paint flaked and peeled off the sides. Several upturned shingles on the roof revealed water damage. And missing spindles on the front porch created unsightly gaps while the buckled wood planks offered a treacherous entrance.

Jessica greeted Kate at the front door and led her into the two-story foyer.

"What's going on?" Kate asked.

"As I told you last night, NaNa got to talking about Renee Verano. She said some things about the Sinclair and Verano families that you need to hear."

"Like what?"

"You've got to hear it from NaNa. But don't be surprised if she just rambles on or falls asleep in the middle of talking. She's just really old."

The women walked through the house to the back sunroom overlooking the garden—a once stately collection of flowers and plants now overgrown with weeds from lack of attention. NaNa sat at the back of the room in a worn wicker chair with yellow and green floral cushions with her feet up on a matching ottoman. Her swollen and callused feet had walked a lifetime. A long white braid of hair cascaded over her left shoulder and snaked down across her chest through a silver necklace with a cross. She sat peacefully with her head tilted to the side and eyelids drawn shut. Her face was ancient.

"Is she asleep?" Kate whispered. "Should we wake her?"

Jessica nodded her head and motioned for Kate to take a seat on the couch next to NaNa. Jessica bent down, put her hand on NaNa's weathered hand and gently patted it. "NaNa. Are you awake?"

The woman sluggishly opened her eyes. Without moving her head, she looked around the room until she focused on Jessica.

"Oh, Jessica. My dear. I must have fallen asleep," NaNa said.

Jessica squatted in front of her. "I'd like you to meet my friend Kate. Kate Crawford." Jessica stood and slowly backed away to give NaNa an unobstructed view of Kate.

NaNa squinted her eyes and swayed her head slowly back and forth as if it would help adjust her vision.

"Remember we were talking about Nate Crawford winning the election? How he used to work for Verano Industries?" Jessica said.

NaNa instantly became alert and slowly sat up in her chair. "Yes. Yes. I knew Jimmy Verano. We went to Oakview High together."

Kate smiled. "And Jimmy was married to Renee?"

"Humph…that woman. More of a chameleon if you ask me." NaNa slowly narrowed her eyes as she focused on Kate. "Jimmy was a great man from one of the original families of Oakview. Mind you they weren't wealthy back then. It was Jimmy who built his real estate empire from the ground up. It was the Depression. He made his money from buying foreclosure properties."

"When did he marry Renee?" Kate asked.

NaNa smiled and let out a hoarse laugh. "Renee wasn't his first wife. Jimmy married his high school sweetheart, Daisy

Jane. They were quite the couple around town, always in the society pages." NaNa looked out the large sunroom windows and the unkempt garden beyond and let out a sigh. "Jimmy always believed in treating everyone equally, regardless of their pedigree. He built a lavish home on Montgomery Ave. You know up in the hills above Oakview. It was too bad Daisy Jane could never fill that house with kids. Such a beautiful home."

"Yes, yes, I know it well. That's one of Renee's homes," Kate said.

"Renee's home? Humph! That was all Daisy Jane. Jimmy and Daisy were married some thirty years. Much longer than Lloyd and I. God rest his soul."

"I'm sorry about Lloyd," Kate said sincerely.

"No need. He was a good man. Lived a good life," NaNa responded.

"Thirty years. That's quite a long time. Why did Jimmy and Daisy Jane separate?" Kate asked.

"Oh they didn't. They would've been together for eternity if the good Lord hadn't had other plans for Daisy Jane. It was such a shame when she died."

Kate leaned in closer. "She died?"

"Something about food poisoning. Not quite sure what from. It was right around the time when that Renee woman or whatever she was calling herself back then returned to Oakview."

"What do you mean returned? Didn't Renee live in Oakview?" Kate asked.

"Of course. She was raised out at the Convent and took her classes there," NaNa said matter-of-factly.

Kate looked at Jessica then back at NaNa. "How did you know her?"

"Oh, everyone knew her. But her name back then wasn't Renee. It was Regan Gallagher."

Kate's jaw fell open as she gasped. "She was the one who brought the paternity claim against Lawrence Sinclair."

NaNa looked at Kate and pursed her dry lips. "Oh, you know about that? We always suspected 'funny things' happened at the Convent but Regan was the first one to come out and say something. And she accused a Sinclair. It was quite the scandal. I'm not saying it wasn't true, that she was lying, but she made a huge stink. Said her mother had an affair with Lawrence Sinclair. And her mother was a nun."

Kate inched closer to NaNa. "What did you think?"

"We didn't know what to think. That was not something that ever came to light back then. You kept it a secret. I think Regan was just after the Sinclair money. When she lost the suit, Regan had to leave town. She was gone for some time. But then she came back as Renee Fisher."

"Renee Fisher? She changed her name?" Kate asked.

"She married some poor bastard back east who'd recently passed away. Left her just enough money. But her name wasn't the only thing she changed. She dyed her hair blonde and changed the make-up and clothes she wore. A little too sexy if you ask me. I kept my Lloyd close when she was carousing the streets looking for her next husband. Poor Jimmy Verano. Daisy Jane was dead. He fell for Renee. He fell for her tricks. They married a year after Daisy died."

"Only a year? That seems like a short amount of time," Kate said.

NaNa looked at Kate and smiled. "Oh, child. When you've been with someone for over thirty years and they die, you miss the companionship. You need someone there with you. Jimmy was in his '50s. Renee convinced him early on that she was the one who could take care of him—by spending his money. And she certainly did."

"Didn't Jimmy die, like, thirty years ago?" Kate asked.

"Yes. Renee and Jimmy were only married for ten years when Jimmy died. Died right here in Oakview driving down the road from their Montgomery property on Ridge Road. They get a lot of fog up there at night. He lost control of his car and crashed into a tree."

"A car accident?" Kate looked over Jessica. "Just like Walter Rudolf."

Jessica jumped into the conversation. "When Jimmy died, is that when Renee took complete control of Verano Industries?"

NaNa looked over at Jessica. "Yes. And that's when her feud with the Sinclairs took off."

"What did you think of the Sinclairs?" Kate asked.

"They were nice enough people. But they were always trying too hard to fit in with the established families of Oakview. My family's been here since the 1850s. We worked hard to get here. We belong."

"But when the Sinclairs leased the land to the O'Connell family and then provided the land for the Altamont Heights Country Club, didn't that help?" Kate asked.

"No matter what they did, they never truly gained acceptance in the community. That paternity suit ruined their chances. You see, they weren't like the rest of us."

"What do you mean?" Kate asked.

"They were new money, always looking to make a quick buck. Taking advantage of people to make money. They didn't have the pedigree of my family. Lawrence Sinclair's son, Stewart, married a nice girl from San Francisco. That was a step in the right direction. But their son, William? His wife, Maria, reminds me a lot of Renee."

"How so?" Kate asked.

"William met her at UC Berkley. That's where all the Sinclairs go to college. Maria wasn't daughter-in-law material. His parents wanted William to marry one of the local Oakview girls, from one of the better families. Like my family. Not that I'd allow any of my children to marry a Sinclair. Maria was a girl from nowhere, with no family."

"But she had to be pretty smart to get into Berkley," Kate said.

"That's why she reminds me of Renee. Maria knew the Sinclairs had money. She sunk her claws into William and never let go. Rumor has it they had to get married."

"Had to?" Kate asked raising her eyebrows.

"All I know is that son of theirs, Logan, was born six months after they got married. Maria loved that son of hers.

Would do anything for him. I don't know what happened to him? He left years ago."

"Do you know why they closed the Convent?" Kate asked.

NaNa slowly put her hand on top of Kate's hand then lightly patted it. "Oh, child. Everyone knows that story."

CHAPTER 69

"I was at the main San Jose library," Courtney said into her Samsung phone as she sat in her black jeep.

"What were you doing there?" Ruby asked.

Courtney stroked the steering wheel. "I was following Kate Crawford and her brother Eric."

"Why were they there?"

"Eric told me yesterday they were heading down there to do some research.

"What were they researching?"

"I don't know. I couldn't get close enough without being noticed," Courtney lied as she looked over at the photocopies on the passenger seat of some of the newspaper articles she had discreetly obtained from Eric after Kate rushed out of the library. How simple it had been to wander in and convince Eric of their random encounter. And because she had completely gained his confidence, he easily shared information on where Kate had gone.

"Where did they go after the library?"

"Eric stayed behind but I followed Kate to Oakview. I'm parked outside the house of a Mildred Roberts?"

"Why the hell would she go there? Has she gone there before?"

"Not that I know of. You know Mildred Roberts?"

"Mildred knows me and might say some unfavorable things."

"Well...that could be a problem for you," Courtney smirked as she briskly pushed the "End" call button. She threw her phone into her purse then grabbed Walters's laptop from the passenger seat. She connected to the Internet, logged into Walter's iCloud account and tried to locate his phone. Nothing. It was not on.

CHAPTER 70

Kate looked back at Jessica then cupped NaNa's hand with her own. "I was only a couple years old when the Convent closed its doors. No one ever told me the real story."

NaNa grabbed Kate's hand and pulled her in closer.

Kate moved forward then knelt down next to NaNa. She was only inches away from her face.

"One of the priests from the Seminary had a tryst with a nun at the Convent." NaNa leaned back to see Kate's reaction.

Kate looked at NaNa but did not show any emotion. "Was there a child from the affair?" Kate asked.

NaNa sighed as she released her grip of Kate's hand. "There was a rumor but nothing ever came of it."

"In the newspapers from back then, it mentioned the Convent was shut down due to earthquake damage. Is this true?" Kate asked.

NaNa laughed. "I remember. Damage from the Coalinga earthquake. Sure I felt that quake but no houses in our area sustained enough damage to make them uninhabitable. I think it was just the Seminary's way of covering up that incident. No one had any proof so the rumor just died away, along with the closing of the Convent."

NaNa had confirmed everything Eric and Kate had discovered at the library. And as long as NaNa was talking,

Kate decided to ask the most difficult question of all. "Do you remember what happened to my sister, Jenny Crawford?"

NaNa slowly grabbed the cross from her necklace and began rubbing it. "Oh, Lord. Your poor sister. Oakview families don't like when something happens to one of their own." NaNa turned to Kate. "If I remember correctly, there was a lot of pressure put on the police to close the case. No suspects. No evidence of foul play. It was best for everyone if that girl just killed herself. I don't know how your parents survived."

Kate sat back and studied NaNa's face. Her eyelids began to droop as she wearily tried to focus on Kate.

"I don't understand why your father went to work for Verano Industries."

"Why?" Kate asked.

NaNa released her grasp of the cross and let her hand fall to the side. She yawned. "Renee is such a bad seed and your father..." NaNa closed her eyes.

Kate looked at Jessica then back at NaNa as she placed her hand on top of the grand dame's hand. "You were saying."

NaNa slowly opened her eyes. "Nate. Your father. He's a good man. Always helping people. Giving back. Not making a quick buck. I don't know how he managed to do that kind of work with that Renee woman watching over him."

Kate looked back at Jessica who shrugged her shoulders then pointed back at NaNa.

NaNa's eyes were closed and she was breathing heavily.

Kate drew back her hand. As she stood, she whispered, "Thank you NaNa. You've been very helpful."

CHAPTER 71

Jessica walked Kate onto the front porch of the house. "I told you, you had to hear it first hand."

"That's some crazy shit." Kate grabbed onto the railing and took a step down.

"Did it help?"

Kate stopped and looked back at Jessica. "Definitely. To think, I started off trying to find more information about Logan Sinclair. Then I discovered he was involved in my sister's death. Now I realize there's much more to all of this. These wealthy families have their own secrets. And they'll do anything to keep it that way."

Jessica grabbed on to Kate's hand. "Wait. I've got something for you." She went back in the house and returned with a white manila envelope.

"What's this?" Kate asked as she took the envelope.

"I did some research. I kept thinking about Walter Rudolf. Something didn't seem right. I used my connections to pull some records."

"Should I read them now?" Kate said as she opened the envelope and looked through the papers. One paper was a spreadsheet listing financial numbers. "How'd you get these?"

Jessica smiled. "You know I can't reveal my sources."

Kate pulled out the spreadsheet and looked over the numbers. "These are Rudolf's?"

"Yep. I was able to get his annual salary and bank records for the last three years. He was a marketing guy. Only made $140K a year. His wife wasn't working. They had a lot of debt including $30K in credit card bills. Then two years ago, his bank account started to increase $9K a month—every month. The money came in from various sources. I bet he was being paid off."

"My dad said Rudolf started to align himself with the Sinclairs about two years ago."

"That's the connection."

Kate shook her head. "But what good is Rudolf dead if he was helping the Sinclairs?"

"Perhaps he had dirt on one of the Sinclairs and was going to talk?"

"Regarding Cross Creek?"

Jessica lightly swatted Kate on her back. "Regarding anything."

"Good theory," Kate said as she pulled out the paper from the envelope. "What's this?"

Jessica leaned in closer to Kate. "A police report."

"For Walter Rudolf?"

"No." Jessica pointed at the date at the top of the paper. "From the night Jenny died."

Kate looked at Jessica and froze.

Jessica smiled. "Let's just say someone owed me big."

Kate read over the report then jumped up and down, giving Jessica a hug in the process. "Oh, my god. You are the best!" Kate placed the papers back in the manila envelope. "Tonight should be an interesting family dinner."

CHAPTER 72
Saturday Night

The two-story craftsman-style Crawford home presented well from the street. A wood-shingled roof, beige smooth stucco walls and a half porch shading a distressed red front door signaled rustic elegance. The lone oak tree in the front yard stood guard with its massive limbs spread across the entire property. Uplighting of the trunk and three limbs illuminated the expanse of the arbor at night and made the entrance to the home feel like a tree house. A blue yard sign with white lettering that read, Nate Crawford for Oakview City Council, was still standing while another sign had fallen over in the front ditch.

A light breeze swayed the tall redwood trees surrounding the rear of the house as branches brushed up against the dining room windows. Nate, Eric, Kate and Vivian sat around the oval dining room table for their weekly family dinner.

Tension from the week's events filled the room. No one said much as they ate their meal.

"It might rain again," Eric suggested.

"It's raining early this year," Vivian added.

Eric looked at Kate then opened his eyes wide as he took a bite of pasta. Under the table, he discretely stretched his legs and kicked Kate's foot.

Kate put her fork down and turned to face her father. "How are things going since the election?"

"Well, I don't officially begin work until I'm sworn in on December 11th," Nate responded.

Vivian looked from Kate to Eric. "So keep the evening of Tuesday, Dec 11th open. We all need to attend the ceremony, as a family, to support your father."

"What else do I have planned?" Eric sarcastically added under his breath.

Kate smiled then returned her attention to Nate. "What happens on the Council between now and then?"

"Actually, quite a bit. I've already had a couple meetings with the current council. We're discussing the open committee positions, who will be Mayor and of course the Cross Creek project. We're supposed to vote on that come June. That's why Eric is helping me do some research."

Nate gave Kate the perfect opportunity to talk about everything Eric and she had uncovered. "I know. Eric told me. I went to the library with him this morning."

Vivian raised her eyebrows.

Nate remained calm and did not react to this comment. He took a bite of pasta then leaned back in his chair. "That's great you want to help, Kate. What did you and Eric research?"

Eric piped in. "The Seminary, the Sinclairs, the Convent–"

"The O'Connell family and Verano Industries." Kate picked up her fork and took a bite of salad.

Nate look at Vivian but remained silent.

"There's a reason I went to the library with Eric." Kate put down her fork, wiped her mouth with the napkin and took a sip of water. "Something happened at work this week. And it may relate to Jenny's death."

Nate leaned forward and put his elbows on the table.

Kate chose her words carefully. "I was assigned a new account. The company is called Fortunato."

"Should we know who they are?" Nate asked.

"No. But you do know the head of the company." Kate leaned back and looked at both of her parents. "Logan Sinclair."

The clank of Vivian's fork dropping on her plate echoed through the small dining room as she blurted out, "I knew it!"

"Logan is really back?" Nate gripped the sides of his chair.

Kate placed her hands on the table. "Sander assigned Fortunato to me on Monday."

Nate clenched his teeth and threw his napkin down on his plate. He looked at Vivian. "I knew working at Obsidian would mean trouble."

"What?" Vivian narrowed her eyes and pointed at Nate. "If you recall, I was opposed to it. You were the one who pushed it. You said it might come in handy."

Kate turned to Vivian. "So you did call Ms. Walker and ask if I could interview with Obsidian?"

Vivian ignored Kate and looked out the window at the grove of redwood trees. She closed her eyes and took a deep breath. When she opened her eyes, she turned back to Kate. "How did you know about that?"

"Logan told me," Kate shot back. "I had dinner with him last night."

Outrage filled the room as no one spoke but the tension on their faces conveyed their true feelings.

Vivian lowered her head.

Nate stared at Kate.

"Why did you make me believe Jenny committed suicide?" Kate asked.

Nate stared down at his food and did not respond.

Without looking up, Vivian mumbled, "It was best for everyone."

"Bullshit," Kate shouted.

"Kate?" Nate reached towards Kate and tried to touch her hand.

Kate withdrew both her hands into her lap. "I've always tried to be perfect. Follow the rules. Do the right thing because I thought Jenny let you down." Kate's cheeks began to turn red. "I didn't want to let you down." Her voice began to tremble as a tear streamed down her right cheek. "You were so over protective." Kate wiped the tear away with her hand. "What really happened to Jenny?"

Eric looked at Nate and Vivian. "I told Kate what I know."

Vivian silently turned and looked outside the dining room window again as a lone tear streamed down her face.

Nate tapped his fingers on the table. "We thought you'd be extra cautious with your relationships if you thought Jenny killed herself over a boyfriend. We were protecting you."

"I couldn't lose another child," Vivian muttered under her breath.

"Congratulations! You succeeded in completely debilitating me. No wonder I've never been able to keep a relationship." Kate stood and wiped her hands over her face.

Vivian looked at Nate as Kate walked out of the dining room, through the living room to the bench by the front door.

Kate grabbed the manila envelop from under her purse and returned to the dining room. She took out the papers and placed one in front of Nate. "Here's the police report from the night Jenny died."

Nate's jaw dropped.

Vivian grabbed the paper.

"How did you get that?" Eric asked.

"My friend Jessica called in some favors," Kate said as she continued to stand next to Nate.

Vivian gasped. "It says the police received a call from the Seminary.

Nate looked up at Kate. "The Seminary was the anonymous call?"

Kate sat in the chair between her parents and pointed at the report. "I think Father O'Connell left on a sabbatical because he made that call."

"The Sinclairs got to him because he's the only one who knows exactly what happened that night," Eric said.

Vivian looked over at Eric but did not say anything.

"Sander benefited the most." Kate leaned back in her chair. "The Sinclairs have taken good care of him. Did you know he received their scholarships for undergrad and graduate school at UC Berkeley?"

236

"And then they invested in every high tech company he's worked for over the last twelve years," Eric added.

"Why would they do that?" Vivian asked.

"The companies were all start-ups. They were probably investing in their future," Kate said.

"But all those companies failed, until Sander landed at Obsidian," Eric said.

"And you're launching your IPO on Tuesday." Nate began to understand the gravity of the situation.

Kate turned towards Nate. "The Sinclairs had to find another way to make money because you and Renee decimated their real estate empire."

Nate pushed his chair back from the table. "What are you talking about?"

"Why did you go work for Renee after Jenny died?" Kate asked.

Nate did not respond.

"Before Jenny died, you worked for yourself." Kate looked over at Eric for support. "You developed small commercial spaces and houses. Then you teamed up with Renee for the Verano Shopping Plaza."

Eric leaned in towards Nate. "After that project, you stopped developing for profit and concentrated on building affordable housing."

"And all at the expense of the Sinclairs," Kate added.

Vivian sat back in her chair and crossed her arms.

"You'd get wind of a property the Sinclairs wanted to buy. You'd come in and take it from underneath them," Kate said.

"It's not like you made a ton of money on those projects. You even lost money on a couple of them," Eric said.

Kate turned her chair towards Nate. "Why do it at all?"

Nate sighed as he looked up at the ceiling and closed his eyes. "I never intended any of you to get involved. That wasn't the plan."

Kate grabbed the back of Nate's chair. "What is the plan?"

CHAPTER 73

Brett ran his fingers through his disheveled hair as his blood shot eyes tried to focus on the document he was reviewing on his laptop. Thank God he had showered and changed his clothes this morning. He was going to be at Obsidian all night. Now if he could just remember to eat, he'd at least have the strength to make it through to Tuesday.

He selected the print option on his word processor application to review the latest draft of the press release for Obsidian's IPO. He picked up the copy from the printer and headed out of his office towards the elevator. Sander wanted to review this draft in person.

Walking out of the elevator onto the 14th floor, Brett realized the only lights on this floor were in Sander's office. He looked down at the press release one last time as he continued down the hallway.

Brett heard voices. He slowed his pace when he realized the voices were arguing.

"You would have loved it. She was so scared. But like all of them, she did exactly what I wanted."

"Why the fuck are you still doing that?"

Brett recognized the second voice to be that of Sander. He stopped just outside Sander's office and looked through the crack between the door and doorframe. Sander was talking with another man Brett didn't recognize.

"You can't just come back here and think you own the place and everyone in it," Sander blurted out.

The other man turned around to face Sander. He was dressed all in black, had dark hair and tan skin. "I can't. Why not? You owe me."

Sander laughed. "I owe you? We both know what happened." He grabbed the man's shoulder. "You should be thanking me for keeping quiet all these years."

The other man shoved Sander's hand away. "I think my dad has thanked you enough. Now it's my time."

Sander smiled. "You have no idea what you're doing, Logan."

Logan turned around and slammed Sander down onto the desk, scattering several papers and pens onto the floor. He used his right knee to pin Sander down by his thigh. His hands pressed down on Sander's chest leaving his head hovering just above his face.

Brett fought back the impulse to run into the office as this was his first chance to see Logan up close. Was he everything Kate had described?

"This is not about you, you fucking asshole!" Logan hissed. "It's my turn!"

Sander did not respond. He lay still on the desk, his glasses shifted up onto his forehead while his arms spread wide above his head.

"You're pathetic," Logan said as he released his hold of Sander and stood. "Just like all those bitches."

CHAPTER 74

Nate opened his eyes. He placed both hands on the dining room table and spread his fingers wide. "We never believed Jenny committed suicide. But the police had no witnesses or suspects because Logan and Father O'Connell took off for Italy. No one was talking. It was so obvious the Sinclairs were using their influence to cover it up. There was nothing we could do."

"Is that when Renee stepped in?" Kate asked.

"Yes. She provided the hope of retribution if we took matters into our own hands," Nate said.

"How?" Kate asked.

Nate shook his head. "We'd buy any property the Sinclairs were thinking of developing."

"Even if it cost a lot of money?" Kate asked.

"Cost was not a problem for Renee," Nate chuckled. "We bled them dry and forced them to sell all their properties to pay their creditors. They don't own anything anymore."

"Except the land they leased to the Seminary," Eric interjected.

"Exactly," Nate said as he looked from Eric to Kate. "We knew the lease would end at some point and they'd want to develop it, make back all that we had taken from them. We hoped the Oakview City Council would change over the years but the same people kept getting re-elected. And those people had a history with the Sinclairs."

Kate pursed her lips. "So you run for City Council, win and then somehow convince two other council members to vote with you against Cross Creek?"

Nate pointed his finger at Kate. "Bingo. And I know two members are on the fence."

"Was Rudolf's death part of your plan?" Eric blurted out.

"What are you talking about? That's a horrible thought," Vivian scolded.

Nate's mouth twisted in a grimace. "That was an accident."

"How well do you know Renee?" Kate asked.

"She's been there for me—for all of us." Nate looked over at Vivian. "After Jenny died, Renee helped us get back on our feet. I don't know what I would have done without her. She saved all of us."

"Not all of us," Eric said.

"And I am sorry for not noticing. I didn't understand everything you had gone through. And then you took off." Nate scooted his chair closer to Eric and put his arm around his shoulder. "You know I wish I could go back and change things."

Eric nodded his head.

Kate continued, "Have you ever thought that Renee may have been using you to get back at the Sinclairs? That she could have had Walter killed to ensure Cross Creek would get voted down?"

Nate widened his eyes. "That's crazy talk."

"Do you know Mildred Roberts?" Kate asked.

"I know who she is," Vivian offered.

Kate looked over at Vivian. "She's the great grandmother of Jessica Knight's fiancé. She's lived in Oakview her whole life."

"What's your point?" Nate asked as he returned his hands back to the table.

"I spoke with Mildred." Kate pushed her plate towards the center of the table. "She told me that Renee Verano's real name is Regan Gallagher."

Eric jumped in. "Regan was a woman who brought a paternity suit against Lawrence Sinclair back in 1928."

Nate and Vivian remained silent as they looked at each other.

Kate sat back in her chair. "Regan Gallagher claimed she was the daughter of Lawrence Sinclair and sued for her inheritance. She claimed her mother was a nun at the Convent."

Vivian gasped.

"The Sinclairs got to the judge who ruled against Regan." Kate threw her arms up in the air. "Regan, or Renee, was discredited and left town."

Eric looked at Kate. "Researching the history of the Seminary, the Sinclairs leased the land to the O'Connell family in 1910. That was the same year Regan Gallagher was born."

"Did you know that Lawrence had a brother, Rupert?" Kate wiped her hands on her napkin. "They worked together to build the Sinclair empire. But Rupert died in 1910."

"Something about an accidental shooting," Eric added.

Nate and Vivian sat transfixed.

Kate looked at Eric who nodded his head. "We think Rupert had the affair with a cousin of the O'Connell family who was a nun. Someone found out and killed Rupert. Lawrence Sinclair ended up leasing the land to Father Edward O'Connell to keep everything quiet."

Nate smiled as he examined his fingernails one by one. "This is a fascinating history lesson but how does this relate to Jenny's death?"

CHAPTER 75

Brett coughed and kept his head down as he walked into Sander's office.

Sander rose from the desk as Logan spun around and glared at Brett.

"Oh. I'm sorry. I didn't know you were meeting with anyone," Brett said as he looked up at Sander.

"Ah…you want me to review the PR draft." Sander said as he adjusted his glasses on his face then reached towards Brett.

"If you're busy, I can come back later?" Brett offered.

"No. No. It's fine." Sander took the paper from Brett then looked back at Logan and smiled. "It's probably time you two met."

Logan walked over to Brett and confidently offered his hand, "Logan Sinclair."

Brett shook Logan's hand. "Brett McCormick."

"Logan is the head of Fortunato. Brett is Kate Crawford's boyfriend," Sander offered as a grin came over his face.

Logan immediately retracted his hand.

Brett suddenly felt uncomfortable. Why would Sander offer personal information to a client? He realized Kate was right to be suspicious of Sander and Logan.

Sander walked over to the small table in the corner of the office. "Brett's my Director of Communications. He knows all about my plans for buying your company."

Logan narrowed his eyes and looked Brett up and down.

Brett joined Sander at the table.

"I'm going to go stretch my legs," Logan said as he abruptly walked out of the office.

CHAPTER 76

Kate looked at Nate and then Vivian. "We think Rupert is Renee's father. Which makes Renee a Sinclair."

Vivian raised her hand. "If that is true, it was decades ago. Why would Renee even care anymore?"

Shaking her head, Kate asked, "Why has Dad helped Renee all these years? Why do you care if Logan is back in town? Revenge! Revenge for something they both got away with."

Nate looked at Vivian then Kate. "So why do you think Logan is back?"

Kate hesitated. "That's confidential."

Nate reached over and placed his hand on top of Kate's hand. "Honey, I don't think confidentially is really a problem with all of us right now."

Kate looked at Eric then Vivian. "Sander wants to buy a product Logan created called Mirage."

"Why?' Nate asked.

"That's where things get complicated." Kate grabbed the sides of her chair. "The product is amazing. It will give Obsidian an edge over our competitors."

"Shit. That means the price of your stock will go up," Nate interrupted.

"Exactly." Kate turned to Nate. "The Sinclairs are going to make a shitload of money, money they can use to fund Cross

Creek. But here's the problem. Logan's product is not unique. Another account of mine, Cayenne, created a similar product six months ago. I think Sander gave Logan the idea for Mirage."

"Wouldn't that be a breech of confidentiality?" Vivian asked.

"It would if we had the signed non-disclosure agreements with Cayenne. But those documents have mysteriously gone missing. Sander is setting up Logan to take a major fall and I'm collateral damage."

"How would Logan not know?" Nate asked.

"And why are you involved?" Vivian asked.

"Logan wants to return to Oakview as the prodigal son. For the past twenty years, Sander has been the son William never had. Logan knows his dad won't accept him back into the family unless he returns as a success and Sander is exposed as a fraud. He saw the potential with Obsidian and probably pressured Sander to help him. But Logan is blind to what really is going on."

"What is going on?" Nate asked.

"Sander doesn't want Logan back to mess up his world. I think Sander stole Cayenne's idea and gave it to Logan."

"But you said Sander is going to buy Logan's product," Vivian said.

"I think that's all for show. He has a meeting with Cayenne on Monday. I don't think he ever intended to buy Logan's product. He'll tell William that Logan stole the idea. Then William will never accept Logan back into the family. He'll expose him as a fraud. And Sander will continue to maintain his position as favorite son and preserve his potential future inheritance."

"But how will he link Logan to Cayenne if Logan's been in Italy this whole time?" Nate asked.

"That's where I come in. I'll be the scapegoat. Cayenne is under my watch. The NDA has gone missing. Sander could easily plant evidence that I supplied Logan with information about Cayenne's product. He never wanted me to work at Obsidian. And now he will be rid of both of us."

Eric looked at Nate. "Does Renee know the Sinclairs are invested in Obsidian?"

Nate shook his head "I don't know. We thought if I got on the council and voted against the project that would be it. Checkmate. But if they have money, they might be able to turn the other council members or go above us to the state level."

"That brings us back to Walter," Kate said.

"Was his death really an accident?" Eric asked Nate.

Vivian looked at Nate. "Tell them."

"The night Walter died his wife Elizabeth called me. What I didn't tell the police was that she asked about Jenny's death. Whether Walter had talked to me about it. I thought this was weird, so I confronted Elizabeth about it the other day."

"You went to her house?" Eric asked.

"Yep. At first she wouldn't say anything. She seemed really scared. Right when I was about to leave, she told me to find Walter's phone, then I'd know everything."

"What could be on the phone?" Eric asked.

"I think it has to do with the Cross Creek project," Nate said.

"Or the Sinclairs," Vivian added.

Kate looked at Nate. "Wasn't Walter driving over here to see you the night he died? I bet he wanted to show you whatever is on his phone."

"But someone got to him before he made it," Vivian suggested.

"Did the police ever recover the phone?" Eric asked.

Nate shrugged his shoulders. "Not that I know of. If they'd found the phone and it had incriminating evidence on it, we would have heard about it by now."

"Wait!" Kate exclaimed as she looked around the room. The words creek and phone had triggered something in her mind. "Oh, my God. Oh, my God!"

"What?" Nate asked.

Kate opened her eyes wide with excitement. "On Wednesday when I went for my run and was attacked?"

Everyone nodded.

Kate raised her arms. "Before the attack, I followed Dillon down into the creek where Walter crashed his car. I found an iPhone."

"That's why you were attacked. Someone saw you with the iPhone." Eric said.

"Where is it now?" Nate asked.

Kate stood. "I took it to Obsidian. I was going to recharge it. Figure out who it belonged to and give it back. Oh my God. I totally forgot about it. It could be Walter's phone!"

"We need to go to Obsidian and get that phone," Nate declared as he stood.

Kate looked at Eric. "No. Dad. It might look too obvious if we run into Sander. Eric can come with me."

"Of course," Eric said as he stood.

Nate grabbed on to Kate's hand. "Be careful! If Walter was killed over this phone, you could be in danger."

"But no one knows I have it," Kate said.

"Except the person who attacked you," Eric said as he walked out of the dining room.

Kate squeezed Nate's hand then looked at Vivian, "We'll be fine." She turned around and walked out of the dining room.

As the front door closed, Vivian shook her head. "Was that the smart thing to do? Let them go on their own?"

Nate turned to Vivian. "What other choice do we have? For now, I'm going to go have a talk with Renee. She's got a lot of explaining to do."

CHAPTER 77

Kate and Eric stepped out of the elevator onto the eleventh floor of Obsidian. The dim lights illuminating the hallway intensified the glow of the Altamont Heights cityscape through the windows. The floor was silent except for the low hum of the HVAC system echoing around them. Kate led Eric down the hallway.

Once in her office, Kate dashed over to the file cabinet and grabbed the silver iPhone. She unhooked it from the charger and pressed down on the power button. Kate hung her purse on the back of the chair then sat down.

Eric sat in the chair across from Kate. The florescent light above slowly illuminated the room.

Kate looked over at Eric. "Are you ready to do this?"

"We don't even know if it's his phone."

"What if it is? It changes everything."

"I know. I'm ready. We need to do this."

Kate pushed down on the Home button. An image of a blonde woman appeared on the display as a screen saver. Kate held up the phone for Eric to see.

"Who's that?" Eric asked.

"Elizabeth Rudolf?"

"Could be. I remember seeing a photo of her in the newspaper. She's blonde but I don't know if that is her."

Kate slid her index finger across the bottom of the screen. "We got lucky."

"Why?"

"There's no password."

Twenty unique square application icons appeared on the display. "At least it seems to work. Where should we look first?"

Eric pulled the chair around the desk next to Kate. "Phone calls."

Kate touched the green phone icon in the lower left hand corner then looked at the Recent setting.

"Oh my god!" Kate pointing at the display.

"This has got to be Walter's phone. Who else would be calling Mom and Dad's number at 7:56 PM the night of the election?"

"That had to be right around the time he...he died."

"If there's something on the phone against the Sinclairs, it's got to be a video or photo."

Kate pressed the Home button then selected the Photo icon. "There are a ton of images. Where do we even begin?"

"Let's start at the bottom."

"Good point. Those are the most recent." Kate selected the very last entry that happened to be a video.

"It's completely black. Skip to the next one," Eric said.

"Wait. It's over five minutes long. It must be important." As the video loaded, Kate looked out into the hallway then turned to Eric. "Shut the door."

CHAPTER 78

Courtney pushed the Off button on the TV remote then reached for Walters's computer. She sat back in bed and adjusted the pillows behind her head as the computer started up. She felt trapped. Her research had been futile. Eric had not offered up any information on the location of Walter's phone. And Ruby still had her by the balls. She needed the phone to be free again. There was nothing else she could do but organize her clothes and hang out in her hotel room, checking Walter's iCloud account every couple hours.

Once the computer booted up, she opened the web browser, logged into the account and waited. The Find My iPhone icon came up. She clicked this option then re-entered Walter's password. As the service was trying to locate the phone, Courtney closed her eyes. She dreamed of her past exploits and how uncomplicated it had all seemed at the time. What had she gotten herself into this time around?

A beep from Walter's computer snapped Courtney back to reality. She opened her eyes and looked down at the monitor. A street map was now displayed. A small blue dot with a radiated circle around it blinked at 4th Street. On top of the circle was a rectangular box containing the words, Walter Rudolf's iPhone.

"Holy Shit!" Courtney blurted out. The phone was on. She looked at the map but could not figure out the location. She moved the cursor over to the navigation buttons and zoomed out. She zoomed out again and snorted a laugh. She saw Highway 101 and then Paseo Grande. The blue dot was in Altamont Heights.

Courtney zoomed in as far as she could go. The blue dot was hovering over the 2000 block of 4th Street. This area was the business district of Altamont Heights. She had eaten at a restaurant somewhere near this location. But which building was the phone inside?

She opened another window of the web browser and in the search field, inserted the words, 2000, 4th Street, Altamont Heights.

Within seconds, the search results came back: Bank of Bay building. Courtney clicked on a link for the building web site. She scrolled down the list of businesses that leased space in the building. Obsidian Technologies.

CHAPTER 79

Kate and Eric hovered over Walter's phone as the video began to play.

Two silhouettes appeared from out of the darkness, backlit by a dim light from above. The sound of heavy rain striking cement echoed in the background.

Kate turned up the volume.

The image came in and out of focus as the operator moved closer. The figures were standing under a trellis with leafy vines wrapped around wood pillars.

Kate gasped.

"What is it?" Eric asked.

"That's Logan and William Sinclair."

The father and son were standing arms length apart. William towered over Logan. Both were wearing black rain jackets.

"What are they saying," Eric asked.

"Shh," Kate said softly as she turned up the volume to the highest level.

William looked around his surroundings. "You need to leave."

Logan pointed at William. "Not until you talk to me."

"I'm expecting someone," William said as he looked behind Logan.

"I know. And I'm not leaving until you answer one question."

William returned his focus to Logan and waited for him to speak.

"Why did you abandon me?"

William lowered his head.

"You never came to visit. You never called."

William edged closer, pointed his finger at Logan then jabbed at his chest. "The night you killed that girl I realized you are no son of mine."

Kate and Eric looked at each other then back at the screen.

William backed up, turned around then disappeared from view.

"That was such a long time ago. Yeah…I pushed her off the roof but it could also be seen as an accident. I mean, she did it to herself." Logan said.

Kate grabbed Eric's hand.

William walked back into view. "You haven't changed a bit."

"Oh but I have. I have changed—"

"You think I am blind? You think just because you haven't heard from me, I don't know what you're up to? You're a liability. I know everything, EVERYTHING you do." William turned away from Logan and faced the camera with an exaggerated wrinkled forehead and an upturned lip. "Don't you even respect women? For God's sake, they're not manikins for you to manipulate."

"Respect women? You're a fine example. Does Mom even know about all your infidelities?"

William immediately turned around. "Don't put this on me. You were the one who pushed her."

"That Crawford girl was obsessed with me. It was her fault."

"You and I both know the truth." William said as he rotated back towards the camera.

"Then you must know why I'm back?"

William shook his head. "I can't even imagine. You know the Crawford's are bound to come after you."

Kate gasped.

"So you don't know that Sander has been helping me?" Logan asked.

A scowl instantly appeared on William's face as he turned around to face Logan. "Sander? Why the hell would he want anything to do with you?"

"Because he owes me. He's the one that got to stay and become the son I never could be."

"What are you talking about?"

"I've come back to claim what is rightfully mine. I'm going to make you proud of me. So that you will write me back into your will."

William shook his head and laughed. He walked past Logan and looked into the darkness behind him.

"I've created a software product that Sander is going to buy. I'm going to make a name for myself and help you with the Cross Creek project."

Kate and Eric looked at each other then back at the video.

William grabbed Logan by the shoulder. "Don't even think about messing with Cross Creek. I've already got things in motion that have taken years to plan."

"Are those plans really working? You're relying on that Rudolf guy?"

William released his grip of Logan. "How, how did you know?"

"Nate Crawford's out for revenge. If he wins the debate tonight, you'll finally realize that your money—what you have left—can't buy everything."

"You don't know what you're talking about."

"Oh really. Mom's told me everything. How you're almost broke. You need Cross Creek."

William did not respond.

"Mom's the one who has helped me all of these years. And what I'm doing with Sander will help all of us. You don't need to do anything except keep pushing your Cross Creek project."

William threw up his hands. "Stop it. You don't know what you're talking about. You need to leave."

"I know. You're meeting with Rudolf. Don't worry. I'll leave before he gets here."

William looked down at the ground but did not say anything.

Kate bit her lower lip and glanced over at Eric.

"I know you never wanted me. You think mom got pregnant so you'd have to marry her. But now I'm back and I was hoping we could be a family again," Logan said.

William laughed. "You've got to be kidding–" He abruptly stopped talking and looked in the direction of the camera. "Did you hear that?"

The video feed turned down and focused on the dark ground.

Logan's voice continued. "No. No one is here. Listen to what I'm saying."

"I think you better leave. I'm done with this conversation."

"Dad! Things can be like they used to–"

"Like they used to be? You've got to be joking. You were a spoiled brat who took no responsibility. You killed that girl. I helped Sander to keep him quiet. But ironically, he's become the son I've always wanted."

The view of the video feed retuned to Logan and William. They were not talking. Just staring at each other.

"How did you know I would be here?" William asked.

"Mom. Mom told me. She knows everything," Logan said as he walked out of view.

William looked around his surroundings while the sound of rain pelting the ground filled the silence.

The video feed turned vertical and then ended.

"Oh, my god!" Kate put the phone down on the desk.

"We've found our smoking gun," Eric said.

"This is crazy. No wonder Walter ended up at the bottom of the creek. But how did Rudolf happen to record it?"

"Maybe he showed up early for his meeting with William and stumbled upon their conversation. But who knew Rudolf recorded their conversation?"

Kate looked at Eric and narrowed her eyes. "Either someone saw him doing it or Rudolf told someone. Either way, Rudolf ended up dead because of this video. We need to get it to the police ASAP."

"No! We need to get it to Dad. He gets to decide."

Kate reluctantly nodded her head as she grabbed Walter's phone and stood.

"Where's the bathroom," Eric asked.

"You've got to be kidding? You can't hold it?"

"Sorry. I didn't get a chance to go before we drove over here."

"Ok. It's down the hall on the right, past the stairwell. Please hurry."

"I'll just be a minute." Eric walked out of Kate's office into the hallway.

CHAPTER 80

Kate sat down at her desk. She looked at the idle desktop computer. She spotted the USB cable for her iPhone lying next to the keyboard. She looked at Walter's iPhone. She could download the video from Rudolf's phone, place it on her private server or even email it Jessica, Eric, or her Dad. The evidence would be in a secure location and the iPhone would be inconsequential.

She placed Walter's phone next to the computer as it powered up. She thought about Brett. Was he still here? Kate reached behind the chair and dug through her purse for her phone. She sent Brett a text:

u stil @ wrk?

I'm here w Eric

levn soon

With in a couple seconds she got a response.

mtg with Sander

he jst took a break

c u 2morro?

Kate responded

y

Kate placed her phone back in her purse then swiveled her chair around and looked out at the cityscape. It was a beautiful evening. The lights from the shops and restaurants reflected brightly into her office with a calming, mesmerizing effect.

She reached over to the file cabinet to grab the USB cable for Walter's phone when she heard footsteps coming from outside her office. Kate immediately turned around and stood. She walked towards the door. "I've got an idea on how we can–"

Expecting to see Eric, Kate took two steps back when she saw it was Sander.

CHAPTER 81

A short, middle aged Hispanic woman dressed in a buttered-colored flannel night gown led Nate down the main hallway to the back parlor of the grand Verano Estate on Montgomery Blvd. The five thousand square foot Georgian style mansion with its barrel vaulted boxed ceiling hallway was a piece of art to be marveled at, but not this evening.

Renee sat reclined in a dark brown leather chair next to a crackling fire. Wrapped in an ornate tan blanket covered in swirling red paisleys, she looked like an over stuffed crepe.

"What's so urgent?" Renee asked.

Nate entered the room and began to pace in front of Renee.

"Thank you Maria. When you exit, please shut the door," Renee said.

As soon as the door closed Nate stopped pacing "You lied to me?

"Excuse me?"

"You've been after the Sinclairs from the day you were born."

Renee looked away from Nate then slowly rolled her tongue over her dry creased lips. "I've never lied to you about anything. I've just never told you the whole story."

"Wouldn't you think I'd like to know why you really wanted to help me? I thought you cared about us, were doing it to help my family find justice for Jenny. Not for your own selfish reasons."

"Nate…dear. I think of you as the son I never had. I would never want to hurt you. That was never my intent."

"Then why didn't you tell me you were the illegitimate child of a Sinclair?"

Renee sighed as she looked down at her ringed fingers. "That's what this is about?"

"Yes. I feel blindsided. I wish I knew all along your motivation for wanting to bring down the Sinclairs. I thought you were doing it for Jenny."

"In a way I was. But at least we were working towards a common goal."

"What do you mean?"

"I knew some day that you'd find out about the paternity suit. It's public knowledge, but a time long forgotten. I really was helping you because of Jenny. The best revenge for people like that is to take away what is most important to them—their money."

"I don't see the significance of Jenny's death to you."

Renee motioned for Nate to take a seat next to her on the butterscotch-colored couch. "You really want to know why I decided to help you get back on your feet after Jenny's death and include you in my plan to ruin the Sinclairs?"

"You're not making any sense."

Renee grabbed Nate's hand. "It was my fault Jenny died."

Nate furrowed his brow and smirked. "Now you're sounding crazy."

"It's true. I was the one who got Logan into drugs."

Nate retracted his hand. "You what? What does that have to do with Jenny's death?"

"I know a lot more about the Sinclairs than they think. I knew Logan was on shaky ground with his trust fund. So I hired someone to introduce him to drugs. It wasn't very difficult. He was a troubled youth. When I learned William was thinking of cutting him off, I had my person point him towards dealing. That way Logan could make his own money."

Nate stood and began to pace. "How do you find someone to do that?"

"Money and the right connections."

"But why did you want to do that?"

"I wanted Logan to get into trouble, to get arrested. I wanted a scandal for the Sinclairs to deal with—a distraction from the Oakview property."

Nate stopped pacing and looked at Renee. "Verano Shopping Plaza?"

"Yes. The land belonged to that senile Ronald Johnston. I partnered with you because you had built his home in Altamont Heights ten years earlier. I thought you could persuade him to sell to us. Then those damn Sinclairs started talking with Ronald's kids."

Nate rubbed his chin. "I do remember. Right in the middle of all the negotiations, Ronald started to change his mind."

"I wanted Logan to get in trouble so he'd be a distraction for the Sinclairs. They'd lose focus and we'd get the property. I never thought in a million years that Eric would show up at the Convent to buy drugs from Logan."

Nate shook his head. "And Jenny would show up to stop him."

Renee bit down on a fingernail and looked up at Nate.

"I never intended any of your children to get hurt."

Nate narrowed his eyes. "You were using me for everything."

"I didn't know Logan would become obsessed with Jenny. We'll never know what happened on top of the Convent, but I'm positive Logan killed her."

Nate did not respond.

"That's why I had to help you. I had no choice. From the day Jenny died, you became part of the family I never had."

Nate stood and walked over to the fireplace mantel. He looked down at the amber flames burning through the stack of wood. "What about Walter Rudolf? Did you have him killed?"

Renee lowered her chin and looked up at Nate. Her dry, translucent eyelids slowly lowered than opened. "I'm sorry for what happened to Jenny. There's nothing we can do to bring her back. Logan is the one you should be angry with. And Sinclairs are the ones you should question…not me."

"I still don't like how this all began but we've got bigger things to think about. Logan's being back in town may hurt us."

"How?"

Nate walked over to Renee. "Remember I told you he was shopping a product to Obsidian?"

"How does that affect Cross Creek?"

"Obsidian will be launching their IPO on Tuesday. The Sinclairs have invested a lot of money in Obsidian. If Sander buys Logan's product the stock will skyrocket."

Renee clenched her hands around her blanket. "And the Sinclairs will make a lot of money. Damn it!"

Nate sat down on the couch next to Renee. "Kate and Eric are on to something right now that could change everything."

"What?"

"Do you remember, I told you Elizabeth Rudolf mentioned something about Walter's phone?"

"Yes."

"Kate thinks she may have the phone. The morning she was attacked, she found a phone down by the creek. We think whoever attacked her is behind Walter's death."

"Seriously. Does Kate have the phone with her? Do you know what's on it?"

"Kate brought it in to Obsidian but the battery was dead. She and Eric are there now picking it up."

Renee sat back in her chair. "If it's Walter's phone, it changes everything."

CHAPTER 82

Sander smiled as he stopped in the doorway to Kate's office and leaned against the open door. "Sorry, Kate. Didn't mean to startle you."

"No worries. I didn't know anyone else was here." Kate backed up and sat down in her chair. She strained her neck to look into the hallway to see if Eric was on his way back from the bathroom. She then glanced down at her desk and saw Walter's phone.

"I was taking the stairs down to the tenth floor." Sander took a step further into the office. "When I passed this floor, I saw a light on in an office. I thought I'd find out who was working late."

"Well, you found me." Kate pointed at herself and forced a smile.

"What are you working on?" Sander asked as he slowly sat in the chair opposite Kate.

Kate felt her hands become clammy and a knot start to form in her throat. She pointed at her desktop computer now displaying a sunflower screen saver while she placed her left hand over Walter's phone. "I was working on my annual review."

Sander creased his forehead and raised an eyebrow. "Reviews aren't due until January."

"I know but Amy wants an early draft by next week."

Sander leaned back in the chair. "Such dedication to come in on a Saturday night."

Kate didn't know if Sander was being sarcastic or genuine. She looked around the room then felt the strap from her purse on the back of the chair. She raised her arms up in a form of surrender. "You got me. I'm just trying to impress you. I actually came in because I left my purse here yesterday." Kate reached back and grabbed her purse and placed it in her lap. "And then I got to thinking about my review. How I should just finish it."

Sander narrowed his eyes as a smug smile spread across his face. "Is that all you can come up with? I thought you were smarter than that?"

Kate felt her face become hot.

Sander leaned forward in his chair. "What are you really doing here?"

Kate pushed her chair slowly back away from the desk.

"I think it's time you and I had a little chat." Sander placed his left hand on the desk and leaned in towards Kate.

Kate pushed her chair a few inches back. *Breathe!*

"I know you've been investigating your sister's death; investigating me—running searches on your office laptop and computer. You think I played a role in your sister's tragic end. But you're wrong. I was just a bystander."

"How? How did you know–"

"I'm the CEO. I know everything my employees do on my computers."

"But you've never said anything to me for two years."

"You have to understand, Logan is callous towards women. He has entitlement issues that stem from his upbringing." Sander leaned in towards Kate and whispered, "He was just born that way." He leaned back and adjusted his glasses. "But Jenny was different. She brought out the good in him."

"You can't be serious," Kate blurted out.

"That night...I never saw what actually happened to Jenny. I left Logan with Father O'Connell. Whatever happened before or after is none of my business."

"You know more than you are saying."

"That's exactly what happened."

"I guess it doesn't hurt that the Sinclairs have been bank rolling you all these years to keep you quiet."

Sander looked down at his hands as a patronizing grin formed across his face. "That's going to be hard to prove."

"How can you live with yourself?

Sander focused on Kate. "I have the best job in the world. Why would I want to do something stupid and mess that up?"

"Is that why you slipped Cayenne's product idea to Logan? So you could buy Mirage instead of Virtual Presence? And then the Sinclairs would profit from the IPO—all of them, including yourself."

Sander shook his finger at Kate. "You have such an imagination. I have no idea what you're talking about."

"I think you do. You gave Logan enough information about Cayenne's product so he could duplicate it in Mirage. You found out I was looking into my sister's death so you decided to let Logan and me fail. You'll say I stole Cayenne's product and helped Logan create Mirage. Then you can be rid of both of us and William will never accept Logan back into his family. That's why you deleted Cayenne's NDA and destroyed my hardcopy."

Sander smiled with admiration. "I wouldn't say it like that. You have to understand. It's just business.

"Who helped you?"

Sander moved his index finger over the desk in a circular motion. "I know lots of people who will do anything to help me succeed and further their own careers. Take for instance the Strategic Accounts Team."

"Amy?"

"I wanted to give you a head start on your career. Amy had her chance to whip you into shape. I thought she was succeeding. But then you had to go stick your nose in all of this shit."

Sander took off his glasses, closed his eyes and rubbed his temples with his fingers. His face became slightly red as he placed the glasses back on his face. Sander was agitated. Kate had never seen him lose his cool.

"Shit that Amy should have taken care of. Shit that could mess things up on Tuesday. Shit that I've been working on for over two, for five years, most of my life. If you'd just gone along with the plan, you may have gotten a promotion. Now you're going to blow your career. Is that what you want?"

"Go along with what plan?"

Logan appeared in the doorway. "I can't find him."

Kate looked up at Logan. "What are you doing here?"

"Kate! Where's your brother?" Logan roared impatiently.

"What are you talking about?" Kate lied as she covertly slid Walter's phone off the desk into her lap and slipped it into her purse.

Logan studied Kate. "What's in your lap?"

Kate felt like a caged animal with its handlers at the door, waiting for her to make a move. She looked down at her lap. "My purse."

Sander and Logan looked at each other.

Kate stood and grabbed her office phone. "Do I need to call security?"

Sander laughed. "Kate put that down. We just want to talk."

Kate hesitated as she returned the office phone. She slung the purse over her shoulder as she backed up to the windows, looking around the room for an exit.

"We just want the iPhone that's in your purse," Sander said.

"Walter's iPhone," Logan interrupted as he walked towards Kate. "I saw you and your brother watching something on it. If it's what I think it is, we can't have that video in circulation."

Kate looked directly at Logan. "Fuck you!"

Logan ran at Kate and grabbed her by the neck, pushing her into the blinds and pinning her against the window. "You cunt!"

Sander stood. "Logan, I think–"

"Shut up!" Logan yelled as he moved his left hand across Kate's chest, brushing against her breast for a moment before continuing down her waist to her purse. "Walter was such an idiot. He tried to blackmail my mom. But she wouldn't have it."

"Where's the party," a voice called out from the hallway.

Logan looked at the doorway and released his hold of Kate.

"Brett, I told you I'd be right back," Sander said curtly.

Brett stood in the doorway looking from Kate to Logan to Sander.

Kate raised her eyebrows straining to get Brett's attention.

Silence filled the room.

"Kate? Everything okay?" Brett asked with concern as he looked at Logan.

"I need to get out of here." Kate said as she started to walk past Logan.

Logan held out his arm in front of Kate.

"It's an emergency! Kate pleaded. "I need to get to my parents house."

"Not so fast!" Logan said as he grabbed at Kate's purse.

Kate hit Logan's hands as she tried to pull herself away from him.

"Kate?" Brett said as he walked into the office towards her. "What's going on?"

"Logan killed my sister!" Kate screamed at Brett.

Brett immediately ran at Logan, pushed him into the file cabinet then held him down with his body. "Go!"

Kate ran for the door. Sander stepped in the way. She kneed him in the groin then pushed him into the chair as she ran out of the office.

Kate sprinted towards the elevator. She pushed the down button and looked back. She heard arguing but did not see anyone. Kate pushed the button again and looked up at the green florescent arrows. She looked back down the hallway.

"Ding."

The elevator doors opened.

Logan emerged from her office.

Kate turned around, ran into the elevator and almost knocked over Eric and Amy.

CHAPTER 83

Courtney looked down at her ringing Samsung phone. The caller ID kept blinking 'Ruby." She shook her head then took a deep breath as she glanced up at the Bank of Bay building. On the fourth ring, she decided to answer the call.

"Where are you?" Ruby asked.

Courtney lied as she grabbed the steering wheel. "My hotel room."

"I haven't heard from you this whole evening."

Courtney looked in the rear view mirror at her reflection and combed her fingers through her long dark hair. "I'm a little under the weather."

"I don't care. I need you to find Walter's phone."

Courtney sighed. "I've looked through Kate's entire apartment and it's not there. I've logged onto Walter's iCloud account. I can't locate it. So the phone is either broken or Kate's never turned it on."

"I can't emphasize it enough that I need to find that phone broken or not before Tuesday."

"Yes. I am quite aware of the importance."

"Once you find it, give it to me…and we are done."

The call ended.

CHAPTER 84

"What's the hurry?" Eric questioned Kate as he helped her up from their collision.

Kate was breathing hard. She looked at Amy then back down the hallway to her office. Logan was walking towards them.

Amy stepped out of the elevator but held the doors open with her hand. "What's wrong Kate?"

Kate lunged towards the elevator control panel and selected the "L" button.

The doors remained open.

Logan smiled when he saw Amy holding the elevator.

Kate looked over at Amy and pleaded with her eyes. "Logan is not what you think. He's a monster! Release the door."

Amy looked back at Logan then at Kate. She pursed her lips, furrowed her brow and narrowed her eyes. She let her hand drop then turned and walked down the hallway.

"No!" Logan yelled as he sprinted towards the elevator.

As Logan ran past Amy, she stuck out her foot, kicked him in the shin, and sent Logan crashing to the carpet, landing within inches of the elevator doors.

The elevator doors closed.

Eric and Kate looked at each other.

Kate took a deep breath. "Sander and Logan know we have Walter's phone."

CHAPTER 85

"Logan Sinclair? How'd you get my number?" Courtney rudely questioned.

"I need your help," Logan pleaded frantically.

"I don't work for you." Courtney was annoyed by this interruption as she glanced over at the Bank of Bay building.

"You don't but I know about the arrangement my mother has with you. Ruby's her damn nickname and she told me to call. Kate Crawford has Walter's phone."

Courtney sat up in her car seat. "You've got my attention."

"She's at Obsidian—"

Courtney smiled.

"She's in the elevator heading down," Logan said slightly out of breath. "I'm going to try and stop her. If she gets out, Kate will head over to her parents."

"Where do the parents live?"

"Creek Drive."

"Ah, that's right." Courtney smirked. "You want me to get to Kate before she gets to the parent's house?"

"Yes. Head over there now and wait for my call."

Courtney rubbed her purse. "Use whatever means to stop her."

"Yes."

"I'll do what I can."

The call abruptly ended.

Courtney looked at the entrance to the Bank of Bay building. No sign of activity. She reached in her purse and grabbed the Glock 26, 9mm pistol. She opened the car door and stepped out. She had plans of her own.

CHAPTER 86

Kate paced back and forth in the elevator as they continued their descent to the lobby. "What happened to you? I thought you were going to the bathroom?"

"I did. But the one on your floor was closed for repairs. I went up a floor," Eric said as he noticed they had just passed the 6th floor. "That gal got on the elevator right when the doors shut."

Kate shook her head and waved her hands in the air. "That's my manager, Amy. I can't believe she helped us."

Eric grabbed Kate by the shoulders. "Stop. Don't freak out. We got Walter's phone. We're home free."

Kate closed her eyes. *Breathe*. "You're right. We're Okay."

"Is Walter's phone in your purse?"

Kate nodded as she opened her eyes.

"We're good. Let's get back to Mom and Dad's then figure out our next steps."

The elevator shook. Kate grabbed onto the handrail as their descent came to a sudden stop. She looked up at the display and saw they were on the 4th floor.

The lights dimmed then went out.

CHAPTER 87

Courtney casually walked up to the Bay of Bank building with the Glock 26, 9 mm pistol discreetly shoved in the back of her True Religion jeans under a black leather Burberry jacket. She had her hair rolled up inside a black baseball cap and was wearing sunglasses. The darkness of the evening illuminated the inside lobby. Only one oversized security guard was working the front desk next to the invisible gate to access the elevator and stairwells.

"Can I help you?" The security guard asked as Courtney approached the security desk.

"Yes. I have a meeting with Kate Crawford of Obsidian," Courtney said as she leaned against the podium and read the guard's nametag, Harold. Harold could barely see the computer screen behind his thick bifocal glasses and his hands were bent and slow from arthritis. She scanned the area behind the security desk. The glass enclosed elevator shaft was twenty feet behind the guard. Ten feet to the left and right of the elevator were two separate doors to stairwells. And tucked in behind the elevator area was the entrance to the garage. It appeared to have another level of security as there was a raised panel next to the door handle with a yellow light in the upper corner. She'd need an access card to enter.

Harold looked up at Courtney then back down at the computer monitor. "What's your name?"

"Why do you need my name, Harold?" Courtney asked a little too harshly.

"If you want to go upstairs dear, I need a name and ID," Harold said genuinely as he looked up at Courtney.

"Oh. Sure. It's Jenny Crawford," Courtney responded with a scarlet smirk plastered across her face.

"And ID?" Harold asked extending his hand towards Courtney.

Courtney reached behind her back with her right hand and clasped the pistol. She fluttered her left hand in the air pointing outside the building, "I forgot it in my car."

The guard leaned forward, following Courtney's gesture and looked outside.

Courtney placed her left hand firmly on the podium, leaped up in the air and smashed the pistol down onto the left temple of the guard.

CHAPTER 88

The red glow of emergency lights illuminated the small, cramped metal walls that held Kate and Eric trapped inside the elevator.

"What the fuck!" Eric shouted as he reached for the emergency phone.

Kate grabbed Eric's hand. "Logan! He's not playing games anymore. He'll do anything to get Walter's phone."

"I should call for help."

"No! We can't get the police involved. They may be on the Sinclair payroll." Kate reached into her purse. "I bet Walter's email account is still active. Maybe I can email the video to dad."

As Kate fiddled with the phone, Eric looked above at the small square escape hatch. He jumped up but could not reach it. He settled on looking at Kate. The glow of the phone display revealed a momentary quiet calmness on her face.

"Shit!" Kate balked.

"What?"

"The file is too large."

"Why didn't you download the video in your office when you were waiting for me?"

Kate returned Walters phone to her purse then looked up at the ceiling, "I was just about to when Sander came in. What about that hatch?"

"It's too high up."

Kate placed her hands on Eric's shoulders. "Give me a lift."

The elevator shook. A loud thud came from the ceiling.

Kate stepped back and looked up at the hatch. "Did you hear that?"

"Hear what?"

The clanking sound of metal on metal echoed throughout the elevator.

"Someone's opening the hatch," Eric said excitedly.

Kate leaned up against the elevator doors. "What if it's Logan?"

CHAPTER 89

Kate sensed movement down by her ankles. She leaped forward to see a crack of light appear between the two closed doors. And then a blunt narrow object materialized at the bottom of the crack.

"What the…" Eric began to say.

The long cylindrical object pushed into the elevator and then pulled to the side, opening the doors further.

Kate and Eric both stepped back to the rear of the elevator as two hands appeared and grabbed at the lower sides of the doors, struggling to push them apart.

"Are you gonna help me," a woman's voice called out.

Kate edged forward and saw a shock of red and auburn hair. "Amy?"

"We don't have all day. If you want to get away from Logan, you've got to help me with the doors," Amy called out.

Eric and Kate ran at the doors, pushing them to the sides. Amy wedged a broom in between the doors to hold them open. There was only two feet of clearance between the bottom of the elevator doors and the top of the ceiling of the 4th floor.

"Pull the stop button on the control panel," Amy said.

A loud clank and twisting sound came from above.

Eric looked up at the ceiling then reached over to the control panel and grabbed the red emergency button.

"Now get out of there," Amy said.

Kate knelt down on the floor, rolled over on her stomach and inched backwards into the opening. She carefully pushed herself up over the broom trying not to dislodge it from the doors. In the hallway below, Amy grabbed onto Kate's legs, then waist and helped her down.

The metal door to the hatch flipped open. Eric looked up and saw Logan's face.

"Crawford!" Logan yelled as his face disappeared from view and two feet started to come through the hatch.

Eric backed out of the elevator, taking the broom with him as he landed on the floor next to Kate. He scanned the hallway and saw the red glow of an "Exit" sign ten feet away. He grabbed Kate's arm and pushed her towards the stairwell. Amy ran off in the other direction.

As they entered the stairwell, Kate turned around and saw the elevator doors close, just as Logan dropped down inside.

CHAPTER 90

Courtney nervously looked around the lobby as she impatiently waited for the elevator. What she initially thought was a good idea to get past security now left her totally exposed. If someone entered the building, they'd know she was responsible for Harold lying on the floor. At least he was still breathing.

She walked up to the garage entrance, looked through the small window in the door then yanked down on the handle. Just as Courtney suspected, she required a special key card to access the garage. She walked back to the security desk and looked outside. It was a Saturday night in Altamont Heights. Several groups of people walked by the entrance but they were heading two blocks over to Alma Ave. Courtney took another look at the elevator and then the two stairwell entrances on either side.

What was taking the elevator so long? From the building directory, Courtney knew Obsidian was located on the 10th through 14th floors. She'd have to make a decision quickly.

Courtney walked towards the elevator. She looked to her left then walked to the right. She pulled back the door to the stairwell and entered.

CHAPTER 91

"We're almost there," Kate said as she continued to jog down the concrete stairs.

A loud muffled clank stopped her forward motion.

"What was that?" Eric said as he took two steps ahead of Kate, stopped, and spread his arms wide in front of her.

"Sounded like a door closing," Kate said as she looked back up the stairwell.

Eric looked down over the handrail, "It wasn't the lobby door. It's right there."

"Forget it. Let's go," Kate said as she grabbed Eric's hand and continued down the stairs.

When they reached the bottom, Eric slowly opened the door as he and Kate edged their way out into the lobby.

"Oh my god," Kate said as she pointed at the security guard on the ground.

The stairwell door behind them closed with a loud clank.

"Keep moving," Eric said as he pushed Kate towards the garage entrance. He pulled down on handle but the door wouldn't open. "What the fuck?"

"My key card!" Kate shouted. She thrust her hand into her purse and produced a black credit card sized object. She rubbed it against the raised panel as the yellow light turned green and allowed her to open the door.

As they ran towards Kate's green mini cooper, they heard a loud metal clank from the lobby. Kate looked over her shoulder to see the lobby door securely close.

From the window within the door, a dark shadow watched their escape.

"Shit!" Courtney blurted out looking through the window to the garage. She turned around and walked towards the security guard laying on the floor. His hand started to twitch as he let out a groan. This was Courtney's queue to leave. It would be better to confront Kate away from the public eye. Courtney sprinted out the front entrance, across the street to her jeep. She turned the ignition and pulled a U-turn. At least she knew where Kate was heading and had a slight lead.

CHAPTER 92

Kate sped onto Elder Drive nearly sideswiping a mailbox. "I still can't believe Amy helped us."

"You okay? Eric asked looking at the road ahead.

"I'm fine." Kate slowed down, quickly looked left then right before rolling through the stop sign and turning onto Creek Drive. She drove around the bend and saw the pedestrian bridge.

"Look out!" Eric yelled.

Kate instinctively hit the breaks as she saw a red flare burning into the asphalt. A black jeep was parked sideways in the middle of the road just past the bridge blocking them.

"What the hell?" Kate came to a stop several feet in front of the flare.

The driver side door of the jeep opened. A woman with dark hair, pulled back in a ponytail stepped out. Kate looked in her rear view mirror and saw the lights from a car approaching.

"Courtney? Is she okay?" Eric said as he carelessly opened his door.

"Wait! What are you doing?" Kate asked.

"It's just Courtney."

Before Kate could respond, Eric stepped out of the car, shut the door and walked towards the jeep.

Kate remained inside the car. She grabbed Walter's phone from her purse. She turned around to look at the other car behind her. It was now stopped a couple feet away from her bumper, blocking any possible chance for Kate to back up unless she made a U-turn and drove into the dense shrubbery along the road. The headlights were higher than her car and blinded her from seeing the driver or make of the vehicle. She turned back and focused on Eric.

Eric gave Courtney a hug and a kiss on the lips. He motioned with his hand for Kate to join them.

Kate put the car in park and put on the emergency brake. She left the engine running as she looked in the rear view mirror again then reluctantly opened her door.

Stepping out of the car, Kate placed Walter's phone in the back pocket of her jeans. She closed the door then looked at the car behind her. Squinting, Kate held up her hand in front of her face to gain a better view. Someone was in the driver's seat.

"Kate, do you have a jack in your car?" Eric asked.

Kate put down her arm and walked towards Eric and Courtney. "What happened?"

"Says her tire just blew," Eric said.

Kate looked at the jeep and saw the two tires facing them were intact. It was a black jeep.

"I was on my way over to see Eric. Can you believe this happened?" Courtney smiled.

Kate noticed Courtney was wearing all black. Eric hadn't inspected the other side of the car. She was not distracted by Courtney's sudden appearance.

"I had no idea you were going to stop by. I'm glad you wanted to see me again." Eric put his arm around Courtney's shoulder.

"Kathunk!"

Kate heard the sound of a car door close. She turned around and saw a figure walking towards them.

"Which tire did you blow?" Kate asked as she looked back at Courtney.

"The front right one," Courtney replied quickly.

"Eric." Kate felt uneasy. She quickly turned around and circled back to the passenger side of her car. "Let me see if I have a jack in the trunk."

As Kate passed the passenger door, she saw the driver from the other car was now standing in front of her car's headlights. Logan. "Eric, run!"

"Not so fast!" Logan ran at Kate.

Kate turned and sprinted past Logan's car. Her footsteps slapped the damp asphalt as she headed towards the pedestrian bridge. She leaped over the steps then heard the "clomp, clomp, clomp" of her 3 inch Tom wedge shoes pounding against the wood boards.

When she reached solid ground, Kate heard Logan call out, "Kate, stop! Courtney, go after her!"

Kate ignored Logan's plea and emerged from the grove of trees surrounding the bridge. She quickly tossed her shoes as she ran across the empty field towards the old cement foundation of the Convent. The clouds parted and a half moon provided just enough light to judge the uneven surface ahead.

When she reached the cement steps, Kate slowed down to assess her surroundings. She was in the middle of the expansive field edged by the surrounding trees. She felt her bare feet but they appeared unharmed. She quickly glanced behind but did not see Logan. Beads of sweat lined her forehead as she tried to hold her breath and listen for any noises. All she could hear was the pounding of her heart.

Off in the distance, Kate spotted a light from behind some trees.

"Bang!"

Kate looked back at that creek. Was that a gun? Where was Eric? Instinctively Kate ran away from the sound and towards the light.

As she got closer, Kate realized the light was coming from the Seminary.

CHAPTER 93

Eric pressed the gas pedal of the Mini Cooper into the floor, turned the steering wheel and burned rubber as he side swiped Courtney's black jeep and made a U-turn. He sped ahead, past the pedestrian bridge and looked anxiously in his rear view mirror. Headlights. Courtney was following him.

He turned onto Elder Ave and then Paseo Grande heading in the direction of Sinclair Shopping Center. Kate had run across the pedestrian bridge. The only place to hide on that side of the creek was the Seminary. Eric felt perspiration dripping down his right ear and then his chin. It dripped down onto his lap before he realized it was blood.

Eric had been stupid. Why had he trusted Courtney? She was only standing a foot away. When Logan ran at Kate, Eric realized he was in trouble. In that moment, he pushed Courtney over then ran for Kate's car. That's when he heard the gun shot. He thought he'd gotten away without injury. At least the bullet had only grazed his ear.

Should he call the police? Eric was more concerned with what Logan might do to Kate should he catch her. He couldn't let that monster do the same thing to Kate as he'd done to Jenny.

Eric turned onto the service road heading towards the Seminary. He looked in the rear view mirror. Courtney was still behind him.

CHAPTER 94

Emerging from the tunnel of trees, Kate saw the light in an upstairs room on the western side of the Seminary. She ran past the dark parking lot and leapt up the limestone stairs two at a time until she reached the dimly lit front entrance.

Kate pounded on the large mahogany doors with both hands.

No response.

She pounded on the doors again.

No response.

Kate looked over her shoulder and saw a figure emerge from the tunnel of trees.

She pounded on the doors again and screamed, "Help! Help! Please let me in!"

The figure was now in the parking lot. She placed both hands again on the enormous wooden doors, pounded and screamed, "Please! Please let me in!"

"Kate. Stop. It's pointless," a winded Logan said from the bottom of the limestone steps. "Just give me Walter's damn phone."

Kate quickly looked from side to side. She was trapped. But then she remembered the hallway on the western side of the building that led to an outer door. Father O'Connell might have left it open.

Logan slowly walked up the steps.

Kate sprinted to the side and jumped into the shrubbery. Landing on the ground, she pushed her way forward along the side of the building. She reached the corner and turned without looking back. Spotting the side entrance, Kate climbed the steps to the door.

She turned the knob.

The door was locked.

Kate peered through the window but only saw shadows in the hallway.

She pounded on the door. "Help. Please help. Let me in."

No response.

Kate had to make a decision. She pounded on the door again and watched the glass ripple with each blow. She saw her dark reflection in the window and then one behind her.

Logan grabbed Kate from behind and pulled her down off the steps. She kicked her foot back, hitting Logan square in the knee as she elbowed him in the groin. He fell to the ground as Kate took off down the side of the seminary towards the rear of the property.

Looking back over her shoulder, she did not see Logan on the ground. He was gone. She kept running, trying to find a way in.

Kate reached the end of the building and turned the corner. She ran through an open clearing of tall dry grass. There was no back-entrance the whole length of this section of the building. When she reached the opposite corner, Kate stopped and looked again for Logan. Nothing. She peeked down the final side of the building and saw at the far end, steps leading up to an entrance.

It was a large metal door.

Kate pushed down on the latch.

The door opened.

She pulled the door back and ran inside.

"Clunk."

The sound of the door closing focused Kate's attention. She found herself in a small room with only two rectangular windows near the ceiling. Light from the moon revealed two benches, a pew, a cross with Jesus Christ hanging on the wall, and a door at the far end of the room.

Kate sprinted towards the door. She placed her hand on the doorknob. It turned.

She raced into a small courtyard. A fountain with four lion heads spewing water into a low basin stood in the center. The splashing noise made for a peaceful setting but did not drown out the "Clunk" of the exterior door closing in the other room. Kate had to keep moving.

An arched corridor was at the far end of the courtyard. Kate remembered her conversation with Father O'Connell. He had mentioned the door behind the altar led out to a courtyard. She ran off towards the dark passageway.

"Kate, where are you?" Logan sang.

Logan was in the courtyard.

Kate blindly felt her way along the dark hallway hoping to find the door into the chapel.

Footsteps. Slow and steady and right behind Kate.

Her hand felt something cold, hard and smooth. A door knob? Kate rotated her wrist. The door opened. Kate flung herself into the back of the altar of the chapel and quietly closed the door behind her.

The stained glass windows came alive with the light from the moon illuminating the encased holy figures. The large silver cross on the altar twinkled as Kate ran down the stairs towards the large oak doors at the end of the aisle.

Kate grabbed the handles and pulled.

The doors wouldn't budge. They were locked.

She surveyed the room. What was she missing? Was there another exit? Kate crouched down on her knees and crawled over to the first row of pews on the left. She sat down and leaned up against the wood post, closed her eyes and tried to catch her breath.

"It's over Kate."

Logan was in the chapel.

"I know you're in here. Just give me the phone."

Kate tried to remember what the chapel looked like when she was there with Jessica. She peeked around the side of the pew. Logan was walking down the center aisle, bending down, and looking under each row as he passed.

Walters's phone. She reached in her back pocket. She tapped the numbers 9-1-1 but hesitated to hit the send button. What would she say? What would the police do? Logan wouldn't hurt her. Would he?

"Kate. I'm going to find you. But this time, you won't be a witness. I know how to deal with you. And you'll give me what I want."

What had he done to her sister? What had she seen?

"You know, in the beginning, I had no interest in your sister. I didn't even know her. It was all my mother's idea. Get close to that Crawford daughter. Become a distraction. It'll help with some business deal. Your sister was so young and innocent."

Kate held her breath and resisted the urge to stand up and confront Logan. She looked at the phone and thought about the Sinclairs and all their business connections. Could they still have an in with the police? The phone wouldn't be safe with the police. She'd do whatever it took to protect that video. Kate returned the phone to her back pocket of her jeans and looked at the wall in front of her.

Her eyes scanned up the wall and made their way to the steel pipes of the organ. There had once been a balcony up there. It was remodeled to accommodate the organ. And the access point to the roof had been left intact. If she got to the roof, there might be another way back into the Seminary.

Kate crawled along the length of the pew to the small alcove. Once concealed inside, she stood and walked to the stairs leading up to the organ.

When she reached the top, a narrow walkway took her behind the organ, past a bench to a small door. Kate slowly turned the knob.

The door creaked as she pushed in. Once inside, she closed the door behind her. It was pitch black. She reached out, felt something cold and hard. She pulled out Walter's phone and held it out in front of her for light. Kate was holding onto a railing of a spiral staircase.

Kate started to climb.

The stairs trembled the higher she climbed.

The door below creaked open. She looked down and saw light from the open door. And then the stairs began to shake. Logan was following her.

Kate took a step and bumped her head on a low ceiling. She took a step back and aimed Walter's phone above her. The light illuminated a short platform up against a brick wall.

Dead end.

No exit.

And then she saw a small metal door above the platform. It had to be some sort of access to the roof. Kate crouched down and crept up to the door. She pulled across the gas spring rod. Nothing. She pulled it again and pushed up. Nothing. Kate put her shoulder onto the damp metal door, pulled the gas spring rod, stood and pushed up. The door opened.

CHAPTER 95

A cool evening breeze swept Kate's hair up into her face as she stepped onto the gravel roof and shut the hatch door. Her feet bristled at the sharp contours of the rock but she had no time for pain. She brushed a strand of hair away from her eyes then assessed her surroundings.

The chapel was an island with a narrow gravel isthmus connecting it to the main rectangular Seminary building. A decorative widow's walk lined the front of the building with a flat gravel roof exposed to the inner courtyards. The roofline pitched on the sides making it impossible to walk to the back of the building.

She headed quickly towards the main building. Kate peered over the widow's walk at the parking lot below and spotted her green Mini-Cooper. Eric was here. But then she saw a car emerge from the tunnel of trees, a black jeep.

Kate quickly scanned both sides of the roof. Midway down the western side, the large octagonal skylight caught her attention. The stairwell was below it. Perhaps she could break the glass to get inside? And then she saw a large square box just beyond the skylight. It was identical to the roof hatch she had just emerged from on top of the chapel.

Kate glanced back at the chapel. Logan was stepping out of the hatch. She kicked up her heels and ran towards the skylight. The granular rocks under her feet gave way. Kate slipped and fell. She didn't feel her jeans tear at the knee nor the abrasion of her skin from the gravel in the wounds. She picked herself up and kept running.

She ran past the skylight to the hatch. She walked around the box looking for a handle. She felt the sides. Nothing. Kate came to the corner and placed her arms around both sides. She crouched down and then lifted. It didn't budge. The gas spring rod to open the hatch was only accessible from the inside.

Logan was now twenty feet away.

Kate was stuck.

CHAPTER 96

Kate was safe. At least that's what Eric thought when he spotted her on the roof as he ran through the parking lot towards the Seminary. When he reached the grand mahogany entrance, he tried unsuccessfully to open the doors. They were locked. He pounded on the thick wood as he looked behind him. A black jeep was in the parking lot. And then he saw Courtney emerge from the darkness and slowly walk into the light. She was holding a gun and it was pointed directly at Eric.

"You're more fun than I thought," Courtney said as she took one last step onto the landing in front of the doors.

"Who are you?" Eric asked as he stepped away towards the side of the landing. He felt the back of his right ear where the bullet had left its mark. A stream of blood made its way down his neck and had stained the back of his shirt.

"Does it really matter?"

"What about the last two days we've spent together? What about last night?"

"Let's just say I owe someone a favor." Courtney walked past the large mahogany doors to within a few feet of Eric. She stopped to assess her surroundings.

"A favor? What kind of favor requires you to sleep with me and then try and kill me?"

Courtney smiled as she slightly lowered the gun and looked at the gleaming metal. "Last night could have been more fun but I had to restrain myself."

"You were holding back?" Eric joked trying to distract Courtney into lowering the gun further.

Courtney cocked her head to the side. "If I had not restrained myself, you wouldn't be here right now."

Eric tried to comprehend what Courtney was saying. Nothing made sense. "Was everything you told me about your life a lie?"

Courtney smirked. "Not everything. I'm from back east. And I do have a controlling family with its own secrets."

"Are you an addict?"

"Yes, but not to drugs." Courtney's eyes narrowed and a devilish grin took over her face. "I don't like to use guns. The ending is too quick and easy. Not my style. But if I have to use one, I know how to." She gripped the gun tighter.

Eric backed up to the edge of the landing and surveyed his options. He could jump down to the shrubbery but what would that get him? As he wiped his forehead, smearing blood from his ear onto his cheek, he saw a figure silently peek out from the entrance of the Seminary. Father O'Connell.

Courtney was enjoying this moment. She took pleasure in being in control once again.

"Do you do this type of thing all the time?" Eric asked trying to keep Courtney distracted.

"It depends on what you mean." Courtney said.

Father O'Connell quietly tiptoed outside the Seminary doors and held up a finger to his lips for Eric to see.

"Befriend recovering junkies, sleep with them and then try to kill them?" Eric said.

"I have higher standards but this was never about you. You were just collateral in all of this."

"Collateral in what?"

"In recovering Walter's phone."

Father O'Connell stood less than a foot behind Courtney.

"Do you know what's on that phone?"

"No. And I don't care. I just need it. It's my ticket out of here."

"Well I care." Eric spread his arms out in front of his chest. "It's video evidence that Logan Sinclair killed my sister."

Courtney lessened her grip on the gun and looked away from Eric.

Eric took the opportunity to make a run at Courtney and knocked the gun out of her hand.

Father O'Connell grabbed Courtney from behind. He wrapped both his arms around her neck and in one violent motion, twisted her head to the side with his enormous hands.

Courtney's body immediately became limp as she collapsed to the ground, eyes open. She never saw it coming. Courtney was dead.

CHAPTER 97

"End of the line," Logan said slightly out of breath as he stood opposite Kate on the other end of the skylight.

Kate slowly rose from her crouched position and turned around.

"If I'd known you were a runner, I would've worn better shoes," Logan joked.

"What are you going to do?" Kate asked as she faced Logan. The skylight stood as the only protective barrier between herself and Logan.

"Kate. I don't want to hurt you but I need Walter's phone."

"Fuck you!"

Logan looked down at the gravel roof and smiled. "That's not nice to say, especially under the circumstances." He looked up at Kate. "There's nowhere to go. Just give me the phone."

"How do I know you won't hurt me?"

"You're going to have to trust me."

"Is that what you told my sister the night you killed her?"

Logan took two steps around the skylight closer to Kate. "You don't know shit!"

Kate glanced down at her feet. She was about ten feet away from the edge of the roof. She glanced behind Logan at the roof hatch. He had left the door open on the hinge. If she could get to the other side of the skylight, she could make a run for the hatch. The only thing she could do now was keep Logan occupied by talking to him.

Logan took another two steps closer to Kate.

"I know enough, you bastard. You became obsessed with Jenny. You didn't like it when she told you No."

"SHUT UP!" Logan took another step towards Kate.

"Your father said it best. You were a spoiled brat who got whatever he wanted. I bet my sister wouldn't give you the time of day. She hated you. Your mother's plan of getting close to Jenny was going to fail because of you."

Logan raised his hands. He was holding something. "You make me out to be such a monster. I tried to reason with Jenny. But she wouldn't listen."

"But why did she come to the Convent?"

"I didn't invite her but she knew what was going on."

"You lie!"

Logan took another step closer to Kate. "Carolyn overheard my phone conversation with Sander. She knew what was going down that night." Logan laughed. "Sweet Jenny thought she'd come to the rescue."

"Exactly, to prevent Eric from buying drugs. But you had an entourage of friends with you. You all pressured him into trying something else that got him wasted.

"I didn't want him to ruin the show."

"The show?"

"De-virginize the local girls. It was a monthly event."

Kate stared at Logan but could not find the words to respond.

Logan smiled. "I was doing these young girls a service. Someone was going to fuck them sooner or later. Why not have a Sinclair be your first. I loved the juxtaposition of fucking virgins on top of the Convent. It really turned me on."

Kate shook her head as she realized there was no point in trying to reason with this monster. He was beyond comprehension. "On top of the Convent?"

"That's the best part. Sander was the one who found it. A vacant utility shed up top. He outfitted it with a mattress and blankets. He even burrowed out a small peep hole to watch me work."

And then it hit Kate like a ton of bricks. "Jenny turned you down, in front of all your fans. Your ego was shot and you couldn't take it. You smacked her around. That ring of yours left a partial imprint on her check. She escaped from your love shack. You went after her and threw her off the roof. You killed her."

Logan smiled. "On the contrary. Jenny had already been the main feature a couple months before. She showed up not to stop Eric from buying drugs but stop the show for that night." Logan took two steps closer to Kate. "You don't remember?"

Kate ignored Logan's question and walked between the edge of the roof and skylight. She glanced down at the courtyard below then focused back on Logan.

"Of course, what happened to Jenny was an accident."

Kate stopped. "If it was an accident, why didn't you tell the police? You were just a teenager."

Logan shook his head. "No! No I wasn't. I turned eighteen that day. Jenny was fifteen. I would have been tried as an adult. And if my father had found out she was…he would've disinherited me."

Kate took another step away from Logan. Her back was now to the roof hatch with the open door.

"If Jenny had just taken care of the situation, everything would have been fine. I had almost convinced her when you got in the way."

"Me?" Kate froze.

"Why the hell did that dumb-ass brother of yours bring you anyways?"

Kate smelled the perspiration seeping through Logan's clothing as she took another step back.

"You ruined everything!"

A sudden deep tightness spread across Kate's chest. Her throat felt clogged as tears began to form in her eyes.

"You don't remember?"

Kate shook her head as she wiped the tears away from her cheeks.

"I was trying to reason with Jenny but you distracted us." Logan took two steps closer to Kate.

An image of Jenny's necklace came to Kate. She saw the jeweled letters lying just below Jenny's collarbone. Kate was touching the letters one by one as her sister held her tight.

Logan drew a line in the gravel with his foot. "You seriously don't remember...what she told me?"

Kate tried to remember but only visualized holding Jenny's necklace in her small delicate child hands. What was Logan talking about? What had Jenny said to him?

"Well that changes everything." Logan took another step closer to Kate. He was now ten feet away from her with his back to the closed roof hatch.

Kate quickly glanced at the open hatch behind her.

"Don't even think about it!" Logan turned his hand in the moonlight to reveal a gleaming metallic gun. "Give me the phone."

Kate looked down at the courtyard below. She couldn't just hand over the phone. "Why did you even come back? You know your deal with Obsidian isn't set in stone."

Logan lowered the gun.

"Sander is meeting with a company on Monday that has a product similar to yours. It's so similar, I'd say you stole their idea to create Mirage."

Logan smiled. "You're bullshitting me." He raised the gun again.

"The company is named Cayenne. I've been managing them since last May when Sander first saw a demo of their product. He told them he'd buy their product if they included an analytics component."

"Analytics?"

Kate took two more steps backwards. "That's what makes your product unique. No one else has anything like it...except Cayenne. They are going to show their finished product to

Sander on Monday. He's going to buy their product over yours."

"You're lying. That's not part of the plan." Logan lowered the gun to his side as he considered Kate's words. He shook his head. "Sander is going to buy my product."

"Why?"

"He owes me and my family. The stock we have in Obsidian will provide us with more than enough money to fund the Cross Creek project. Obsidian will lease one of the buildings for its corporate headquarters. And then Sander will retire a wealthy man and I will take over Obsidian. The name Logan Sinclair will finally mean something."

Kate threw up her arms. "You really think Sander is going to do all the grunt work and then step aside and let you take over?"

Logan lowered his head and his body seemed to cave in with this bit of information.

"Why would Sander need you if he has Cayenne's product with no strings attached? Sander is playing both of us. He wants you to fail. He wants people to think you stole Cayenne's product idea. The NDA we have with Cayenne has mysteriously disappeared. He'll place the blame on me for giving you Cayenne's product idea. And then he'll be rid of both of us."

"He wouldn't dare. The press around that would ruin the IPO."

"It wouldn't even get to the press. He'd quietly go to your father. Tell him that you stole Cayenne's idea. He'd position himself as the victim who discovered the problem before it infiltrated Obsidian. Your father will finally have a reason to be done with you and write you off forever. And Sander will then buy Cayenne's product. And since your father invested in Obsidian—not you—he will make a lot of money."

Logan crossed his arms. "But that's not how we planned it."

"Isn't it possible that Sander and maybe your father have simply gone behind your back?"

The distant sound of a train horn interrupted Kate.

"Kate are you up there?" A voice called out from the courtyard below.

CHAPTER 98

Kate strained her neck to look over the side of the roof. From the dim light, she saw a man with white hair. Father O'Connell? "Yes. I'm up here. Help!"

"Kate. It's Father O'Connell. Is Logan with you?" Father O'Connell asked.

"Yes. And he's got a gun," Kate shouted.

"Logan! Don't do anything stupid!" Father O'Connell called out in a stern voice.

"This is none of your business, old man. I don't even know why you came back. You should have stayed right where you were," Logan said.

"My mission has always been to help you—to save you. I've lived with my mistakes for too long," Father O'Connell said.

"Don't bullshit me. I know why you agreed to take me to Italy. And why you stayed for so long," Logan said.

"I should have had the police take you that night. I've lived with both our sins for too long," Father O'Connell said.

Logan snickered and pointed the gun over at Kate. "No, you came back because of Kate."

"That's not your place," Father O'Connell argued.

Logan took one step closer to Kate. He was now five feet away from her. "Why not? She's almost figured everything out."

"Please don't do this," Father O'Connell pleaded.

"I need that stupid phone, Kate. It contains my future. Nothing else matters." Logan moved his finger down over the trigger and turned the gun sideways.

"Why don't you and Kate come downstairs? We can talk through everything," Father O'Connell urged.

"Logan won't let me," Kate said.

"Why not?" Father O'Connell asked.

"There's a video on the phone. It proves Logan was responsible for my sister's death. If I give it to him, he'll destroy it," Kate called out.

"Since you want to destroy my life, I might as well destroy yours," Logan shouted at Kate.

"Logan, please!" Father O'Connell roared.

"Silence, old man!" Logan yelled.

"What are you talking about?" Kate asked.

Logan lowered his gun. "You know why they closed the Convent?"

Kate shook her head.

"They closed it down because of you," Logan said.

"Me?" Kate was completely confused.

Logan pointed the gun down into the courtyard at Father O'Connell. "That man. He's a priest. He's supposed to be all holy and moral. So how come you, Kate Crawford, are his daughter?"

Kate couldn't breath. Everything around her moved in slow motion. She could only hear the pounding of her heart reverberating in her ears as her face became hot. The rapid beats slowly decreased as her body became numb.

"C'mon, O'Connell. Do you deny it?" Logan laughed.

Father O'Connell sat down on the edge of a stone bench in the inner courtyard.

"Sander's mom lived at the Convent and worked for the Seminary. She knew all about its secrets. She told my mom about the affair hoping it would somehow save Sander since he was with me that night."

Kate looked down at Father O'Connell sitting on the stone bench.

Father O'Connell cried out. "If you hadn't gotten Jenny pregnant, none of this would've ever happened!

Kate felt the wind knock out of her lungs.

"Fuck you, O'Connell" Logan placed the palms of his hands on his forehead. "Why'd you have to say that?"

Kate gathered her thoughts as she took two steps back. "That's why you killed Jenny. You got her pregnant? You bastard! You were only concerned about your inheritance."

Behind Logan, Eric poked his head up through the now open hatch.

Logan pointed the gun directly at Kate as he took a step towards her. "That's the one thing my father wouldn't tolerate. Another forced marriage due to a pregnancy. I would've lost everything. That's why I need that fucking phone!"

Kate took a step back. She slowly reached in her back pocket and took out Walter's phone. "Ok. Here it is. You can have it." Kate bent down and placed the phone on the gravel roof by her feet. She took a step back.

Eric quietly lifted himself out of the hatch and softly stepped onto the gravel roof.

Kate continued to creep backwards as she glanced behind Logan at Eric.

Logan smiled. He lowered the gun and started to walk towards the phone. "Oh Kate, I knew you'd come to your senses."

Eric took another step closer to Logan.

"Maybe you can get down on your knees and show me how much your life means to you, and I'll—"

The gravel beneath Eric's shoes kicked up and hit the metal frame of the roof hatch.

Logan immediately turned around.

Eric ran at Logan, grabbing him around the torso, sending them both to the gravel roof. The two men fell in a heap of twisting legs and turning arms rolling towards the skylight.

Logan's gun hit the metal frame of the skylight, fell on the gravel then bounced over the edge of the roof.

The men rolled from side to side as they each struggled to take control.

Kate watched from a few feet away trying to figure out when to intervene. And then a memory came back to her. She was with Jenny the night she died.

The men rolled within inches of the edge of the roof.

Logan wrestled Eric onto his back and straddled his torso, pinning his arms down with both knees. He smiled as he reared his back and raised his arm, readying to throw a punch.

"Eric!" Kate screamed as she instantly recalled an image of Jenny on top of the Convent.

Logan looked over at Kate as he sent a punch.

Eric managed to free his right arm, deflecting the jab by grabbing onto Logan's fist and pulling his arm across his chest, shoving his knee up into his groin.

Logan groaned in pain.

Jenny had been holding Kate in her arms. Someone was trying to wrestle Kate away. She remembered being told to run. And then looking back...she had seen Logan push Jenny off the roof.

"Go to HELL!" Kate yelled as she ran at Logan and pushed him off of Eric.

Logan had a look of surprise on his face as he fell backwards, arms flailing in the air trying to find balance. He extended his arms, straining to grab onto anything then found Kate's shirt with both hands.

Kate's feet slid along the gravel roof, taking her entire body towards the edge.

Logan's backwards momentum was too strong. Kate was going over the edge with him. She instinctively placed her arms up between Logan's chest where he held on to her shirt and thrust her arms out.

Logan let out a high-pitched scream as his hands were ripped away from Kate's shirt. He fell towards the courtyard with his arms and legs thrashing the air.

Kate turned around in midair as her chest and chin hit the gravel roof with force. Her pelvis and legs dangled off the edge. She clawed at the gravel surface as her body slipped further off the roof.

"Eric!" Kate screamed as her arms slid towards the edge. Her hands feverishly worked into every crack until she felt a cool, wet channel. The gutter. She forced her hands into the narrow opening and tried to gain some leverage by inserting her elbows inside but the crevice was too small. She kept slipping.

Kate's fingers began to lose their grip. Her muscles ached. Her right hand started to cramp.

And then Kate sensed a heavy weight on her back. It was grabbing at the back of her shirt and bra pulling her up.

Eric lay on his stomach, reaching down over the edge of the roof. He took his other hand and clamped down on Kate's forearm.

"I've got you. Don't worry. I'm not gonna let go," Eric said.

Kate looked down into the courtyard. Father O'Connell was kneeling over Logan. Logan lay on his back, face up in a pool of dark blood.

"Can you grab onto my shoulder then kick your feet up onto the side of the building?" Eric asked.

Kate nodded. She took a deep breath, grabbed onto Eric's shoulder and kicked the side of the building. She was now eye to eye with Eric.

Eric wrapped both arms around Kate's waist and lifted her up over the edge of the roof.

Kate crawled over Eric's body then threw herself onto the gravel roof.

The siblings came to rest, lying on their backs next to each other. A light breeze blew over the roof. Their lungs took in the cool evening air as their breathing gradually decreased.

Eric rolled onto his side and reached under his back. He lifted Water's phone off the gravel. It was intact and undamaged.

CHAPTER 99

"How'd you get away from Courtney?" Kate asked Eric as they sat down on the couch in the parlor of St. James Seminary. The portrait of Father Edward O'Connell stared down at them from the fireplace mantel, observing their conversation.

"Luck, I guess." Eric held a bloodied cloth up to his right ear.

"But how did you end up here?" Kate asked.

"I took a guess that you ran to the Seminary. And Courtney followed me."

Father O'Connell came into the room and placed a hot cup of Earl Grey down in front of Kate. He then sat on the couch across from them.

"How did she die?" Kate asked.

Father O'Connell and Eric looked at each other.

"She took a fall and broke her neck," Father O'Connell said.

"I should call Dad and find out where he is." Eric took his iPhone out of his back pocket. "He should be here by now with Logan's car."

Kate took a sip of the tea and looked at Father O'Connell. "Thank you, but I may need something a little bit stronger."

Father O'Connell smiled.

"Damn!" Eric said looking down at the display on the phone. He shoved his other hand in his pant pocket and took out a crushed pack of cigarettes.

"What?" Kate asked.

"Can't get any cell service," Eric said.

"It's pretty spotty when you're inside," Father O'Connell said as he stood and pointed to the entrance of the Seminary. "You reached your dad last time when you were outside. Go take a smoke and try him again."

Eric immediately stood and walked to the foyer. He stopped, looked at Father O'Connell and then Kate. "Kate…will you be okay?"

Kate nodded.

Eric walked out of the parlor.

The sound of the large mahogany door closing ushered in an unbearable silence.

Kate took another sip of the tea as she scanned the room trying not to look at Father O'Connell. She felt numb. Why hadn't they called the police? What would happen with Logan's body? What could she possibly say to Father O'Connell? Bending down to place her teacup on the saucer, Kate glanced up at Father O'Connell. He had been staring at her every since Eric left the room. Kate felt her cheeks flush as their eyes locked.

"I didn't want you to find out like that," Father O'Connell began. "It's not how…it…was supposed–"

"Then it's true. You're my father?"

Father O'Connell looked down at his hands as he rubbed them together. He crossed his legs and leaned back into the cushions of the couch. He threaded his fingers together and rested them on his knee.

"Was I ever supposed to know?"

Father O'Connell looked up at Kate. "That was my fault. If I had just stayed in Italy, you would have never found out."

"Then why'd you come back?"

"I knew the Sinclairs were trying to push through the Cross Creek project. But being in Italy, there was very little I could do. Then I discovered Logan had returned to Oakview.

I knew the type of person he had become. He would only come back for a specific reason."

"And what would that be?"

"Revenge."

"Revenge?"

"When I found out he had been speaking with Sander since the summer, I knew his plan had to involve Obsidian. And I worried they would pull you into whatever they were doing."

"Me? Obsidian? How do you know anything about me?"

Father O'Connell closed his eyes. "Do you know I was the one who found you wandering on the grounds of the Seminary that night?"

Kate shook her head.

Father O'Connell opened his eyes, stood and walked over to the couch and sat next to Kate. "You lead me back to the Convent. And that's when we found Jenny, together. You kept playing with that necklace around her neck."

Kate stared through Father O'Connell trying to remember. Is that why she had always kept the necklace, something of Jenny's to hold on to?

"When you were born, I didn't know how I would ever be in your life. But from that night forward, I had to know what you were up to and be prepared to come back to help you if necessary."

How?"

Father O'Connell shook his head. "I paid an investigator to keep tabs on you. I had to know about your life. I just wanted to know that you were safe. That's how I knew you had taken a job at Obsidian."

Kate closed her eyes. She tried to comprehend the enormity of the situation. A Catholic Priest was her biological father? She was already on edge with Logan's death and now a hot seething anger began to well up inside of her. She squinted her closed eyes and shook her head. How could she have been so blind all these years? Kate sat up and pointed her finger at Father O'Connell. "How irresponsible can you be? You're a priest! You took advantage of my mother. And you've known I was your child this whole time? What kind of man are you?"

Father O'Connell stood and walked over to the fireplace mantle. He rested his arm on the ledge and looked out the front window into the dark night. "I've asked myself that many times. As humans, the one flaw we have is to feel. It's a very powerful emotion that is uncontrollable. But the way I felt in the presence of your mother was…incredible. I had never experienced anything like that. And because of that feeling, I've ruined my life."

Kate laughed. "How?"

"I'm a priest. I gave my life to God over fifty years ago. And the day I met your mother, I almost ended my life with God. I tried to resist these feelings for her but I couldn't. I asked God for guidance and forgiveness but never found it. I knew what I was doing. I knew it was wrong. That it was a sin."

Father O'Connell walked over to the coffee table, picked up his teacup and gave it a swirl. "But I thought I could live in both worlds—with God and your mother. My punishment came swift and hard. Jenny confided in me about her pregnancy. When I heard it was Logan, I should have reacted quicker. I didn't and Jenny died. I knew your mother would never be the same. I knew our lives would forever change."

He gulped the last of the tea and set the cup down. "When William and Maria told me I had to take Logan to Italy or they'd tell the world about you, I had no choice. I had to go. I looked at it as a way to redeem myself and live a solitary life with the prodigal son." Father O'Connell shook his head. "I shouldn't try to hide my guilt in biblical metaphors but I did try to nurture Logan and turn him into a respectable person but he had so much resentment and anger inside."

Kate's agitation started to subside. Father O'Connell's words had a calming effect. "Does Renee know about me?"

Father O'Connell looked at Kate. "We've never discussed you. But Renee knows everything."

"What was it about my mother that made you want to forsake your vows?"

Father O'Connell closed his eyes. He took a deep breath then looked at Kate. "It started innocently enough. Your mother helped manage our books. But we'd end up talking for hours, about life, your brother and sister, your dad. I became her confidant. The feelings I had for her, I couldn't shake. At the time, your father was always working. He wasn't around much. And then it just happened. We knew it was wrong but we couldn't resist."

Kate put up her hands. "Stop. I don't need all the details."

"But I want you to know that you were born out of love–not lust, not something cheap. A love that I can't even put into words as I'd never felt anything like it. Even the power I feel from God was masked by these feelings."

"Is that why the Convent closed down?"

"Unfortunately, yes. Laura Walker found out about our affair but I kept her quiet by providing a place for her to live at the Convent. When you were born, rumors started to surface about a nun having an affair with a priest. I had no choice but to close the Convent. After five years of silence, I didn't think Laura would use information about you to save her son especially since Sander had told them he'd go public with Logan's love nest." He looked down and shook his head again. "No one was supposed to know."

"The Seminary seems to have a lot of secrets. Why is Rupert Sinclair buried out back in that pauper's graveyard?"

Father O'Connell stared at Kate without answering the question. He walked up to the front window where he pulled back the beige curtains. "That's a story for another time." He looked back at Kate. "Your dad's here. They're walking up the steps right now."

"Does my Dad know about you and my Mom?" Kate asked as she stood.

"I never said anything. That's really not my place." Father O'Connell turned around and walked up to Kate. He placed his hand on her shoulder and looked down at her. "And it's not your place to say anything to your dad until you talk with your mother."

"Does my mother know about Jenny being pregnant?"

Father O'Connell shook his head.

Kate looked up at Father O'Connell and tried to find the words to tell him she understood. But the words didn't come because they were beyond her.

CHAPTER 100

Sitting on the sage couch in their living room, Nate and Vivian remained paralyzed by what they were viewing on Walter's phone.

"It's all here," Nate said looking at Kate and then Eric.

"I'd say that was a confession," Vivian added.

"Now what do we do?" Kate asked as she and Eric sat across from their parents in the two brown leather chairs.

"We need to back up the video." Eric reached towards Nate for the phone. "I'll do it right now on Dad's computer." He grabbed the phone and walked out of the room.

"What do we say happened to Logan and that woman?" Kate asked.

"Father O'Connell is dealing with the police," Nate said.

"What's he going to tell them?" Kate asked.

"I'm not quite sure. He said he was going to call the police after we left. But you and Eric were never there," Nate said.

Kate thought about Logan falling. Could she have stopped herself from pushing him over the edge?

Nate sensed Kate was struggling with her feelings. "You didn't kill Logan. He did that to himself. He fell off the roof."

"I know. I just keep replaying it in my mind?"

"He got what he deserved," Vivian blurted out.

"Should we take the video to the police?" Kate asked.

Eric came back into the room. "It's downloading. So what do we tell the police?"

Nate looked at his hands but did not respond.

Eric looked at Kate and then Nate. "We're going to the police—aren't we?"

Nate looked at Vivian and squeezed her hand. "That's something we'll have to decide as a family."

"What good will it do to take it to the police?" Vivian said looking from Kate to Eric.

Kate couldn't believe her ears. After twenty years, they finally had proof. Logan killed Jenny. Why not tell the world and make things right. "What are you talking about? Hasn't that been the plan all along?"

"With Logan dead, isn't it pointless?" Vivian asked.

"We go after William and Maria, Sander and Father O'Connell," Eric said.

Nate looked at Vivian. "Logan paid the ultimate price with his life. Sander took advantage of the situation but I don't think it would be fair to the employees or the stock holders of Obsidian if we exposed their CEO as an accomplice to this whole scenario."

"What about William and Maria? Maria pressured Logan to form a relationship with Jenny to help their business. That relationship ultimately got her killed. These people are sick," Kate said.

"I feel your anger. I know it's not the right thing to do. But I think we can use the video to our advantage," Nate suggested.

"How?" Kate asked.

"They won't want this video to come to light. I think we can use it to get what I've always wanted."

"And what is that?" Kate asked.

"To make the Sinclairs accountable for their actions. There are consequences for living in a Sinclair world."

Kate was confused by her father's words. What was he planning? She'd had enough of hidden agendas. "But what are you going to do?"

"Renee and I want to stop the Sinclairs from developing

317

properties that destroy neighborhoods and towns. They've always been in this business to make a quick buck, regardless of how it will affect people. They will make a lot of money from Obsidian's IPO. There is nothing I can do about that but now I want them to become more generous with the community and give back." Nate looked around the room. "But we all have to be in on this decision. We don't ever talk about this with anyone. Just the four of us here—our family."

Vivian and Eric both nodded their heads. Kate stood idle not knowing what to think or say. The room was quiet for several seconds.

"No one is going to get hurt," Nate said looking at Kate.

"What about Jenny?" Kate asked.

"I agonize over Jenny's death every day but nothing I do now will bring her back." Nate stood and paced in front of the mantel. "If we go to the police, the Sinclairs will have this case tied up in court for years. It's not the correct nor just thing to do but I say we take things into our own hands and make them pay, the Crawford way."

Kate thought about her dad's words. She had been raised to always do the right thing. She had wanted to set things straight with Cayenne and in the process figure out what really happened to Jenny. But through it all, she had been the target to take the fall if things went wrong. She thought about Logan killing Jenny over her pregnancy. Perhaps her dad would set things right without using the criminal justice system. Kate stood and walked over to her father and took a leap of faith. "Whatever you're going to do, I want in. I want to help."

Nate smiled as he took Kate in his arms. "Of course. I'd love nothing more."

Kate stepped back from her father. "What about Walter Rudolf?"

"The Sinclairs have got to be behind his death," Eric added.

"I agree." Nate sat down on the edge of the coffee table. "But where's our evidence? The police already ruled his death an accidental drowning. I hate to say it but I don't think there's anything we can do except use it as ammunition for this plan Renee and I have cooked up."

"Renee's plan? Didn't she use you?" Kate asked.

"In a way she did. But I spoke with her. We were both after the same goal," Nate said.

"What was that?" Eric asked.

"The truth. The Sinclair secrets have finally come back to bite them and will now be their downfall. But don't worry, we won't let them fall that far, just far enough," Nate said.

"So what can I do?" Eric asked.

Nate pursed his lips. "I'm definitely going to need your help. You still want to do some research for me?"

"Absolutely," Eric said.

"Let's go into the den. I can show you what I'm thinking." Nate and Eric walked out of the room.

CHAPTER 101

Kate stood next to the mantel and looked over at her mother sitting on the couch. How could she have kept the affair with Father O'Connell a secret for all these years? And why did she now look content and relaxed sitting on the couch. Kate hadn't seen her like this—ever.

"How are you doing through all of this?" Vivian asked.

"I guess, ok. I didn't expect Logan to die. But I do see his death as payback for what happened to Jenny."

"What about Obsidian? Will you be able to manage working with Sander?"

Kate shook her head. She hadn't even thought about Obsidian. Work was the last thing on her mind. "I can't go back."

Vivian patted the couch cushion next to her signaling Kate to come sit. "Don't rush to any decisions just yet. Remember that you have all those stock options."

"I'm not even thinking about the IPO. I just can't face Sander after everything that's happened." Kate sat down next to her mother.

"Your father has a plan. It'll all work out."

Kate put her arm on the back of the couch and turned in towards her mother. "I'm not really concerned about my work. I'm worried about you."

"Me? Why?"

"Why have you been so bitter all these years?"

"Can you blame me? You know now what really happened. Imagine having that bottled up inside all these years and not being able to prove it."

"That's what I've always thought. But now I realize it's something else."

"I don't know what you're talking about," Vivian said airily as she looked over at the photos on the mantel.

"Have you ever told Dad about what you've suspected?"

Vivian looked at Kate and raised her right brow. "What are you referring to?"

"Up on the roof, before he fell, Logan told me about Father O'Connell."

Vivian did not change her expression. Instead she calmly said, "And?"

"Does Dad know about your affair with Father O'Connell?"

Vivian held her breath.

"Is Father O'Connell really my biological father?" Kate asked.

Vivian looked away.

"If it's true, I think it's time you came clean. At least tell me the truth. I think you owe it to me."

Vivian closed her eyes. Tears began to stream down her face. "I hoped you'd never find out."

"Well, I did."

"That was a long time ago–"

"And you've made yourself miserable ever since."

Vivian's demeanor instantly changed. She clenched her fists and her body became tense. Her eyes darted around the room searching for something she could not find.

"Mom, he didn't leave because of you."

Vivian focused on Kate.

"He was blackmailed."

Vivian relaxed her hands and wiped the tears from her face.

"Laura Walker knew about your affair. She knew about me. The night Jenny died she told William and Maria Sinclair."

321

"What are you talking about?"

"The Sinclairs blackmailed Father O'Connell. They'd tell the world about your affair and me if he didn't help get Logan out of the country."

Vivian looked off at the mantel with the photos of her children. She became relaxed once again. "Why would she say anything?"

"My guess is Maria wanted to set Sander up, blame him for Jenny's death. Laura panicked and played this card, hoping it would save her son." Kate thought about Jenny's pregnancy. Should she tell her mom how Sander probably used this information to secure his future? "I think William used Jenny's death as an excuse to send Logan far away from him."

Vivian looked at Kate but did not respond.

Kate scrutinized Vivian's face. Was she hiding anything else? "Why didn't you leave Dad?"

"It's complicated."

Kate leaned back on the couch. "I've got all the time in the world."

Vivian stood and walked to the mantel. She selected a frame containing a photo of Jenny.

Jenny was around ten years old. Her long brown hair was swept back in a ponytail, her blue eyes glistening in the sunlight, and she was laughing.

"Your father and I were going through a rough patch. Patrick was there for me. We never intended anything to happen but it did and God punished me by taking Jenny." Vivian reached her hand out to steady herself on the mantel.

Kate thought about her mother's words. Vivian had never been a loving mother. She'd never shown the affection typical of her friends' mothers. But she had been there for Kate and had raised her. "I'm also your daughter. And I'm here. I'm alive."

"I know. Understand that you're the reason I never left your dad."

"Me? I don't believe you."

Vivian placed the frame back on the mantel. "You have to understand that I was a mess after Jenny died. Patrick left suddenly for Italy and Eric took off. The time I spent at the hospital made me realize I had to stay with your dad. I needed stability and I needed to take care of you. I loved you."

"Does Dad know?"

Vivian looked off towards the stairs down to the den. "Your dad knew about the affair. He found out a couple days before Jenny died. But he never asked about you, whether you were his. He doesn't want to know and frankly I don't think it matters to him anymore."

"Why did Dad stay?"

Vivian sat down on the couch and tapped her long bony fingers on the armrest. "I think Renee got to him."

"Renee?"

"She got your dad to think about his future. Renee gave him a new job and a new life. And you. It's always been about you."

"What do you mean?"

"Your dad could never leave you. He loves you."

Kate closed her eyes.

"It was never easy. But we came to an understanding how to live our lives, together."

Tears began to stream down Kate's face. "Do you think all of this didn't come at a price?

"You seem to be doing great. I don't understand."

"You were so strict with me growing up. Never allowing me to date. Sending me to the all-girls school. I always thought I had to be perfect. And I've spent years trying to figure out why I can't bond with anyone."

"You probably haven't found the right person."

"No! It's this fear of abandonment. Fear that they'll leave me. So I'm the one who ends it. Do you know that I was at a point of breaking up with Brett when Eric returned?"

"Having Eric back in our lives has helped everyone. Your dad and I are trying to make another go at it. Vindication for Jenny's death has kind of given us a second chance. We both want to make it work."

"Even with Father O'Connell back in town?"

Vivian stared at Kate but did not respond. She walked back to the couch and sat down next to Kate. "We're all different people now. It can never be like it was between Patrick and me. What made it possible, the possibilities that might have been ours, had we not been derailed are now long gone. We were reckless and now realize the error of our ways."

"Will you ever tell Dad about me?"

Vivian looked down at her wedding band. "After all this time, I'd ask whether it changes anything. Who do you consider your real father?"

Kate sat back and looked up at the photos on the mantel. "I'm not the same person I was a week ago. My life's been completely turned upside down."

Vivian leaned in closer to Kate and whispered. "You haven't told Eric or anyone else, have you?"

"About Father O'Connell?"

"Yes."

"No. Father O'Connell told me to talk with you first."

"Good. Thank you." Vivian spread her arms out on top of the armrest. "Is this something you can live with? Our little secret?"

Kate hesitated to respond. She had uncovered too many secrets over the last week. Should she tell her mom about Jenny's pregnancy? It was all too much for her to comprehend. "I'm going to need some time to think about it. I can't make any promises."

CHAPTER 102
Sunday

Kate slowly stepped off the elevator onto the 14th floor of the Bank of Bay building. She cautiously looked from side to side before walking forward. The floor was silent except for the beating of her heart. Kate felt flush as she pushed herself to place one foot in front of the other. She was still in a daze over what had transpired the night before, but a call that morning had changed everything.

She heard voices coming from Sanders office.

"Why the fuck did you want to meet this morning. I have more important things to deal with today." Kate could tell that was Sander's voice.

"You'll want to hear this," Amy said as she turned around and spotted Kate walking towards them.

Sander took one look at Kate as a scowl appeared on his face. He returned to his desk and shook his head. "Now what?"

Kate looked at Sander and then Amy.

Amy closed the door then ushered Kate to take a seat opposite Sander. She reached down to her dark leather Coach valise and produced a plastic manila envelope. She handed it to Kate. "I called Kate this morning. I thought we should all meet to discuss what's in that envelope."

Kate accepted the envelope.

"Open it," Amy instructed.

Kate pealed back the Velcro. Inside was the NDA for Cayenne; date, names and signatures. It was all there.

"What is that?" Sander asked.

Amy turned around and walked up to Sander. "It's the original NDA for Cayenne. You know the one you had me take from Legal. The digital copy you had me erase, the photo copy you had me take from Kate's office."

"Take? I never asked you to do anything?" Sander argued.

"Bullshit! You've asked me to do a lot of things for you. Do I need to even mention Mirage or Fortunato?"

Sander looked down at his hands.

Kate remained silent not wanting to disrupt their conversation.

"You almost had me there. Almost positioned me perfectly as your inside man to do your dirty work." Amy jabbed her index finger into Sander's chest. "It would've worked if that fucking asshole friend of yours hadn't…"

"I warned you about him—"

"He humiliated me!" Amy interrupted

"Why is she here?" Sander asked pointing at Kate as he stood. "She doesn't need to hear any of this."

Amy placed her hands on Sander's chest and pushed him back down into his chair. "I don't know what you and Logan did to her family. But you got me tangled in this mess and I'm not going to take the fall. Clive and Russ will figure it out soon enough. I took Russ for a ride to steal their code. I know you gave it to Logan as 'inspiration.' If Cayenne sees Mirage, they will know it was me. Now I realize, you wanted all of us to fall."

Sander remained calm without showing any emotion.

Amy leaned in towards Sander and scoffed, "You fucking bastard. I thought we had something…something special. Now you're going to do something for me."

"And if I refuse?"

"I know the number of a good reporter," Amy said looking at Kate as she took a step back. "One call from me and your precious IPO will be history."

Sander looked at Kate and then focused back on Amy. "What do you want?"

CHAPTER 103
Four Weeks Later
Tuesday

Four hundred people crammed into the small Oakview City Council Hall to witness the changing of the guard. The crowd sat in twenty rows of wooden benches, divided by a center aisle facing the elevated council member chairs. These five chairs surrounded a curved mahogany table that held five metal microphones for each council member. The name of each council member was etched on a plaque on the wall behind each respective chair. A large silver Arne Jacobsen-inspired clock hung above the names.

Renee Verano held court in the back right corner of the hall as she did for every Oakview City Council meeting. Tonight she wore a navy blue Prada pantsuit with an excessive amount of jewelry dripping from her neck, wrists, and fingers.

Nate sat in the front row to the right of the council with Vivian by his side. They were holding hands, making conversation with the people seated next to them.

Kate stood at the back corner of the hall, her fingernails freshly painted the color Barefoot in Belize. Brett had his arms wrapped around her waist. He rested his head on her shoulder and said, "It's almost show time. Where's Eric?"

The crisp evening air entered the hall as the door opened behind them.

Eric walked in and made his way over to Kate and Brett.

"Thought you were going to miss it," Kate said quietly to Eric.

"Wouldn't miss this for the world," Eric whispered back.

Kate surveyed the room and noticed William and Maria Sinclair sitting in the front row center. Father O'Connell and Father di Luca sat on either side of them.

As the clock struck 7 PM, the crowd became quiet while the City Attorney, Manager, and clerk took their seats at desks in front of the council. Four council members appeared from the inner chamber behind the elevated platform and took their seats. From left to right sat John Stewart, Mayor Wendy Rodriguez, Madison Stone, and Randy Steele. Walter Rudolf's seat on the far right remained conspicuously empty.

Wendy Rodriquez was a short, stout woman in her early fifties with dark hair. She dressed immaculately in a Tahari tweed suit that was making its premier. She looked around the room, picked up her gavel and rapped it twice. In a monotone voice she said, "Welcome. As the clock has indicated, it is 7 PM on December 11. The Oakview City Council is now in session."

As she placed the gavel next to her notes, Rodriquez continued adjusting the microphone and brought it in closer to her face. "Let's do a quick roll call. All members present?" Rodriquez caught herself and remorsefully said, "except for Rudolf. May we have a moment of silent please, in memory of Council Member Walter Rudolf."

The crowd became silent. No one moved.

After a minute, Rodriquez continued "All Council members present?"

The other council members raised their hands.

"Good," said Rodriquez. "Before we get to the real business tonight, I would like to acknowledge some of our guests. Rodriquez pointed towards the front center of the audience. "We are especially privileged to welcome William and Maria Sinclair. Not only is the Sinclair family one of the founding families of Altamont Heights but also they own one of the largest commercial real estate businesses that has helped revitalize many of the communities around the Bay

Area. With their Cross Creek project, Oakview will become the next great city in the Bay Area."

Kate smirked and elbowed Eric. It was quite obvious Rodriquez sided with the Sinclairs.

Rodriquez looked at the other council members. "Now on to council business. Are there any council, commission, committee, or staff reports?"

No one from the council or city staff replied.

"Now on to regular business. I believe this is what all of you have been waiting for. There has been a canvas of votes of general municipal election consolidated with the gubernatorial election held on November 6. The Oakview City Council action tonight is to adopt the council resolution 5128 declaring the canvass of returns and results of the general municipal election." Rodriquez turned to the council members. "Do I have a motion?"

Councilman Steele saluted the motion.

"Do I have a second?" Rodriquez asked.

Councilwoman Stone raised her hand.

"Any further discussions?" As no one uttered a word, Rodriquez concluded, "Let's vote."

A large board displaying the names of each council member with a green "yes" and red "no" option hung to the right of the council members.

"Seeing that all members have voted "yes", for the record, the motion passes 4-0. Please note that Rudolf is absent." Rodriquez looked at the audience, "In passing this council resolution 5124, by law, the election which was held in November is now law. In other words, the person who was elected has officially been accepted into the Oakview City Council."

There was silence as Rodriquez gathered the papers around her space and organized them into one neat pile. "As a final act as Mayor, I would like to take a moment to reflect on my past year of service and give advice to the new member."

Rodriquez moved the microphone to the edge of the table then sat back in her chair. As she spoke of her responsibilities over the past year, Nate looked back at Kate and nodded his head.

Kate smiled. As predicted, Rodriquez included the Sinclairs in almost all of her remarks.

"With that said, I would like to continue the meeting," Rodriquez said glancing down at her notes. "Tonight represents the novel transition of our local governing body as part of the finest tradition of the democratic process, welcoming a new member of the city council."

Rodriquez looked up and around the room. "Does the City Manager or staff have anything they'd like to add?" When no one responded, she continued, "At this moment, I would like to turn over the meeting to the City Clerk, Alice Brown for swearing in of the new council member and the selection of the Mayor."

"New member, Nathan Crawford, please join me at the podium in the front of the council," Alice Brown said.

Nate released his hand from Vivian and stood. He made his way up to the front, and stood next to Brown.

"Please turn around in front of the podium and face the audience," Brown said to Nate.

Nate faced the audience.

"Raise your right hand," Brown said.

Nate raised his right hand.

"Do you Nathan Crawford solemnly swear that you will support and defend the Constitution of the United States and the constitution of the State of California against all enemies, both foreign and domestic? That you will bear true faith and allegiance to the Constitution of the United States and the Constitution of the State of California? That you take this obligation freely without any mutual reservation or purpose of evasion and that you will well and faithfully discharge duties upon which you are about to enter?"

"I do," Nate said.

"Congratulations," Brown said as she shook Nate's hand.

"Thank you," Nate said.

"Welcome Nate Crawford to the Oakview City Council," Brown said as she turned to the audience.

The entire hall stood and cheered.

Nate smiled and waved his hand.

Brown pointed towards Walter Rudolf's empty chair and said to Nate, "Please take your seat."

Nate walked over and sat down in the black leather chair.

Brown cleared her throat. "The next order of business is to select the Mayor."

Kate whispered to Brett. "This should be interesting."

"Why?" Brett said.

"It'll show who's teamed up with my dad to oppose Cross Creek," Kate said.

"We do not need a second on the nomination but we do need a motion and someone to close the nominations," Brown said.

"I nominate John Stewart for Mayor," Nate said.

Rodriguez blurted out, "I nominate Stone."

After a brief pause, Stone said, "I say we close the nominations."

"Since the new member does not yet have his name on the voting board, I will simply ask for a show of hands," Alice said. "All in favor of John Stewart for Mayor, please raise your hands."

Crawford, Stewart and Steele raised their hands.

"All in favor of Stone, raise your hands."

Stone and Rodriguez raised their hands.

"May the record show John Stewart is the new Mayor of Oakview."

Kate smiled. "Just as my dad predicted."

"John, I mean, Mr. Mayor, it appears that you need to switch seats with Rodriguez as she is sitting in the seat traditionally reserved for the Mayor."

Rodriguez stood and reluctantly changed seats with Stewart.

"Mr. Mayor, I return the meeting to you," Alice said.

The audience applauded.

Once the clapping subsided Stewart continued. "Good evening council members. And welcome new colleague.

Before we finish the meeting, I would like the opportunity to speak about my plans as Mayor moving forward."

Kate looked around the room as the audience cheered at Stewart's remarks. Everyone involved with the Cross Creek project was present. She smiled at the thought of what was about to happen.

Stewart ended his remarks by asking, "Would the new council member like to make a statement?"

Nate immediately raised his hand.

"I now turn over the meeting to Nate Crawford," Stewart said.

Nate adjusted his microphone, took a folded piece of paper out of his breast pocket and cleared his throat. "I would first like to thank my family for supporting me through the election." He looked directly at Vivian and said, "I will need your love and support more than ever as I move forward in this new adventure."

He looked on to the audience. "Everyone in this community deserves the right to be heard. I am your voice. Do not hesitate to call me any time even on the most trivial matter. I promise that I will represent your concerns and needs. Any decisions I make will be for the betterment of the community."

Nate paused and looked around the hall.

"Lastly, I would like to thank all of my supporters. I truly believe I would not be here today, sitting in front of this microphone if it were not for all of you."

Stewart looked out onto the audience and said, "Any further comments? Any written communications?"

From the front center row, a hand slowly emerged from the sea of people.

A low murmur spread through out the hall as everyone began to whisper.

Stewart looked over at Nate who was smiling.

"I see that William Sinclair has something to say?" Stewart breathed into the microphone.

"Yes…Yes…I…do...do," William uncharacteristically stuttered as he stood.

"Please approach the podium," Stewart said.

William slowly made his way up to the podium. The normally tall and tan man looked pale and hunched over. He adjusted the microphone. "Good evening."

The council responded in unison, "Good evening."

William forced a broad smile. "This is not really my thing to get up in front of all of you. But I have something important to say. And it has to come directly from me."

The hall fell silent.

"There's been a lot said about my Cross Creek project." William pointed his finger at the council. "You're supposed to vote on my proposal come June."

William looked back at Maria and then turned and faced the council. "We have decided to withdraw our development proposal for that land."

Gasps and murmurs from the audience filled the hall.

"After much consideration, Sinclair Enterprises has decided to subdivide the land." William looked back at Father O'Connell. "We have decided to donate half the land to St. James Seminary."

Several claps and a couple cheers came from the stunned audience.

"The other half of the property that has sat dormant since the Convent was torn down will be donated to the City of Oakview."

The audience gasped.

William looked at Stewart and then Rodriguez. "I hope I am not speaking out of turn but I believe Oakview plans to keep the garden and develop the rest of the land for recreational use."

Stewart looked at Nate and smiled.

Rodriguez sat back in her chair. Her eyes became as wide as teacups with her mouth open in a look of shock. Stone had the same expression on her face.

"Sinclair Enterprises and St. James Seminary believe this proposal is the best use for the land."

Brett squeezed Kate and kissed her neck.

Eric grabbed Kate's hand.

"This act of generosity is simply the Sinclair family giving back to the community. Now it's up to the people of Oakview to work with the city council to make it become a reality."

With those closing words, William turned around and walked back to his seat as the majority of the audience stood and applauded.

John Stewart grabbed his microphone. "If there is no other business to discuss, this meeting is adjourned." He rapped the gavel twice and the meeting ended.

CHAPTER 104

As the crowd filtered out of the council chambers, Kate turned around and gave Brett a hug. "My day is getting better by the minute."

"How'd your dad get the Sinclairs to scrap their project?" Brett asked Kate and Eric.

Kate looked at Eric then closed her eyes. She hated lying but had promised her family not to tell anyone what had really transpired—even Brett. "I think Logan's death really hit the Sinclairs hard." Kate opened her eyes and looked up at Brett. "They realized that in death, life can come. The land will now become a community park and live on forever for the people of Oakview. In a weird way, I understand their situation. I've finally been able to put the past behind me."

"But you never got confirmation on whether Logan or Sander played a role in your sister's death," Brett said.

"I think the truth was too painful for any of us to accept," Kate said as she took a step back from Brett and looked at Eric.

"I filled Kate's mind with a hope we could blame someone else for Jenny's death," Eric countered.

"In the end, Logan and Sander had nothing to do with her death," Kate concluded.

"It's unfortunate but Jenny committed suicide," Eric said as he walked away.

"As long as you are okay with everything," Brett said to Kate as he reached in his pant pocket. He took out his vibrating iPhone and looked at the display. "Shit. I've got to take this. I'll be back in a sec."

As Brett walked away, Kate saw her mother at the front of the council chambers, standing next to her father. Their eyes locked.

Vivian smiled.

Over the last month, Kate and her mom had come to their own understanding of how to move forward without delving into the past. Kate wanted to move forward in life. Move forward with Brett. She knew she was taking a big leap of faith to put the last month behind her, but she was willing to take that chance. And then she spotted Father O'Connell.

They had not spoken since that horrible night at the Seminary. Kate had not decided if she would include him in her new life. Now, staring at the elder priest in his black suit, Kate realized there was no need for any kind of relationship with a man she never knew. She already had a father.

Kate spotted Eric standing alone in the corner next to the council member chairs. She walked up and tapped him on the shoulder.

Eric turned around and smiled.

"Can you believe what just happened?" Kate asked.

"I know. Weird to think the Crawfords were able to stand up to the Sinclairs," Eric said as he stood tall and pumped up his biceps.

Kate turned inward towards Eric and whispered, "I never thought they'd go for that deal."

Eric looked over Kate's shoulder at the sea of people and lowered his voice. "I think the Sinclairs wanted to protect their name more than anything. If we leaked that video, it would've destroyed them. Are you still cool with how Dad handled it?"

"Yes and no. I still have reservations about not going to the police, but I've come to understand that sometimes you have to take things into your own hands for justice to be served."

Eric nodded his head in agreement.

Kate turned around and joined Eric against the wall as they watched the remaining people slowly file out of the council chambers.

Eric spotted Father O'Connell and nudged Kate, "I can't believe Father O'Connell lied to the police."

"It was a good story. Logan killed Courtney over a lover's spat and then threw himself from the top of the Seminary."

Eric leaned into Kate. "You'd be surprised what Father O'Connell is capable of. I just feel like such an idiot for thinking someone like Courtney had feelings for me."

Kate grabbed Eric's arm and squeezed it. "Don't beat yourself up. That woman was just using you to get information."

"That's what I'm worried about. Will I ever be able to trust another woman?"

"I doubt that situation will ever repeat itself."

"I guess you're right." Eric smiled.

Kate felt her phone vibrate. She looked at the display. "Sorry Eric, I need to take this call."

Eric gave Kate a hug. "Rodney's Wednesday 9 AM?"

Kate gave Eric a thumbs up as she turned and walked back towards the exit. Once outside, she pushed the answer button on her phone. "I was wondering when my favorite Seattle developers were going to call."

"Hey, Kate," said an excited Russ.

"What have you done?" interrupted Clive.

"What are you guys talking about," Kate smiled as she twisted a lock of her hair around her finger.

"We just got off a call with Sander Walker," Clive said.

"Why is Sander, some lawyer and a PR guy flying up to Seattle to meet with us tomorrow?" asked Russ.

"Our meeting last month went really well," Clive said.

"But we didn't hear back from Sander or you," Russ said.

"We assumed you'd lost interest in our product," Clive said.

"Or that you were waiting for the quiet period to end?" Russ asked.

"Yes," Kate replied.

"Yes to what?" Clive asked.

"Is the quiet period now over and you can officially tell us something?" Russ asked.

Kate smiled. "Sander loves your product. But our meeting was the day before Obsidian went public. We couldn't tell you that Virtual Presence is the perfect product to complement Obsidian's product line. Sander's flying up to tell you in person. Welcome to Obsidian boys!"

Silence.

Kate couldn't understand their anxiety. "Guys! The visit tomorrow is my gift to you. If you want to accept the gift and have Obsidian buy Virtual Presence, I think...no...I know Sander will give you whatever you want."

Silence.

"Are you guys still there?" Kate asked.

"Yeah," responded Clive.

"I'm in shock," Russ said.

"When we last met, you were off. You didn't seem like yourself. I know you said Obsidian was in this quiet period and we couldn't talk any deals but we assumed the deal was off." Clive said.

"A lot was going on in my life. I'm sorry if you felt I was acting weird. All is good now," Kate said.

"I can't believe what you're saying," Clive said.

"Believe it. And don't be surprised if Sander wants to issue a press release tomorrow announcing Obsidian is buying Virtual Presence," Kate said.

"Why aren't you coming up tomorrow?" Russ asked.

"Will you continue to work with us as our account manager?" Clive asked.

Kate spotted Brett walking towards her.

"Let's just say I'm going to take a break from the high tech world. As soon as my last round of stock options vest, I'm going to go work for my dad," Kate said.

"Your dad?" Russ asked.

"He's starting a philanthropic foundation to redevelop urban areas and help families in need," Kate said.

"Where did he get the funding?" Clive asked.

"He canvassed the local business community but our largest donors will be William and Maria Sinclair and Renee Verano," Kate said.

"Wow. What a great opportunity," Russ said.

"I know. It was an offer I couldn't refuse," Kate waved at Brett as he approached.

"We'll be sad not to work with you," Clive said.

"Oh you won't miss me. You'll be so busy working with our engineers to ensure Virtual Presence is Obsidianized."

"That's a new word. I like it," Russ said.

"If you need any more help, I'd highly recommend an engineer by the name of Hashim Abbasi. Sander knows how to reach him," Kate offered.

Brett walked up to Kate and took her hand in his.

Kate smiled at Brett. "Look guys. I have to go."

"What about our meeting tomorrow?" asked Russ.

"What do we say?" asked Clive.

"What do we ask?" asked Russ.

"Ask for the world and you just might get it. Good luck!" Kate ended the call and put the phone in her purse. She turned to Brett and gave him a hug.

Brett released Kate and stepped back. "I just got a call from Sander. Looks like everything is going as planned. No violation of the quiet period. He's heading up to Seattle tomorrow to talk with Cayenne about purchasing Virtual Presence. And he wants me to come along. I still don't understand exactly what happened with Logan's Mirage product."

"When he died, the product and the use of it died with him."

"Lucky that Cayenne's product was ready to go. Looks like everything worked out for you in the end. That missing NDA didn't even come into play."

Kate looked down at that ground and bit her lower lip. "I'm just glad I get to leave on a good note."

"What? What do you mean leave? Are you leaving Obsidian?" Brett asked.

Kate looked up at Brett and smiled. She had wanted to tell him for the past week but her dad wanted to wait until after he was installed. "We've got a lot to talk about. I've decided to reprioritize things in my life."

Brett grabbed Kate's shoulders and looked at her with concern. "You're not changing your mind about us?"

Kate grinned from ear to ear. "I am definitely not changing my mind about moving in with you."

Brett leaned back from Kate. "Then what are you doing?"

"I'm taking a break from high tech."

"Oh really. Now that you're moving in with me, you're expecting me to support you?" Brett joked.

"No. I'm going into a new line of work—with my dad."

"Your dad? You've got some explaining to do."

"I know. And I'll explain everything." Kate's eyes glimmered with a confidence she had never felt before. Everything was right in the world. Eric was back in her life, her parents were the happiest she had ever seen and now she was moving forward with Brett.

"Tonight?"

"Sure. But only if you help me pack up the last boxes from my place and take them to your condo."

"Definitely."

Brett picked Kate up off the ground and spun her around. "Are you sure you're ready to take this next step in our relationship?"

Kate opened her eyes wide and gave Brett a sensuous kiss on his mouth. "I've never felt more ready or sure about anything in my life.

ABOUT THE AUTHOR

Ursula Ringham was born and raised in Palo Alto, California with a family immersed in real estate development and local politics. She got her start in high tech through a summer job at Adobe. Systems, Inc. After graduating from UC Davis with a degree in International Relations, she worked for over a decade at Adobe and Apple in Developer Relations. Today, Ursula stays actively engaged in the high tech industry through her consultative work helping marketing organizations build better brand identity through her writing. Ursula's love for writing began when she was 13 years old and entered a short story contest. She lives in San Jose with her husband and two children. This is her first novel. www.ursularingham.com